The Book That Matters Most

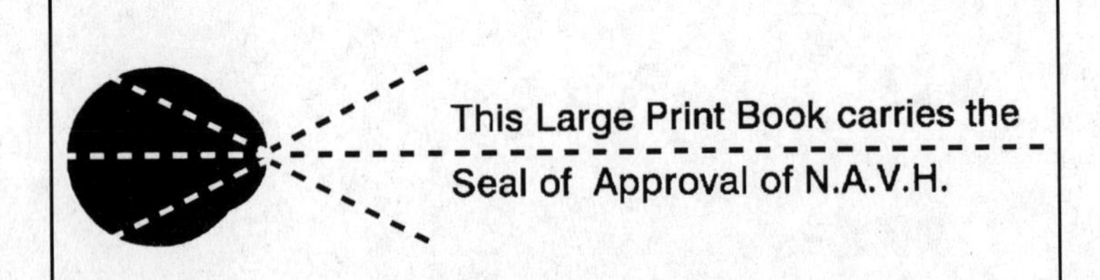
This Large Print Book carries the
Seal of Approval of N.A.V.H.

THE BOOK THAT MATTERS MOST

ANN HOOD

THORNDIKE PRESS
A part of Gale, Cengage Learning

GALE
CENGAGE Learning

Farmington Hills, Mich • San Francisco • New York • Waterville, Maine
Meriden, Conn • Mason, Ohio • Chicago

The Book That Matters Most is a work of fiction. Names, characters, places, and incidents are the products of the author's imagination or are used fictitiously. Any resemblance to actual events, locales, or persons, living or dead, is entirely coincidental.

Thorndike Press® Large Print Core.
The text of this Large Print edition is unabridged.
Other aspects of the book may vary from the original edition.
Set in 16 pt. Plantin.

LIBRARY OF CONGRESS CATALOGING-IN-PUBLICATION DATA

Names: Hood, Ann, 1956- author.
Title: The book that matters most / by Ann Hood.
Description: Large print edition. | Waterville, Maine : Thorndike Press, 2016. | Series: Thorndike Press large print core
Identifiers: LCCN 2016022336 | ISBN 9781410490261 (hardcover) | ISBN 1410490262 (hardcover)
Subjects: LCSH: Parent and adult child—Fiction. | Mothers and daughters—Fiction. | Large type books.
Classification: LCC PS3558.O537 B66 2016b | DDC 813/.54—dc23
LC record available at https://lccn.loc.gov/2016022336

Published in 2016 by arrangement with W.W. Norton & Company, Inc.

Printed in Mexico
2 3 4 5 6 7 20 19 18 17 16

This is for you

▪ ▪ ▪ ▪

Part One: December

▪ ▪ ▪ ▪

It's a long, long way, it grows further by the day
It's a long way from Clare to here . . .
— "From Clare to Here" by Ralph McTell

Ava

Ava saw it as soon as she turned the corner. She stopped, squinting as if that would change what she was looking at. It was a week before Christmas on Weybosset Street in downtown Providence. The Christmas lights already shone, even at five o'clock, because the day was so dark and gray. The air had that festive holiday feeling that came from people bustling about with oversized shopping bags, cold air, tired decorations, a guy selling Christmas trees on the corner.

But Ava felt anything but festive.

She stood staring at the Providence Performing Arts Center marquee. She knew it was backlit in white with black letters announcing *The Lion King,* because she'd come here just last night, the tickets given to her by a colleague from the French department trying to cheer her up. But she couldn't actually see the marquee. No. The marquee was covered in red and green cable knit yarn, almost like it was wearing a sweater. Except Ava knew that it *wasn't* wearing a sweater. The PPAC marquee had been yarn bombed.

Beneath it, her best friend and neighbor, Cate, stood looking miserable in a matching hat and scarf and gloves the color of Christmas trees. Her gloved hands flailed about nervously.

"I didn't know," she was saying into the cold air, her breath coming out in puffs. "I'm sorry!"

Ava had come to hate those words. *I'm sorry.* How many times had she heard them in the past year? A thousand? Ten thousand? What had her kids thought was the biggest number when they were young? A gazillion. That was right. A gazillion. Had she heard *I'm sorry* a gazillion times?

Cate was moving toward her now. But Ava stayed put, as if she were stuck in place. Unlike Cate, she had forgotten gloves and a hat, and she was cold. Really cold. She was always forgetting things these days. She'd go to the bank without her debit card. Walk out to her car without her keys. Find herself at the grocery store without any idea what she'd come for.

"I'm sorry," Cate said again, standing right in front of Ava and clutching Ava's cold bare hands in her warm gloved ones. "If I'd known," she began, but didn't finish because she didn't have to. It was clear what she meant. If she'd known the PPAC marquee had been yarn bombed, she would have had them meet somewhere else. But she hadn't known and here they were.

"It's all right," Ava said, even though it was anything but all right.

Ava was looking up at the marquee again. The stitches were so perfect, the colors so vivid against the gray afternoon, those cables twisting defiantly upward.

"Why don't they arrest her?" Cate said, turning to look.

A small crowd was forming, everyone staring at the marquee. Everyone amused, impressed. Impressed by what? The woman's audacity? Ava had seen that firsthand and was anything but impressed. By her talent? Even Ava had to admit that it must be hard, seemingly impossible, to knit such huge objects. And to knit them so well. But was that really impressive? Curing cancer was impressive. Scoring a ten in the Olympics was impressive. Making a soufflé that didn't fall. Saving people from a sinking ship. Even getting 800s on your SATs was impressive. But this? This was ridiculous.

Cate had Ava by the elbow, and was leading her back in the direction from which she'd come.

"I had no idea," Cate kept saying.

"It's okay," Ava said, even though nothing had really been okay since the day Jim left her. *Left her for that yarn bomber,* Ava added silently as she glanced back over her shoulder where the flashes of dozens of cameras looked like something hopeful — fireflies or shooting stars.

Cate smiled and said, "I've heard this place down here has good martinis. Pomegranate, maybe?"

"Uh huh," Ava said.

"I'm going to try one," Cate said, opening the door of a bar.

Inside it was dim and noisy and crowded.

"Cozy," Cate said cheerfully.

Ava followed her friend, watching her sturdy back and broad shoulders. Even in winter, Cate woke early every day and went to the Y to swim. She was a bike rider, a touch football player, someone always ready to pick up a racket or throw a ball. Since Jim had moved out, Cate had convinced Ava to join her at the pool or a yoga class. But Ava had never been good at things like that. When she and Jim went to the beach, they lolled together on striped chaise lounges instead of riding the waves. Or walked slowly along the shore at low tide searching for shells and sea glass, which still filled various bowls and vases around the house.

Remembering these things — the coconut smell of sunscreen and the feel of her hand in Jim's large warm one — sent a sharp stab of pain through her as Ava squeezed in at the crowded bar.

Cate was trying to get the bartender's attention. "So crowded," she murmured, and Ava agreed, looking around at the tattooed and pierced people.

How had she and Jim got from there to here? Ava thought. She pictured him bending to pick up a sand dollar, intact but fragile. He'd held it out to her in the palm of his hand. "See the star in the center?" he told her. "That's the star that led the Wise Men to the manger. And the holes represent the nails on the Cross." Gently, he turned it over. "On this side, there's a poinsettia." She'd stood on tiptoe to kiss him on the lips. "My own personal encyclopedia," she'd said. And he was. Or had been, she corrected herself. A lover of arcane information and strange facts that she never tired of hearing. That sand dollar crumbled when she picked it up at home later that day, Ava remembered, as if it were an omen of what was to come just a few months later when, one night, unable to sleep, Ava wandered downstairs and found a text message blinking on her husband's cell phone: *Miss u babe.*

She'd stared at it, struggling to make sense of what she saw. The use of *u* instead of *you,* the word *babe,* all of it confusing and mysterious, until she went upstairs to the man she'd thought she could trust, whose trust she had never even doubted, and shook him awake, and waved his cellphone in his sleepy face, and screamed for an explanation. And then came the awful explanation — "I love her. I'm in love with her." Even that terrible night she had heard herself saying, "We can get through this. We can fix this." But Jim, all bedhead and sleepy eyes, shook his head slowly and said, "I think I want to be with her," as if he had just discovered something too.

Cate was nudging her gently now, the bartender looming impatiently in front of Ava.

She ordered a Grey Goose martini, up, with a twist.

"I'll try the pomegranate one," Cate told the bartender. "Frozen," she added.

That was the special holiday cocktail. Ava saw it handwritten in red chalk on a board above the bar: FROZEN POMEGRANATE MARTINI!!!!!

It arrived, all slushy and pink, garnished with cranberries on a bamboo skewer. Cate lifted her drink and clinked her glass against Ava's.

"Here's to tonight," Cate said.

"Yes!" Ava said, clinking her glass to Cate's.

Ever since Cate had announced to Ava that Paula Merino was moving to Cleveland and a spot had opened in the book group Cate ran at the library, Ava had been looking forward to this night. Due to space at the library and a desire to keep the group at just ten members so that everyone had a chance to choose a book selection and have a voice in the discussion, getting a spot was difficult. For over twenty years Ava had listened to Cate describe the book group and how special it was. They went to one another's weddings and brought casseroles when someone lost a loved one and threw baby showers. From time to time, if someone moved away or dropped out — which was rare — Cate asked Ava if she'd like to join. But Ava had never felt the need. Until Jim left.

In fact, Ava had been the one to ask Cate — beg, practically — that if anyone dropped out, could she please, *please* take that spot. She'd tried not to sound desperate, though of course she was. Desperate for company, desperate for conversation, for a way to pass the empty hours that had appeared suddenly when Jim moved out. She was surprised by how much she longed for company. No, she thought as she sipped her drink. Not just for company, but for something more, a deeper connection to people. How easily she'd come to rely on Jim for that. And how woefully she longed for it with others now.

Years ago, before her little sister Lily and her mother died within a year, books had been Ava's refuge. "There are perhaps no days of our childhood we lived so fully as those we spent with a favorite book," her mother used to quote when she'd discover Ava lost in Narnia or on the prairie or at the March household. She would say it with pride. It was the one thing Ava had that Lily didn't. Lily had the lovely blonde blue-eyed looks of their mother, the kind of sweet temperament and charm that made people stop in the street to admire her. But Ava, with her unruly brown hair and blue spectacles, her tendency toward pouting and sarcasm and a generally sour personality, only pleased her mother by being a voracious reader.

There are perhaps no days of our childhood we lived so fully as those we spent with a favorite book. Who said that? Ava wondered. Her mother had been gone long enough now for Ava to have forgotten its source.

"We've changed over the years," Cate was saying. "It used to be all young mothers, desperate to talk about something other than potty training and temper tantrums. We'd meet in the afternoon, during nap-time. Then we went through a phase of meeting at each other's houses in the evening, and cooking food that was in the books. It's evolved nicely, I think. I still try to make the snacks fit with the books we read. And sometimes I dress from the time period of the novel, just for fun. It's really a good mix of people of different ages now." Cate smiled at Ava and added, "You're going to love everyone. You'll see."

Ava wasn't worried about that. She worried the group wasn't going to love her. She was not a group person. Had never been. She was thrown out of Girl Scouts when she was ten because she couldn't make a curler bag out of a Clorox bottle and therefore earn the sewing merit badge. Lily, a year younger, filled her green sash with merit badge after merit badge, for sewing and cooking and botany. She'd even received a special one for selling more cookies than anyone else in New England. When Ava refused to go to the award ceremony, the Girl Scout leader, Mrs. V, had told her she was a bad sport and that Girl Scouts were good sports, easy to work with, and cheerful. Like Lily. "You possess none of these traits, Ava," Mrs. V had said. If Mrs. V could see her now, she would feel vindicated. *I told you so, Ava!*

A string of lights twinkled across the mirror, alternating pineapples and palm trees blinking back at her. Above the bar a small television played silently, and a familiar face came on the screen. Ava recognized everything: the PPAC marquee covered in red and green cable knit yarn; Hayley Morrow, the *News Team 10* anchor, shivering in a too thin pink coat, wearing the wrong color lipstick for her pale skin; and beside her, in full color, a woman with her hair in a messy tumble down her shoulders, wrapped in a fake leopard coat and over-the-knee boots, her kohl-lined eyes smirking at the camera through her over-sized thick black librarian glasses. Her name flashed across the screen, but Ava didn't need to read it. She knew exactly who she was looking at. DELIA LINDSTROM, YARN BOMBER. Husband stealer, Ava added silently.

"Oh, sweetie," Cate said. "Don't look. In fact, let's just leave. Okay? What do you say?" She motioned to the bartender, writing with an invisible pen in the air.

But Ava couldn't stop looking. Because there, right behind Delia Lindstrom, Yarn Bomber, stood her husband — her soon-to-be *ex*-husband — Jim, grinning like the idiot he was. Proud of his yarn bombing, home-wrecking girlfriend. He even had his hand on her shoulder. Possessively, Ava thought with a sickening feeling. And that hand was in a leather glove that she had given him last Christmas, when Ava was blissfully ignorant, and happy.

"Check? Please?" Cate was saying desperately.

Or if not exactly happy, happier, Ava amended. Was it possible to be really happy after so many years together?

"Bartender!" Cate shouted.

Ava finished her martini in one swig. Then she rested her forehead on the brass railing of the bar, and cried.

The Athenaeum in Providence had sat perched high on Benefit Street since 1838. These days it overlooked the comings and goings of Brown and RISD students, lawyers and criminals at the courthouse across the street, museum docents, hipster fathers escorting kids dressed in leather or tulle, harried mothers pushing double strollers, and the eclectic array of filmmakers, artists, writers, and professors who populated the neighborhood. Below, colonial Providence with its lopsided eighteenth-century houses painted in the blues and reds and yellows of that era; above, the grand Victorians of the city's industrialists and bank presidents. The street was all cobblestones and bricks and faux gas streetlamps.

Ava followed Cate into the library's side entrance, across from the Hope Club, one of the two private clubs on Benefit Street. Cars for an event there crowded the streets. As they sidestepped BMWs and Mercedes and the occasional Porsche, Ava vowed silently to be good-natured, amiable, positive. She would not drink too much wine, another vice she'd acquired post-Jim. She would make friends, or at least not offend anyone.

"O-kay," Cate said, shifting from best friend role to head librarian. She opened the door into the room where the book group met, and said, pleased, "It looks like everyone is here!"

Cate's assistant, Emma, pierced and

plump, with colorful tattoos of scenes from *Winnie the Pooh* blazoned across her arms and chest and back, hurried to Cate. Every time Ava saw Emma, the girl had a different color hair. Tonight: an ice blue that brought to mind fjords and icebergs. Despite the cold — they were calling this frigid weather the polar vortex, a new weather term that Ava and Jim would have delighted over; they had shared a love for all things meteorological — Emma had on a black tank top, maybe to show off those tattoos. Or her large, soft breasts that seemed about to tumble out.

"Hi Ava," Emma said. "How are you?"

Before Ava could answer, Emma had already turned her attention away from Ava and back to Cate, talking in her flat tone about the wine and cheese laid out on the white linen tablecloth with the Christmassy centerpiece — holly, red berries, red and white flowers, lots of greenery.

The book group ladies were at that table, plastic glasses of wine in their hands, munching on Camembert and grapes.

Relax, Ava told herself. She took a deep breath and went to join them.

As soon as Ava got a glass of wine, a slender, ancient blonde in a beige Chanel suit came up to her and said, "Are you the one taking Paula's spot? Cate's friend?"

"I am," Ava said.

"Glad to have you. I'm Penny Frost, the grande dame here. Which just means I'm older than everyone else."

Penny shook Ava's hand, surprising her with its firm grip.

"I'm Ava —" Ava began.

"Ava! You're Maggie's mom, aren't you?" a young woman exclaimed. "I'm Honor! Honor Platt? I used to babysit for Maggie and Will, remember?"

A vague image from a decade ago of a serious Brown student toting an impossibly large backpack floated across Ava's mind.

"Honor," Ava said. "How are you? It's been —"

Honor interrupted again. "Maggie was like seven or eight? And Will was maybe eleven? I always liked coming to your house," she added softly.

"You did?" Ava said, feeling that ache of loss creeping in. *Damn you, Jim. See? People liked us. They liked coming into our home.*

"There was always good food in the fridge and you guys were so fun. You and Mr. Tucker." Honor smiled as if remembering. "Will was the sweetest boy. And Maggie . . . well, let's just say she kept me on my toes."

"Honor Platt," Ava said softly. In college, Honor had worn baggy jeans and loose sweatshirts, her hair tied up in a ponytail. She'd played Ultimate Frisbee, and taught Will and Maggie how to throw a Frisbee in a perfect arc. But here she was, a grown woman with soft auburn hair grazing her collarbone and a small blue stone glistening on her left nostril.

"How are they?" Honor said, grinning. "Maggie and Will?"

"Great, great," Ava said, trying to ignore the feeling of worry that always accompanied that question. No, she told herself, they *were* great. Or at least Will was. Maggie — Ava pushed away the doubt that kept threatening to take over. Maggie was fine, she reminded herself, or they wouldn't have sent her to Florence for this school year.

"Grown up," she added.

"I can't believe it," Honor said. "Maggie's almost as old as I was when I babysat her."

Ava nodded and sipped her wine, trying not to let concern about her daughter intrude, which was difficult considering how many times she'd let herself believe that her troubled child was finally on track, only to get surprised or disappointed. This time Maggie *was* on track. Finally. Blessedly.

"What are you doing these days?" Ava

asked, happy to change the subject.

"I'm teaching at Brown now. English department. Women's studies. Tenure track."

"What? That's impressive."

"I'm so glad you joined the book group," Honor said. "When I moved back here after grad school, it was a godsend. A way to connect with people, and get out of my apartment and away from my thesis."

She gave Ava's arm a quick squeeze before moving away from her.

"It's going to be hard to fill Paula's shoes," Penny said.

Ava had forgotten Penny was still standing there.

"Last year our theme was 'The Classics,' and Paula's pick was *Remembrance of Things Past.* Can you believe that?"

Ah, Proust, Ava thought, remembering that he was the writer whose words her mother had repeated. *There are perhaps no days of our childhood we lived so fully as those we spent with a favorite book.* She considered reciting the quote to the woman staring up at her to prove herself worthy to be here, in Paula's shoes.

"I think she's the only one who read it," the woman continued. "All three volumes."

Suddenly, this book group sounded like

more than Ava was up for. Three volumes of Proust?

"Yikes," Ava said.

"You know what I say?" Penny said. "Mark Twain claims a classic is a book people have heard of but never read. Well then, Mr. Mark Twain, you've never met Paula Merino."

Ava attempted a laugh, but it came out as more of a grunt.

Had she even forgotten how to laugh? Ava chastised herself. That did it. She would finish her wine and then apologize to Cate, to all of them, and go home. She thought almost longingly of her new sheets, pink flowered ones. The kind a single woman would have. That's what she'd thought when she bought them. When Jim moved out, she'd thrown out the pewter ones that had covered their marital bed. *Marital bed!* She sounded positively Victorian. It was Jim who liked serious linens, pewter and charcoal and taupe. If he knew she'd stuffed the sheets in the trash instead of donating them to Travelers Aid or some other worthy cause, he'd be furious. He was the kind of person who actually went through their garbage and rescued stale bread — "What about the birds?" — and broken appliances — "What about the tech school?" — and scraps of cardboard — "What about recycling, Ava?" She used to find it endearing, this need of his to make the planet a better place. When the children were little they'd all four go off armed with buckets and clean up the little beach on the bay or the run-down park on the corner. And Ava had to admit that it *had* felt good, her small family doing these small things together. But then his good deeds got larger and more time-consuming, and Ava often felt left behind.

Ava lifted the plastic glass — it really was tiny, wasn't it? — and discovered it was already empty. One more, she thought as she refilled it again, and then home to my own bed. Just as quickly as that thought came to her, she refuted it. The last thing she needed was to be in bed, alone. No, goddamn it. She'd begged to be here. She was desperate for it. Even the smell of books that permeated the room felt familiar and comforting. And all these faces, looking open and ready for something. She needed most of all, the comfort of people who wanted nothing more than to sit together and talk about books.

Cate was asking everyone to find a seat, reminding them that there would be a chance to socialize after the meeting. Her eyes landed on Ava, and Cate looked so pleased that Ava was here that Ava had no choice but to smile back at her, shove a cracker with a slab of Havarti on it into her mouth, and take a seat.

"Welcome," Penny said, and she patted Ava's arm with her liver-spotted hand.

To her surprise, Ava saw that there were two men in the group. One had on a flannel shirt and one of those porkpie hats every man under thirty wore these days. He also had long sideburns, something Ava hadn't seen since her college days. The other was older, Ava's age, wearing a lime green fleece vest and worn Topsiders without socks despite the winter weather. His hair was blond turning to gray, and he had an aging boyish face that had probably melted hearts once. He sat twirling the wedding band on his ring finger, looking down at it, then away.

Ava sighed and ate her Havarti, a cheese she'd always thought tasted like absolutely nothing.

"We'd like to welcome two new members to our group," Cate was saying. "John and Ava."

Heads seemed to swivel in unison to look at them.

"John?" Cate said. "Do you want to tell us a little about yourself?"

The man in the lime green fleece vest shot

to his feet, like he'd been called on in school.

"Sure, sure," he said, and he really did sound affable, like a nice guy. "I live in that building that used to be a school? Over on John Street?" He smiled ruefully. "Moved there just a couple of months ago, from East Greenwich. See . . . uh . . . well, my wife died last year and I'm trying to get out more, you know. Try new things. Meet new people."

Everyone nodded sympathetically.

"So here I am," he said with a laugh. "Nervous," he added, and sat down.

"We are so happy to have you here," Cate said in her super nice person voice. "Ava?"

"What?" Ava said, caught off guard.

"Can you tell us a little about yourself?" Cate prompted.

Ava stood because John had, sending her small paper plate onto the floor. She felt a slight whoosh of nervousness in her stomach.

"Well, so, I'm Cate's friend Ava and Cate is one of those friends, a true friend, a real friend. I mean, my life has fallen apart and Cate . . . Cate . . ." Ava felt herself struggling to hold back tears. Her humiliation at being left by her husband loomed enormous.

Someone cleared her throat. Ava took a

breath, told herself to move along, pull it together.

"And Paula moved to Cincinnati —" she began.

"Cleveland," someone corrected.

"Cleveland," Ava said. *Come on,* she told herself, *you know how to do this.* "So here I am, in an effort to move on. Try new things. Meet new people."

Wait. Wasn't that exactly what John had said?

"Like John," she added.

John looked up, surprised.

Ava laughed, nervously.

"I don't mean I'm here to meet John, though I'm happy to meet him. I mean you," she said, shooting a smile in his direction. John went back to staring at his lap.

Ava took another breath. She talked to her students all the time, standing in front of the classroom, confident and in charge. Why was she so nervous here?

"I love to read," Ava continued. "Or at least, I used to. I mean, my mother and my aunt owned a bookstore. Orlando's? On Thayer Street?"

Not one flicker of recognition passed over anyone's face. Why should it? Orlando's had been gone for over forty years.

Ava took another breath and continued,

"And my mother even used to write. She had a couple stories in *Redbook* back in the early seventies. Domestic stories, nothing very literary, but still."

She searched for where she was going with this. Why had she brought up her mother? Cate looked somewhat horrified, and the guy in the porkpie hat was smirking at her.

"I love to read," Ava said again, weakly.

"Well, good!" Cate said. "Because this is a book group!"

Everyone, thankfully, turned their attention back to Cate. The guy in the hat smiled at Ava, but it seemed like a smile of pity, a *you poor thing* smile. She decided she hated him.

"Here we are," Cate said, "at our December meeting, which is the one in which we choose our reading list for next year. John and Ava —"

She frowned. "Ava, you can sit down now," she said in her schoolmarm voice.

Ava hadn't even realized she was still standing. She sat quickly, kicking over her plastic glass. Luckily, it was empty.

"Anyway," Cate said, taking a calming breath like they did in yoga, another activity she forced Ava to do with her. *Yoga will help you feel better,* she'd promised, but it didn't. "John and Ava, I gave you both next year's theme . . .”

She had? Ava tried to remember a theme, or even a conversation about a theme. But all she could remember were her own persistent inquiries about joining the group. Couldn’t Cate bend the membership limit just this once? she’d kept asking, and Cate would patiently explain how too big a group prevented everyone from getting to choose a book, and that the room wasn’t big enough to accommodate more people, and this way all the members had ample time to contribute their thoughts. When she got the email from Cate with the subject line *A spot has opened in the book group!,* she’d felt such relief and gratitude that it was possible she never actually read the entire email.

Honor turned in her seat in the row in front of Ava.

“You okay?” Honor whispered. “You’re kind of flushed.” She swept her hands over her own cheeks as if Ava didn’t understand the word “flushed.”

“I’m fine,” Ava said. “Thanks.”

Honor shrugged and turned back around. She had on layers and layers of clothes. An enormous, vaguely ethnic scarf, several blouses, and lots of bracelets.

“I have to say,” Cate said, “I love next year’s theme.”

Her cheeks were flushed too, Ava saw, either from a hot flash or real excitement about next year's theme.

"Of course I loved reading the classics last year," she continued. "The *Odyssey* and *Canterbury Tales* and even Proust."

She paused so that everyone could nod and smile and laugh a little.

"God bless Paula," Penny said.

Cate continued. "And the year before, most of you were here then, I loved reading nineteenth-century American literature, all that Twain and Poe. But this year's theme really allows us to reveal something about ourselves, to learn more about each other, doesn't it? It's more personal, and I like that."

Again, she waited for everyone to agree with her. Ava eyed the wine and cheese table. Tattooed, ice-blue-haired Emma was standing guard over it, but surely she wouldn't stop Ava from getting a little more wine, would she? As if she'd read her mind, Emma frowned at her.

"Just a reminder," Cate was saying, "and I think I emailed this to Ava and John too, but we take August off. And we don't read a book for our December meeting. That's when we choose the books, like we're doing tonight."

Ava walked as quietly as she could over to the table. Cate was saying they had to choose ten books for next year, and that she didn't choose one but she did read all the books — even *Proust!* — and led the discussions.

Ava remembered she'd knocked over her glass and it was somewhere under her seat, so she took a fresh one and reached for the red wine.

Emma whispered, "I'll get it," and picked up the bottle and poured. Her arm was close enough that Ava could see on her tattoo the lines around Tigger's feet indicating he was jumping.

"Thanks," Ava said.

She sensed someone behind her and looked up to see Mr. Porkpie Hat also getting more wine. He had one of those ridiculous short goatees running from his bottom lip to his chin. He smiled, showing beautiful teeth. She didn't smile back, but returned to her seat, noisily crushing her dropped cup under her boot as she did. Someone sighed.

"Our theme, of course, is 'The Book That Matters Most,' " Cate said happily, and the group applauded. "Everyone chooses a book that mattered the most to you in your life and each month we read that one book.

John? Ava? I thought you two could go last, if that's okay?"

Ava straightened. *That's* what she was supposed to do? Choose a book? Not any book, but the book that mattered the most to her? She couldn't even remember the last book she'd read that mattered at all. In fact, she purposely chose books that *didn't* matter. In summer she enjoyed sitting on the beach with a paperback while Jim worked his way steadily though Robert Caro's thick biographies of LBJ. But those paperbacks she read — mysteries and travel stories and novels with banal, forgettable plots — did not stay with her. She'd plucked a few off the shelf at this very library, read them, and forgot about them. They didn't *matter.*

Around her, everyone was taking pens out of their pockets or purses and opening those expensive Moleskine notebooks. Was that another thing she had missed? Bring a Moleskine notebook and the book that matters most to you? She thought of when Maggie and Will were young and she made a trip every September to buy their school supplies, the lists long and detailed, requiring three ring binders of various sizes, and all kinds of pens and markers and pencils. She missed the rituals of her young family, of slicing cucumbers and carrots, checking homework, folding the warm laundry, making hospital corners on the beds — all of it. And for the tenth or hundredth or thousandth time that day she thought, *Damn you, Jim.*

Sounds of everyone settling in and Cate's voice announcing yet something else brought Ava back to attention. Who knew book groups were so complicated? Cate had a big bronze urn that reminded Ava of the kind that held a dead person's ashes.

Cate stuck her hand inside, pulled out a folded piece of paper, and grinned.

"Penny," she said, "you get to choose our January book."

The elderly blonde in the Chanel suit stood.

"As many of you know, I was Radcliffe, class of '47," Penny said proudly. "And while there I fell in love with a certain Miss Jane Austen. I read her novels in order, *Sense and Sensibility* first, which was published in 1811, then . . ."

Ava couldn't concentrate on what Penny was saying. All she could think about was that she had one month to read a Jane Austen novel. To date, she'd never read even one.

"Which of her novels is the book that matters most to you, Penny?" Cate was asking.

"The book which the contemporary writer Anna Quindlen said is the first great novel to teach us that the search for self is as surely undertaken while making small talk in the drawing room as it is while pursuing a great white whale."

As Penny paused for dramatic effect, Ava watched several people, including Mr. Porkpie Hat, writing down the quote by Anna Quindlen. To her relief, John looked confused.

Penny announced, *"Pride and Prejudice."*

A few people clapped and at least one murmured with delight. Not having a Moleskine notebook, Ava scribbled the title on the palm of her hand.

Cate reached into the urn and pulled out the next name.

"Luke, you've got February."

Mr. Porkpie Hat stood and faced the group.

"The Great American Novel," he said matter-of-factly. *"The Great Gatsby."*

He seemed to say it directly to Ava, who immediately looked down and wrote the title on her palm. Someone tapped her on the shoulder and thrust a piece of paper at her. Emma. Ava mouthed a thank you, but Emma was too busy awaiting the next name to notice.

"March," Cate said. "What book matters the most to you, Diana?"

A woman about Ava's age stood. She looked vaguely familiar. Dressed in black cigarette pants and an oversized black turtleneck sweater, she had dramatically lined eyes and dark red lipstick. On her head she wore a brightly colored scarf, tied with a big knot in front. Ava could see that Diana was bald beneath the scarf, and she remembered Cate telling her that someone in the book group had breast cancer. They were taking turns bringing her to chemo, Cate had said.

In a deep smooth voice, Diana said, "I asked Cate if I could choose a play. Something by Shakespeare. He is, after all, the writer who matters most to me. But she said no, it had to be a novel. So the *book* that matters most to me has to be *Anna Karenina.*"

At this point, John looked terrified.

"You were a magnificent Anna," Penny said.

Diana took a dramatic bow, reminding Ava where she'd seen her. Diana was one of the actresses at the local repertory theater. For years Jim and Ava had had a subscription, never missing a play. They'd enjoyed those Friday nights, often with Cate and her husband, Gray. Why had they stopped? Ava wondered. When had they stopped?

Cate was already onto April, calling out the name Ruth.

As soon as Ruth stood, Ava recognized her. She was a mother from Maggie's elementary school, one of the ones always in charge of things. Ruth had seemed to be a fixture in the classroom, helping the kids with projects, assisting with school plays, monitoring the lunchroom. Ava could picture her happily running off copies at the printer, checklists and reminders and permission slips and programs. Once, when the music teacher got food poisoning, Ruth even played the piano in her place at the holiday concert.

"I know it's a fat one," Ruth said, "but the book that matters most to me is *One Hundred Years of Solitude.* Sorry," she added playfully. She still had the same soft round body, cheerful face, and neat blond bob that Ava remembered. In her corduroy jumper and clogs, she looked just like a sitcom mom. In fact, Ava thought, Ruth had four kids. Or was it five?

"No, no, that's a wonderful book," Cate assured her.

"Very interesting," a woman said, nodding with approval. "I actually met Márquez once, when I was in Chile." She pronounced it *Chee-lay.*

"I want your life, Jen," Ruth said with a sigh. She laughed and pointed at Jen, who had long straight brown hair and a long serious face with a strong jaw and sharp cheekbones. "And don't say you want my life! No one wants all these kids I have."

Turning to Ava, Honor said, "She actually made a quilt by hand for each one of them, *while* she was pregnant."

"Oh, I know. I only had to get two kids to school on time," Ava said, "and I would get there right before the bell rang to find Ruth on her way out already, all five of her kids delivered to their classrooms. Early."

"Guilty as charged," Ruth said.

"I guess you haven't seen Ruth in a while," Jen said. "She actually has six kids now."

Ruth nodded. "Cameron. Our oops. He's almost eight."

"God bless you," Penny said, shaking her head. "Three was more than enough for me."

Cate reached into the urn and picked the name for May. "Honor?"

Honor stood and said, "This took me a very long time. Should I choose the book that made me fall in love with reading, and led me to my life's work? Should I choose the book that challenged me to think the most?"

Silently Ava prayed that Honor did not choose that one.

"Ultimately, though, one book truly is the one that matters most to me. Thank you, Cate, for giving us this theme. It's been a difficult but enormously rewarding exercise." Her eyes sparkled, and her hands fluttered over her heart.

"To Kill a Mockingbird," Honor said.

"I've read that one!" Ava blurted in surprise.

John shouted, "So have I!"

"You have to reread it," Cate teased them.

She reached into the urn and selected the name for June.

"Monique," she announced. "And welcome back, by the way."

"One of our original group," Penny explained to Ava. "But she got married and moved to France —"

"I know her," Ava said as Monique got to her feet. Her once jet-black hair was now salt-and-pepper, but she still wore it in the same asymmetrical haircut, and her low-cut silky blouse revealed the impressive cleavage she'd boasted years ago. "She taught French with me." One of the best and worst things about Providence was that it was impossible not to run into people you knew.

Without any fanfare, Monique said, "*A Tree Grows in Brooklyn* is the book that mattered most to me," and sat back down.

The next name Cate called was Kiki.

Kiki looked young, maybe the same age as Ava's son Will, who was twenty-three. She reminded Ava of Ava's students, which gave Ava a soft spot for her immediately.

Kiki chose *Catcher in the Rye,* another novel Ava had read years ago. Maybe this wasn't going to be impossible after all.

Jennifer, who had met Márquez in *Cheelay,* had the September book.

"When I was in the Peace Corps in Guatemala," she began, "there were, of course, limited books available."

Jim had been in the Peace Corps too, in Honduras, long before Ava ever met him. He still returned once a year with school supplies or eyeglasses, flying into San Pedro Sula and then driving hours on unpaved roads to the neediest villages. He came back with photographs of grinning children, newly planted avocado trees, chickens in newly built chicken coops. Sitting here now, Ava wondered if she should have accompanied him. Would that have made a difference? Would Delia Lindstrom go to Honduras with him and yarn bomb the avocado trees?

"There was one book that I read over and over," Jennifer was saying, "and that book was *The Unbearable Lightness of Being* by Milan Kundera."

"I love that book," Kiki said.

Luke nodded. "Good choice."

"And that brings us to our newcomers," Cate said. "John?"

John got awkwardly to his feet, rocking slightly in his Topsiders.

"My wife was the reader in our family," John said. "So this was kind of hard. But one book does matter to me. A lot. *Slaughterhouse-Five?* By Kurt Vonnegut?"

"That's a wonderful choice, John," Cate said.

"Good one, man," Luke said.

"I've never read Mr. Vonnegut," Penny said as she carefully wrote the title in her notebook. "It's about time I did."

As soon as John sat down, Cate said gently, "Ava?"

"Last but not least," Ava said, stalling.

She felt everyone's eyes on her. She did not have a book that mattered to her, she thought, suddenly having to fight back tears. Her life mattered to her, her heartache, her losses, piling up with resounding thuds.

Then she heard herself say, *"From Clare to Here."*

She hadn't thought about that book since the summer after Lily died, when Ava read it over and over again, as if it had been written just for her. Someone had delivered it to their house, Ava remembered now, shortly after the first anniversary of Lily's death and just two weeks after her mother left them to jump off the Jamestown Bridge. A woman drove up in a big black Cadillac and handed the book to Ava. "This is for you," she'd said.

"Isn't 'From Clare to Here' a song?" Kiki asked Ava, who was grateful to stop the onslaught of memories threatening to be released.

"Nancy Griffith sings it, doesn't she?" Honor asked. " 'From Clare to Here'?"

"A lot of people have recorded it," Ava said, the song reverberating in her mind. *It almost breaks my heart when I think of my family . . .*

Ava swallowed hard, thinking of Jim and the family she'd lost this year. And thinking too of those other long-ago losses — her sister and mother — that still sat like rocks in her gut.

"But there was a book with the same title," she said softly. "By Rosalind Arden.

That's the one," she said, her voice stronger now. "That's the book that matters most to me."

Maggie

When she first arrived in Paris, with the vague notion that she would become a writer, she went to all the cafés that she'd read Hemingway had frequented. Les Deux Magots and Café Flore, La Closerie and La Rotonde in Montparnasse. "No matter what café in Montparnasse you ask a taxi-driver to bring you to from the right bank of the river, they always take you to the Rotonde," he wrote in *The Sun Also Rises.* But as far as she could tell, only tourists went there now. Or to any of the other cafés she'd so carefully marked on her *Street Wise Paris* map, finding the best route by Métro or on foot. She spent most of the afternoon and into the evening sitting in the cafés, drinking house wine and waiting for her life to begin, for something to happen.

But nothing did.

She managed to leave drunk and disappointed, but not inspired. Not feeling alive, which was what she needed. She had been dead inside for too long, and she had come here with her worn paperbacks of everything Hemingway wrote, and her knapsack, and her little notebook to jot down things she saw and ideas for stories and clever phrases. She'd come here — escaped, really — with all the hope she could muster. Of course, she'd followed a boy. Thomas, a sullen German philosophy student who had never said he would see her if she came to Paris. Thomas, who had promised her nothing and, when she showed up at his apartment in an ugly building on the outskirts of the city, had reminded her of that. "I did not invite you," he said, though he had let her in and had hurried sex — her bent over his desk, him behind her with his pants around his ankles and the buttons on his shirt scraping against her.

She'd gone back to him again, hopeful. Didn't Paris make people fall in love? Find kindred spirits? Find themselves? But it was more of the same, this time on the scratchy rug. Afterward, as they shared a joint, she tried to remember why she had thought it was a good idea to leave Florence and follow him to Paris. She studied his face — long and narrow and impassive. "Maybe tomorrow we could meet at a bar?" she'd offered. He'd nodded vaguely, lit another joint, talked about a philosopher she'd never heard of. His voice buzzed pleasantly around her, his v's sounding like w's. *Willage,* he said. And *wery.*

When he didn't show up at the bar the next night, she didn't even cry. She would stay in Paris, she decided. She would spend her father's money that he'd deposited into her bank account for her year studying abroad, as if that could buy her forgiveness and make everything all right. In her small room in the hostel — a hard cot, a bare bulb hanging from the ceiling, a broken chair — she'd taped a black and white postcard of Hemingway and Fitzgerald drinking in the Café Flore on the wall beside her bed, so that when she lay on her left side, she could stare at it, at them. She'd bought the postcard at one of the kiosks that lined the Seine, along with another one of the Eiffel Tower under construction. That one she taped above the bed, so she could see it as she lay on her back, which she did far too often when Paris was waiting for her outside. She liked the idea of looking at something that magnificent when it was only half-finished. Like her, she thought. Half-finished.

She tried to find Ganymede's, arguably

the best bookstore in Paris for English-language books, the one her *Lonely Planet* and *Let's Go* said not to miss. But it was in a maze of streets near the Pompidou Center and every time she decided to go, she got lost. *"Où est Ganymede's?"* she'd ask, pointing to the map or the guidebook. Everyone knew the store, and they directed her, pointing and showing with their hands the confusing parts of the route. Still, she'd get lost, and instead of persevering she'd go back to her small room in the hostel. *Don't miss Ganymede's Books, a quirky cluttered bookshop in the hip Marais section. The American owner, who goes simply by Madame, is a mercurial dragon who opens and closes the shop at her whim,* said *Frommer's.* She tore that page from the book someone had left behind at the hostel, with the store's address and phone number on it, and kept it in her pocket. Once she even tried calling, but the number had been disconnected and she thought perhaps the iconic bookstore had actually gone out of business.

Sometimes she met men in the cafés. Germans with architectural hair and perfect English. Australians on their walkabout, living out of one giant backpack on a heavy metal frame that they hoisted easily onto their backs. Brits who had come for a long weekend, driving through the Chunnel — she loved that word, *chunnel,* and loved how they said it in their Beatles' accents — and staying with friends from school. Skinny Japanese students wearing thick platform shoes. She tried to avoid Americans. She hadn't come to Paris to meet Americans. But out of boredom or loneliness, occasionally she found herself letting an American guy buy her more wine, share his cigarettes, and brag about all the museums he'd visited in a ridiculously short amount of time, as if there were some kind of race on.

She took them back to her tiny room, shushing them on the narrow stairs if it was after the hostel's curfew. They brought a cheap bottle of wine from the market on the corner, drugs if she was lucky, cigarettes, and enough condoms to get them through the night. She liked their tattoos, the intricate dragons and goofy leprechauns and leaping dolphins and quotes from poetry and full sleeves that wrapped up their skinny arms. She liked their smells — sour wine, stale cigarettes, Dr. Bronner's in peppermint, almond, coconut. She liked their foreignness, how they struggled to find a particular English word or called sweaters *jumpers* and hoods *bonnets,* how they liked techno music that made her cringe, how they used too many hair products and needed orthodontia and didn't go to the gym. Except the Americans, of course. The Americans she hated for their familiarity.

When she woke up, usually around noon, the guy gone, she wandered, hungover or still slightly stoned, her *Street Wise Paris* map in her hands. She tried to remember when different museums were free, but she always managed to mix up the days or times. She walked in the rain, she walked in the sunshine. She walked, searching for inspiration. But late every afternoon she found herself back at one of the cafés filled with tourists, ordering her first *vin maison* of the day. She opened her small notebook and stared at the mostly blank pages there, writing something, anything, just to try and fill it. *Vin maison,* she'd write. Or: *Musée d'Orsay is not free on Thursdays.* Or: *Woman in the purple coat. Possible character for story?*

Too much drinking and walking, too many drugs and too much sex, had made her thin and gaunt. Her hipbones jutted pleasantly against her jeans, the outline of her ribs showed through her threadbare sweater. She liked it, liked to trace her hand along the sharpness of her bones. When she looked in a mirror, she didn't recognize herself — the shadow of dark circles beneath her eyes, the tangled bed hair, the sharp cheekbones above hollow cheeks.

Then one night she left Les Deux Magots alone. It had been unusually empty, possibly because of the hard rain falling. The rain was cold and relentless, and she had no umbrella, so she decided to take the Métro. The night stretched hopelessly before her. She would buy a bottle of three-euro wine, and go to her small room, and stare at those postcards until she drank all of it and, hopefully, passed out.

The Métro too was oddly empty. For a moment, as she settled into a seat, dripping rain onto it and the floor, she wondered if something had happened. A terrorist attack or a madman on the loose. How would she ever know?

A man's voice interrupted her rising panic.

"Tu es trempée jusq'au os." You are soaked to the bone.

Across from her, the man smiled.

She didn't smile back.

"Prends mon parapluie," he said, holding out a black umbrella, folded up neatly like a gift.

The man was a man, not a boy like the ones she picked up in the cafés. He had a full head of longish, dirty blond hair, a hooked nose, a trench coat belted tight around his impressive girth. He looked like Gérard Depardieu, her favorite French actor, Maggie thought. Except not as big and not as old.

"Ah!" he said, smiling again and revealing adorable crooked teeth. "You don't speak French!"

She answered in perfect French that she did, in fact, speak French, but she wasn't in the habit of taking umbrellas from strange men on trains.

He laughed, obviously delighted.

"How did you acquire that accent?" he asked her, sticking to English.

"I went to a *lycée* in the States for eight years," she told him, sticking to French. "And my mother teaches French."

"Alors," he said, using the word the French used to mean *then* or *so* or a million other things, and nodded appreciatively.

She glanced around. Their car was empty except for the two of them.

"Où est tout le monde ce soir?" she wondered aloud.

The train was slowing and the man stood, sweeping one arm toward the door as if to invite her to join him.

"Everyone has left tonight so we can have

the world to ourselves, perhaps?" he answered.

She could hear her mother's frustrated question, *Do you ever, ever think before you act?* She stood too, without hesitating, and followed him off the train.

They walked silently through the rain, their legs bumping beneath the small umbrella, until they reached a place called Willi's Bar. When he opened the door and stepped aside for her to enter first, she found she couldn't move. Here was a bright, well-lit place, filled with happy people. The room buzzed with life. She felt his hand on her back, urging her inside. She stumbled slightly, and he took hold of her elbow with one hand as he smoothed her wet hair with the other.

The maître d' greeted them, grinning and making small talk. It was clear the man was a regular here, and although she tried to listen to their conversation as they walked to a table, she was too overwhelmed by the light and the noise, by *Paris,* because she had finally, after all these weeks and weeks, landed there.

He ordered a bottle of wine, garnet red and tasting of leather. Steak tartare arrived, and artichokes with morels, and crab croquettes. She was starving, she realized as she ate, shoveling the food in her mouth, hearing her mother again: *You eat like it's your last meal! Slow down!*

He ordered a second bottle of wine, a cheese plate.

"How old are you?" he asked her. "Sixteen?"

"Twenty-one," she lied. She had just turned twenty.

He nodded. "And you are here why?"

"I'm a writer," she said.

At night, with the strange boys in her bed, she told them the same thing. But the boys just said *Cool,* or nothing at all. This man nodded again, appreciatively.

"Paris is for writers," he said. "What do you write? Poetry?"

Maggie shook her head. "I'm writing a novel," she said. Not a lie exactly, she decided. She did want to write a novel. She had ideas for a novel.

"Like Hemigway, *oui*?"

"Hemingway is my hero!" she said. It was as if this man was looking right into her soul.

He smiled at her. "This was his city," he said.

"Yes," she told him. "I've been literally walking in his footsteps."

He raised an eyebrow. "So you've been to

the Hôtel d'Angleterre then? In the fifth?"

She shook her head.

"But you must see it!" he insisted. "It is where he and Hadley spent their first night in Paris. December 1921, I believe. Room 14."

"Wow," Maggie said. Somehow she had randomly met the perfect man for her. A man who knew where Hemingway spent his first night in Paris, right down to the room number. A man who looked like Gérard Depardieu.

"It was called the Hôtel Jacob back then," he was saying.

"I've walked by his apartments," she said. Then, to impress him, she added, "Both of them."

But he waved his hand dismissively. "Everyone sees those. There are commemorative plaques on the buildings to be sure no tourist misses them. But a writer" — he lowered his voice and placed a hand briefly on her cheek — "a writer needs the whole story, *n'est-ce pas?*"

Maggie reached in her bag and pulled out her notebook.

"What was the address?" she said, holding a pen above a blank page. "I'll go first thing tomorrow."

"Nonsense!" he said, getting to his feet.

"We'll go immediately."

"Now?" Maggie said.

"Of course now," he said.

Hadn't she come here for adventures? For experiences that she could write about in stories or even a novel? What was grander than an older French man who looked like a movie star taking her to see the very place Hemingway stayed on his first night in Paris?

"Je m'appelle Julien," the man said softly.

"Maggie," she said, her mouth stuffed with cheese made from the milk of cows in the Pyrenées.

On Sunday he took her to Marché Mouffetard. They nibbled freshly baked bread as they walked through the crowded market past fruit and cheese and charcuterie vendors.

"It's still just like he described it in *A Moveable Feast,"* Maggie said, taking in all of the grocers and the rich smells of ripe cheese and meats. How many weeks had she wasted in her tiny room? And smoky bars? Now she was discovering Paris. Hemingway's Paris, she added.

Julien took her hand in his and gave it a gentle squeeze.

"I'm so happy to show you these things,"

he said. He didn't let go of her hand until they reached Marché Monge, where he bought her a *pain au chocolat.*

"My favorite!" she said. "How could you know?"

Still, he didn't kiss her when he left her at the hostel. He just touched her cheek lightly, and asked if she would meet him on Wednesday at the Jardin du Luxembourg.

"I don't believe your Monsieur Hemingway really strangled pigeons for food there and hid them in his baby's pram, do you?"

"Did he claim to have done that?" Maggie asked, delighted.

"So he did," Julien said. "He said he had to since there was no food from the Place de l'Observatoire to the rue de Vaugirard."

Maggie laughed. "Was he right about that?"

"I'm afraid so," Julien said with a sigh. He raised that eyebrow and asked again, "Wednesday?"

Maggie agreed, wondering how she could possibly wait three whole days before she saw him again.

Finally Wednesday arrived. The entire way to the Luxembourg Gardens, Maggie wondered if today would be the day he would finally kiss her. Or perhaps she should kiss him first? She imagined leaning in to him beneath the eyes of the statues of the queens of France. Or perhaps at the Medici Fountain. Maggie smiled imagining it — the kiss, his surprise.

By the time she reached him she had a severe case of butterflies in her stomach at the anticipation of that perfect kiss. When he spotted her walking toward him, he dropped the cigarette he was smoking and crushed it beneath his heel, then opened his arms wide. Without hesitating, Maggie rushed into them.

"What do you like? Besides Monsieur Hemingway?" he asked her later, after he'd kissed her beside what seemed like all one hundred and six of the gardens' statues and then pleaded with her to come to bed with him. He didn't need to plead with her. After the very first kiss, coincidentally by the small model of the Statue of Liberty, Maggie was hoping they would become lovers. By the time he'd pressed her against the statue of Baudelaire, his hands running along her ribs, his tongue deep in her mouth, she was almost certain she had fallen in love with him

Now they were naked, on a large bed in an apartment on rue Saint-Antoine in the

Marais. They had climbed one hundred steps to reach this apartment. Maggie had counted them, *"Quatre-vingt-dix-huit, quatre-vingt-dix-neuf, cent!"*

The last — *cent!* — she'd announced out of breath as she half fell through the door.

Julien caught her, and laughed, and said, "I never counted them."

They drank a bottle of champagne on the big pink couch, kissing and kissing until her lips felt swollen. Julien opened a second bottle, his long hair tangled and wild.

"Shall we take this one to bed with us?" he asked her, almost shyly.

The bed was up a ladder like the kind on boats, steep and narrow, and he guided her up it from behind, his hands on her waist. She had the spins, and when she reached the top of the stairs, she threw herself onto the bed with its white pillows and white duvet, miles of white. Ever since the first time she got drunk, back when she was only what — thirteen? fourteen? before Outward Bound and the farm camp in Vermont and all the things her parents had tried to fix her — she'd loved the spins, loved being drunk or high, feeling the world fall out from beneath her.

The sex was sloppy and fast, a drunk girl and an older man too excited by having sex with someone half his age to do it any other way.

But now he traced her ribs, one by one, and whispered again, "What do you like?"

"Do you have cigarettes?" she asked him.

He did.

"Drugs?"

He hesitated, his fingers pausing halfway down her ribs.

"What sort?" he asked.

She named her favorites. Oxycontin. Vicodin. Adderall. Coke. Pot.

"My parents spent thousands of dollars protecting me from myself," she said, "but I'm just a bad seed, I guess."

She meant to sound flirty, sassy, but somehow the words came out wrong.

Without replying, Julien got out of bed.

She closed her eyes, and let the room spin around her.

"You fell asleep," she heard him say, a minute or an hour or many hours later.

There was a skylight above her, and rain still pounded it.

Julien offered her a cigarette and cognac in a snifter. She sat up, took them both from him.

"I want to make you a proposition," he said. Then he said her name, not Maggie but Marguerite, like it was the most delicious thing.

The cigarette was a Gitane, one of the strong types, and she coughed.

"You may stay here —"

"Here?" she repeated, unable to believe her good luck. Maybe he loved her too.

"And I will bring you food, and cigarettes, and even drugs, if you like."

Maggie took a big swallow of the very good cognac, enjoying the feeling of it burning inside her.

"You want me to be like a kept woman. Your mistress?"

"But you must be here whenever I want you," he said.

He took the cognac from her, and sipped.

He began giving her details. He would get her a cell phone, keys, some clothes for when he took her out to dinner.

Maggie smiled. She would do it, live in this apartment high above the Marais and she would fill her little notebook with keen observations and pithy remarks. At the edge of her brain, her mother's voice threatened to intrude with logic or warnings or both. But Maggie wouldn't let it. I'm in Paris and I'm in love, she told herself, and a shiver of excitement spread through her.

"Alors," he said. "You look happy."

"Oui," she said. *"Très heureuse."*

Maggie got on her knees and inched her way across the vast ocean of the bed. When she reached him, she kissed him full on the mouth.

■ ■ ■ ■

Part Two: January

■ ■ ■ ■

"I could easily forgive his pride, if he had not mortified mine."
— *Pride and Prejudice* by Jane Austen

Ava

"Your mother was here last night," Ava's father said over their sad Christmas dinner in the dining room of Aged Oaks, the assisted living facility where he'd moved that summer.

Soon enough, Ava realized, her father would take the next step down in this system. He'd already moved from independent living to assisted living at breakneck speed. With his dementia growing worse, in no time he would be sent off to the Memory Ward, as they called it here, even though no one in the Memory Ward had their memory anymore.

"She looked good," her father said, nodding and gumming his turkey. Lately, he'd stopped wearing his false teeth, which made him look like the dolls her kids had made out of dried apples. "Boy, has she gotten old!"

Even though the doctors had told Ava that

she should go along with his confusion rather than challenge it, she said, "Dad, Mom died a long time ago." The doctors had instructed her to gently remind her father of facts, so she added, "Remember? Lily died in 1970, and then Mom in 1971?"

He laughed. "But she came in last night, Ava! 'Merry Christmas, Teddy,' she said. And she kissed me right here." He pointed to his cheek, also sunken and spotted with stray gray whiskers from a hasty shave by a nurse that morning.

"Sometimes," Ava said, moving her mashed potatoes around on her plate, "sometimes I dream about her too. And it seems real."

"Me too!" he agreed, finally swallowing his turkey and putting a forkful of gelatinous cranberry sauce into his mouth. "That's why this was so remarkable. Not a dream. *Her.*"

Ava put her fork down. The food was not terrible, just basic institutional food. Could it have been just last Christmas that she was with Jim and Maggie and Will, making a vegetarian lasagna — Maggie had been in yet another phase, vegan this time — and drinking champagne and dancing to "Build Me Up Buttercup" and "Jingle Bell Rock"? How had Jim managed to seem so happy?

He'd already begun seeing Delia Lindstrom, though of course Ava didn't know that. *Seeing.* That made it sound like he was casually dating her, when in fact he was having an affair.

"I told her too," her father was saying. "I said, 'God, it's good to see you, but you've gotten so old.' And she said, 'You don't look so good yourself, Teddy.' "

Ava tried to think of what to say.

"Where's Jim?" her father asked suddenly, as if he'd just noticed Jim wasn't there.

"He left me. Remember?"

Her father nodded and speared more turkey. "That's right. Like your mother left me."

"Well," Ava said, "if you call dying leaving."

"No, she left us."

"Okay," Ava said.

"Everyone left us," he said, turning teary eyes to Ava. "Didn't they?"

"Yes," she said, covering his hand with hers, and those memories she tried so hard to keep at bay flooded her. The angle of Lily's neck. Sirens. The face of that policeman.

"Where's Jim?" her father asked her again.

"Gone," Ava answered.

■ ■ ■ ■

A November night, thirteen months ago. Ava hated herself for being able to point to how many months and weeks and days and even goddamn hours it had been since that night when everything changed. She and Jim had been sitting together after dinner, watching the local news on TV. Ava had her feet in Jim's lap as she corrected student papers. She'd been teaching French at the university for years now, a job she loved. Years earlier, when she was a French major with dreams of working at the UN or perhaps at a publishing house where she would translate novels into French, she would have never believed that she'd be happy teaching students French grammar and conjugations, listening to them stumble as they awkwardly read newspaper articles aloud or recited poetry. But she was happy doing it. She loved how their faces brightened when they actually understood what they read or when they had conversations with one another in French.

That night, Ava graded their French 101 quizzes on conjugating *-er, -ir,* and *-re* verbs while Jim reviewed college essays for Pathways to Success, the nonprofit company he ran. Pathways to Success helped underprivileged students in the lowest-performing high schools gain academic success and get scholarships to college. Periodically he blurted things like, "You nailed it, Thida!" Or: "Way to go, Felipe!" She liked this too, their quiet nights together. Sometimes they played backgammon, or spirited games of Pitch, the card game that the whole family used to play together, splitting into two very competitive teams.

They didn't usually watch the local news, but yet another snowstorm was predicted for the next day, and they both had become obsessed with storm tracking this snowy winter. Ava tried to concentrate on *parler, finir,* and *admettre.*

If Cate or anyone had asked, Ava would have said they were in an especially good phase. Maggie, who had given them plenty of trouble as a teenager, seemed to have finally turned herself around. That's why Ava had felt confident about sending her to Florence. And Will, who had inherited Jim's do-gooder gene, was happily working for a nonprofit in Africa. Ava and Jim had even been making love again, more than they had in years. That too had ebbed and then returned, albeit without its former gusto.

They'd been making plans for the summer just that morning. She'd sent in the deposit on a beach house in Westport, Massachusetts. For one glorious month, they'd leave the heat of Providence and spend their days on the beach.

"I wish it was already July," Ava said, putting down her red pen and the last paper she'd corrected, which had a plethora of red Xs on it. "No conjugating verbs. No correcting papers. Just beach and sunshine and thou."

When Jim didn't answer, Ava followed his gaze to the television, where a reporter stood beneath the statue of Roger Williams that overlooked the city from Prospect Park.

"What is that?" Ava asked. She narrowed her eyes to see the screen better, her glasses only good close up these days.

Jim was grinning.

"Someone has dressed him up," he said, amused.

The screen came into focus. Sure enough, Roger Williams had on a blue and white scarf with a matching hat and gloves.

Ava picked up the next quiz. Already she could tell that the student had completely confused the *-er* and *-ir* verbs.

"Kind of a waste of time, isn't it?" she muttered as she lifted her red pen and began marking Xs. "Dressing statues?"

"Wait a minute," Jim said, leaning forward enough that Ava's feet dropped from his lap. "I know her."

"Of course you do. That's Hayley Morrow. She's been reporting forever," Ava said.

But Jim wasn't listening. He was leaning forward, his eyes shining, as if to get as close as possible to the television.

"My God! It's Delia Lindstrom!"

Ava looked at the television again, this time taking her glasses off. Beside short, squat Hayley Morrow, wrapped in a dowdy wool pea coat, stood a tall auburn-haired woman wearing a fake leopard coat and very high black boots.

"Ms. Lindstrom," Hayley Morrow was saying, "some people believe you dressed Roger Williams here."

Delia Lindstrom did not look at Hayley Morrow. She did not look at Roger Williams. No, she looked right at the camera. Later, Ava would remember it as she looked right at Jim.

"Well," she said, "he did look cold."

"I *slept* with her!" Jim said, as if he'd done something truly marvelous.

Years ago, back when they'd first started sleeping together, they'd told each other everyone they'd had sex with. The lists were woefully short, and Ava was certain she'd remember a name like Delia Lindstrom.

"You did? When?"

"In Greece, of all places. The summer of my Eurail pass."

"Yarn bombing is a type of graffiti," Hayley Morrow was explaining to the viewers, "that uses colorful displays of knitted yarn rather than paint or chalk. Although these may last for years, they're considered temporary, and, unlike other graffiti, can be easily removed if necessary. Nonetheless, the practice is still technically illegal, isn't it, Ms. Lindstrom?" she added, gazing up the full length of Delia Lindstrom.

"Technically, yes," Delia said. "Though one would have to be caught and then prosecuted."

"Ms. Lindstrom," Hayley Morrow said in her serious reporter voice, "other forms of graffiti are considered political commentary or self-expressions or even vandalism. What is the point of yarn bombing?"

"Yarn bombing is about reclaiming and personalizing sterile or cold public places," Delia answered, again looking straight at the camera.

Those words still replayed in Ava's mind, even all these months later. *Yarn bombing is about reclaiming and personalizing sterile or cold public places.* That was just what Delia

Lindstrom had done with Jim — reclaimed him.

Aged Oaks had gone overboard with the decorations. Everywhere Ava looked she saw smiling Santas and snowmen, shiny gold or silver garlands, twinkling multicolored lights. The staff all wore Santa hats with their names written in glitter across the front, and Muzak Christmas carols played nonstop over the intercom.

Ava was relieved to get away from the holiday assault and inside her own house. At the last minute she'd relented and bought a pre-decorated tabletop tree with small gold balls hanging from its branches and a string of tiny starburst-shaped white lights. As she entered the dark house, those lights glowed at her. The sight of that little happy tree made her sit down right there in the front hall and cry.

For some reason, her father had given her a bottle of Bailey's Irish Cream for Christmas, something she'd never liked. It came in a decorative gift set, with two shot glasses with green shamrocks on them. Once she'd composed herself, she opened the box and pulled out one of the glasses and the Bailey's, poured it and took a sip. Chalky. Too sweet. But oddly comforting. She unbuttoned her winter coat, a tweed one that Jim had always liked.

"Merry Christmas," she said out loud, holding the ridiculous glass up in a toast.

Ava sighed. How had she ended up here on the floor in her foyer, drinking Bailey's Irish Cream alone on Christmas night? She should get up, make herself some dinner, have a glass of good wine, for God's sake. But she seemed frozen to that spot, as if her broken heart weighed her down, made it impossible to move.

Her cell phone buzzed, deep in her coat pocket.

"Merry Christmas!" her daughter's voice rang out.

"Maggie!"

"Did you have a good one?"

"I spent it with Gramps."

"I hope you gave him a big smooch from me," Maggie said.

"What did you do to celebrate?"

"Oh, they gave us a big dinner and like, a little party. Secret Santas. You know."

"What did you get?"

"What?" Maggie said, distracted.

"What did your Secret Santa give you?"

"Oh. Um. You know, one of those wooden Pinocchios that are all over Florence. We had a five-euro limit."

"Remember in third grade when your Secret Santa was that boy? His father was a famous actor or something? And he gave you a Game Boy? Everyone else was getting holiday socks and Beanie Babies and —"

"I'm so glad you had a great day, Mom! I'll call on Sunday."

"Oh. Okay," Ava said. In the background she could hear party sounds, happy sounds. "Send me some pictures?"

"I put them on Instagram," Maggie said.

She blew a noisy kiss, said "Ciao," and was gone.

Ava sighed again and reached to turn off her phone when she saw that she had two voicemails.

The first one was from Will. It always surprised her how clearly his voice came through from so far away, and in such a remote place. "All is well, Merry Christmas, I love you." She smiled at her son's no-nonsense tone.

The next one had a number she didn't recognize.

"Hi, Ava," came Jim's voice. "Sorry I missed you. Just wanted to say Happy Holidays. We're in Peru until after New Year's, finally getting to hike up to Machu Picchu."

There was a pause long enough to make

Ava wonder if he'd hung up.

Then his achingly familiar voice again.

"Merry Christmas, kiddo."

And a click.

Peru?

She thought of the casual *we* he'd used. And had he actually called her *kiddo*?

Forgetting it was Christmas, Ava called Cate.

"You are not going to believe this," Ava began without even giving her friend any holiday wishes. "Jim actually called me. From Peru. He said *we're* in Peru. He called me *kiddo.*"

"Ew," Cate said.

"He said he's finally getting to hike up to Machu Picchu. Finally? He never once mentioned wanting to hike up to Machu Picchu. I mean, did you ever hear him say anything like that? Ever?"

"I'm sorry, sweetie," Cate said.

Ava heard the sounds of people laughing, distant strains of music.

"You're having a party," she said.

"No!" Cate said. "Not a party. It's just . . . well, it's Christmas. And Gray made his eggnog."

Gray's eggnog. Last year — every year — Ava and Jim had gone over and drunk Gray's eggnog. Too much bourbon. Gray in a ridiculous Christmas sweater with a reindeer whose nose lit up red. The disgusting dip Cate made in her crockpot with cream cheese, Rotel tomatoes, and breakfast sausage.

"You got the invite, didn't you?"

Ava's eyes drifted to the pile of unopened mail sitting on the bottom step.

"We'd love to have you. Really," Cate was saying.

"I have a date," Ava said. "With Jane Austen."

"Are you sure?"

Ava squeezed her eyes shut. She could picture Gray in that stupid sweater, his shaggy hair, his eyes behind his wire-rimmed glasses. And Cate urging that dip — mommy crack, she called it — on everyone. And couples, wives with their husbands, arms crooked together, ironic eye rolls, jokes, snipes, private signals, all of the intimacies of marriage.

"I'm sure," Ava said.

The afternoon of New Year's Eve, Cate convinced Ava to walk downtown for Bright Night, the city's way of ringing in the New Year with live performances and fireworks. Without hesitating, Ava agreed. She and Jim had hated New Year's Eve, with its forced gaiety and resolutions and silly hats. They'd always stayed home together and cooked something complicated: cassoulet or duck à l'orange or beef Wellington. Sometimes Cate and Gray joined them for dinner. Last year Will and Maggie had both still been home, and Cate and Gray's kids came too, the eight of them moving through the kitchen, chopping and tasting and stirring. After they ate, they'd played charades, a game choice that struck Ava now as both ironic and fitting. Jim had been fucking Delia Lindstrom for over a month by then.

Happy to get out, she put on enough layers to make the buttons on her coat strain. Before she left, unable to keep from worrying about Maggie, she checked her email. Just Maggie's usual cryptic messages. *The Uffizi is always so crowded!!!* Followed by a row of angry red faces. And: *Someone told me in Naples they throw all their old furniture out the window on New Year's Eve. Should I go to Naples? #wearahelmet.* Ava sighed and went to Maggie's Instagram page. Maybe she had gone to Naples. But no. There was only shot after shot of the Duomo from every possible angle. A photograph of a group of girls standing in front of it, arms draped around one another's shoulders and mugging for the camera, was taken too far away for her to make out Maggie from the others, especially with their winter hats and oversized sunglasses. Will's Facebook page proved just as disappointing. A trek to see the mountain gorillas had produced closeups of the gorillas and none of Will.

Ava tucked her phone in her pocket, pulled on her gloves, and headed down the street to meet Cate. The clouds hung low and gray, heavy no doubt with the snow the weatherman had promised. Ava shivered despite her layers, and hurried to Benefit Street where Cate was already waiting for her, stomping her feet to stay warm.

"Thanks for suggesting this," Ava said, her breath leaving a trail of puffs of cold air. "The thought of being home alone —"

"It'll be fun," Cate interrupted cheerfully. "Who doesn't want to hear a klezmer band and watch giant puppets terrify children?"

"Before I left I was remembering how last year —"

"They're going to have food trucks too," Cate interrupted again. "I've been dying to try Mama Kim's. Korean food."

Ava stopped abruptly.

"I get it," she said. "Your mission tonight is to get me to stop talking about Jim, or how my life has fallen apart, or anything related to those topics."

Cate sighed. "Sweetie, it's been almost a year."

"It doesn't work that way," Ava said. "Your heart doesn't have a calendar that turns the page at a year and then, voilà! you're over it."

Cate kicked at some dirty black snow with the toe of her boot.

"Why, I'm still not over —" Ava stopped herself, surprised at what she'd almost blurted.

"What?" Cate said, looking at her.

Ava shook her head. She didn't talk about that summer. Ever.

"I just mean that grief is more complicated than you think," Ava managed.

They continued on in silence, but Ava's mind was anything but quiet. She worked hard the rest of the walk, trying to push the terrible noises away. Trying to avoid the still, lifeless face of a little girl that threatened to appear.

It was Ava who suggested they go ice skating.

They'd listened to the klezmer band, and the all-trumpet concert. They'd found Mama Kim's truck and eaten bulgogi sliders and a pork kimchee rice bowl. They'd watched a modern dance performance and a tap dancing show. There was really not much left to do, which meant that they would have to head back up the hill toward home.

Then Ava saw the skaters gliding across the outdoor rink, scarves flying behind them like a postcard-perfect winter scene. In one corner, a teenaged couple skated a routine together, with fluid spins and twirls.

"I haven't skated since I was a kid," Cate grumbled as she laced her skates.

The line to rent them had been long, and the line to get on the ice even longer. For Ava, the wait was a relief, another way to stall her inevitable night home alone. But she did see Cate glance at her watch several times.

It was almost their turn to enter the rink when a man appeared beside them, grinning. He had on an enormous plaid fake fur hat with earflaps.

"Shouldn't you two be home reading?" he said.

"I've finished already," Cate said. She pointed her thumb at Ava and added, "This is the one we have to watch."

"I've been standing right behind you, but didn't recognize you with all the cold weather gear," the man continued.

Ava almost admitted she didn't recognize him still, when Cate said, "Ava, you remember Luke, don't you? From the book group?"

Ah! Mr. Porkpie Hat. He'd traded that one in for another ridiculous one.

"I wanted to ask you," Luke was saying, turning his full attention to Ava now, "you said your mother owned a bookstore? On Thayer Street?"

"A long time ago. Before you were born," Ava said, caught off guard.

"Cool. And a writer too?"

"No, not really," Ava said. "I mean, she wrote stories but nothing really ever came of it."

"By the way," Luke said, "that book you picked? I can't find it anywhere."

Cate nodded. "I meant to tell you, Ava. We don't have a copy at the library either. Which is odd because we do have a card for it in the old card catalogue, but no book."

The man at the entrance to the rink motioned them forward.

Awkwardly, Cate stumbled ahead onto the ice, leaving Ava beside Luke. She wanted to skate away from him, but a woman came from behind and wedged herself between them before Ava had the chance.

"This is Roxy," Luke said. "Roxy, Ava. Ava

just joined the book group."

Roxy had dyed platinum hair, very black eyebrows, and Hollywood-red lipstick.

She surveyed Ava dismissively. "Luke loves it," she said, also dismissively, Ava thought. "Maybe because he's the only guy."

They were at the edge now, being pushed forward by the people behind them.

"He's not, though," Ava said, her eyes scanning the ice for Cate.

"Right," Luke said. "Some widower. Kind of a sad sack, poor guy."

Just when Ava spotted Cate dead center, Cate's legs shot out from under her and she fell hard on her butt.

"Uh oh," Ava said, relieved to have a reason to get away. "Someone needs assistance."

She skated toward Cate, her legs wobbling at first, but growing steadier with every stroke. The sound of the blades against the ice was exciting, as if she were actually going somewhere. When she stopped, cutting the edges of her blades into the ice and sending up a small spray of snow, Ava had to keep herself from smiling down at Cate.

"Why did I let you talk me into this?" Cate moaned, trying unsuccessfully to stand up.

"You owe me," Ava said, reaching her hand to Cate. "I have to read Jane Austen."

"At least it won't hurt," Cate grumbled as she let Ava hoist her up.

Luke skated by, his arm around Roxy's waist, their legs moving in unison.

"You okay?" he called.

"I hate ice skating!" Cate called back.

"Stick with me," Ava told her.

Cate clutched Ava's arm, and let her drag her across the ice for a bit.

"See? You're getting the hang of it," Ava said when Cate relaxed her grip.

"You know what I realized?" Cate asked. "I knew you grew up here, but I never knew your mother was a writer —"

"She owned a bookstore, that was her real job. She's been dead a very long time," Ava added.

"Well, I bet she'd be glad you joined the book group," Cate said.

"I think you're doing fine now," Ava said. "Okay if I skate alone for a bit before they kick us off?"

She didn't wait for Cate to answer. Instead, she pushed easily from one foot to the other, gliding past the blur of other skaters. She circled once, twice, and still again, faster each time, focusing on nothing but her skates on the ice, the wind on her face, the steady beating of her heart.

■ ■ ■ ■

It is a truth universally acknowledged, that a single man in possession of a good fortune must be in want of a wife, Ava read.

She groaned. Was everything about marriage? Was she really meant to read almost three hundred pages of a book about a man wanting a wife? And on New Year's Eve, no less?

The ice skating and the hot chocolate afterward had brought her more pleasure than she'd had in a long time. Enough to let her curl up on the sofa under her favorite quilt with the damned book. She'd even lit a fire in the fireplace for the first time since Jim moved out, and its crackling mixed with the soft lamplight warmed Ava.

She glanced down at the book, closed now with her finger holding her place. The cover — a woman dressed formally in white, sitting on a mauve fainting chair — should have tipped her off that this was a book about love and marriage and romance and everything Ava did not want to think about, never mind read about for hours and hours.

Maybe, she thought, maybe just this once she wouldn't read the book. Surely there was a movie of *Pride and Prejudice.* She remembered Cate's teasing: No cheating. She vowed to read every other book, from *The Great Gatsby* to *Slaughterhouse-Five.* Every word. Then she went to Netflix, and scrolled down to P.

The book group met on the second Monday of every month, in that same downstairs room. Emma always set up a table of snacks related to the setting of the book. For *Pride and Prejudice,* there were scones and clotted cream and small triangles of cucumber and egg salad sandwiches. When Cate called everyone to their seats, which were arranged in a circle tonight, Ava saw that instead of her usual loose tunic over black leggings with moss green or dark red Australian walking shoes, Cate stood in front of the room in a white Empire-waist dress with a small floral pattern, her pale blonde hair pulled into a bun with stray ringlets around her face.

Ava glanced at the circle of chairs, already almost all occupied. How could she be inconspicuous with this seating arrangement?

"Hey there, Peggy Fleming," Luke said, holding a chair out for her.

There was nothing for her to do except sit.

"You looked good out there," he said. He had the porkpie hat on again, and the same flannel shirt.

"Peggy Fleming?" Ava said, balancing her plate of sandwiches on top of the book in her lap. "A little before your time, wasn't she?"

"My mother loved her," he admitted.

"Ah," Ava said. So she was old enough to be his mother?

Luke tilted his chin at the book. "How'd you like it?"

Ava swallowed, feeling a little guilty. "I enjoyed it," she said.

She had enjoyed the movie, enough to wonder if she might have actually liked the book too. She'd even gone to the bookstore and bought all of the other books. She lined them up on the night table on Jim's side of the bed, waiting for her to open them.

"Just so John and Ava don't think I've lost my mind," Cate began, "as an homage to the beginning of this book club when we would actually recreate meals from the books —"

"I cooked for a week when we read *Like Water for Chocolate,*" Diana interrupted.

Penny and Ruth laughed.

"Not funny," Monique said. "I had to make the food for *Angela's Ashes.*"

"You can see why we stopped doing that," Ruth explained.

"I dress vaguely related to the book —" Cate began, but was interrupted by Ruth.

"You refused to wear an antebellum gown when we read *Gone With the Wind.*"

"True," Cate said. "But I do try. We are serious readers, of course. But we like to have fun with the books too. That's why Emma works so hard on our snacks."

"I like it," John said softly. "Every Halloween my wife made us elaborate costumes. Like once, she constructed an electrical outlet costume for her, and I was a plug."

"I should do that for my twins," Ruth said. "They've been Tweedledee and Tweedledum too many times."

Cate started giving background about the book and Jane Austen, and the group settled into a comfortable silence.

"For someone who wrote behind a creaky door so that she would know when visitors approached so she could hide her manuscripts, Jane Austen has certainly given up her anonymity," Cate said.

Ava tried to concentrate on Cate's description of the social milieu of Regency England and the class divisions, but her mind kept wandering. Jim was back from Peru. She knew because she'd spotted his reliable blue

Prius on her way to the library, parked just two blocks from home. What had he been doing on Williams Street? For a silly moment, she thought he'd parked there and then walked to their old house, maybe to see her, maybe to reconsider his moving out. Out of the house, out of their life. All of it so swift that she was still reeling from it. But as soon as she had the thought, she dismissed it. There were countless reasons for him to be in their neighborhood, more than she could list.

Ava had to work hard to blot out the image of the bumper of Jim's Prius wrapped in pale pink yarn.

"I think it's important to say," Penny said, standing and peering at the group through thick bifocals, "that although Ms. Austen is critical of the upper crust, she also does a good job of satirizing the lower class."

Ava sat up straighter. Apparently she'd daydreamed through Cate's introduction and the discussion had begun.

"Well, in her lifetime England did restrict social mobility, didn't they?" Ruth said.

"In her lifetime?" Jen said, shaking her head. "We restrict social mobility today too."

"I suppose that's true," Penny said. "But I was from old Boston stock and I married the son of mill workers."

"Was your family okay with that, though?" Kiki asked.

Penny smiled. "Yes. Once he became president of the bank."

Ava tried to come up with something to say, but all she could think about was that damn yarn-bombed bumper.

"Let's not forget she was also funny," Honor said, and launched into a PhD-sounding argument about humor versus drama.

Ava forced herself to focus. In the movie, she'd liked the overly romantic scene when Elizabeth and Mr. Darcy met up in the rain. But that didn't seem to add anything to the conversation.

She sensed a pause.

"The character of Elizabeth is curious," she said into the space of quiet. "She's so ill-tempered and rude, yet I think we're meant to like her."

Jennifer was frowning at Ava.

"Actually," Cate said carefully, "Elizabeth is quite sweet-natured."

Now Ava was frowning. Had she mixed up the characters somehow? No. Keira Knightley was Elizabeth, she was sure of that.

The discussion got directed to another topic, about Austen's relevance today, but

Jennifer kept giving Ava sidelong glances.

The actress, Diana, said she hadn't been able to stop reading, to see if Elizabeth would end up with Darcy after all.

"Oh, I knew they'd end up together from the start," Ava said, happy for another opportunity. "The way Elizabeth looks at him at that first ball, you just knew."

"At the first ball?" Kiki said. "You're talking about the movie, aren't you? With Keira Knightley?"

Ava squirmed in her seat.

"In the movie," Kiki said to the group, "Elizabeth totally telegraphs her interest in Mr. Darcy as soon as they meet."

Ava heard Luke chuckle beside her.

John stood and cleared his throat. "Now, I'm not going to say I didn't have some trouble with this one," he said. "But it seems to me that men during that time had lots of options. But women had only one: a good marriage."

Without warning, perhaps from her embarrassment or the wine, Ava burst into tears.

"Oh my," Penny said, her heavy, cluttered gold charm bracelet clanking as her hand shot to her mouth.

"I'm sorry," Ava managed. "It's just . . . I lost my husband last year, and all this talk of marriage and love is hard."

John, in his lime green fleece and Topsiders, strode across the room and wrapped her in a big hug. He smelled good, like coconut and lime, like a tropical island. And the fleece was soft against her cheek. Ava thought she could stay just like this forever.

But eventually John released Ava, and went back to his seat.

There was talk about the motifs of courtship and journeys, the meaning of Pemberley, Mr. Darcy's estate, as a symbol. Ava didn't even try to participate. She'd been caught cheating, there was no need to pretend.

"Before we return for some more wine and British treats," Cate said, "I want to remind you that next month's selection is *The Great Gatsby,* the book that matters most to Luke."

"I have a dreadful reminder," Diana said. "Chemo Thursday."

"It's my turn, D," Honor said. "Pick you up at ten."

"And I'm going to watch the movie *Clueless* Friday night, if anyone's interested in coming over," Kiki said. "It's a modern retelling of *Emma.* Thought it would be fun."

"That sounds divine," Diana said.

Jennifer's hand shot up.

"Cate, remember I emailed you about Ava's choice?" she said.

Ava felt her cheeks growing hot.

"That's right," Cate said. "Ava? I'm sorry but remember? We're having trouble finding copies of *From Clare to Here.*"

Ava said, "I have one. I could maybe pass it around?"

"How about choosing another book?" Ruth said.

"That's a thought," Cate said.

"But it's supposed to be the book that matters most to us," Ava said. "And that's mine."

Ava looked at everyone, their faces turned toward her.

"And besides," Ava added, "the writer has agreed to come and speak to our book group."

As soon as she said the words, she wanted to take them back. What was she thinking? For all she knew, Rosalind Arden was dead. The book had come out ages ago. And even if she were alive, she could live far away, or be too old to travel. She could refuse.

"We've never had the writer come before," Penny said. "That would be interesting."

Cate was studying Ava's face. Did her friend know she was lying? Did she understand it was out of desperation?

"I'll call the intra-library exchange folks," Cate said finally, "see if they have a copy or two."

"We have until November," Luke said. "We'll be able to find some by then."

Relieved, Ava thanked everyone. As they turned from her and their chatter filled the air, Ava felt a spark of something inside take hold. She would find Rosalind Arden. She would tell her how, as a sad little girl, she'd read *From Clare to Here,* over and over for an entire summer. She would explain to Rosalind Arden how her sister had died on a beautiful June morning, and how her mother had spent the next year grieving until she couldn't stand it anymore and drove away from Ava and her father, straight to the Jamestown Bridge, where she'd jumped to her death. Could a writer understand how her book had saved someone long ago, when the world was a fragile, scary place and the people she loved weren't in it anymore? Could a writer understand that her book had mattered more than anything? Ava didn't know the answer. But she was going to find out. She would find Rosalind Arden and tell her everything. And just the thought of that lifted her spirits and allowed her to join the people beside her who were happily talking about books.

When Ava stepped outside into the cold January night, she paused to look up at the clear sky. Despite the lights from the city below, stars cluttered it.

"Pretty," came a voice from behind her.

Ava turned to find John standing, hands in pockets, also looking up.

"Do you ever think maybe they're up there looking down at us?" he asked.

"Who?" Ava asked, then quickly realized what he meant: his wife and her husband.

"Maybe," she said. She tried to think of how to explain about Jim. But she couldn't embarrass herself twice in the same night, could she? Next time, she decided.

John stayed quiet, staring up at the sky.

"Well," Ava said finally, "goodnight."

"Wait," he said, taking a step toward her. "There was a quote in the book that I really liked. So much, I wrote it down."

She waited as he retrieved one of those Moleskine notebooks from his inside pocket and carefully tore out a page.

"Here," he said.

Before she could read it or even respond, he nodded a goodnight and walked off.

Ava stepped under the one light beaming

above the door and read what John had written.

Think only of the past as its remembrance gives you pleasure.

"John?" she called into the darkness.

But he was gone. She folded the paper in half, and placed it in her coat pocket.

Maggie

Of course, he was married.

Although she didn't learn it that first night, it became clear soon enough. The apartment on rue Saint-Antoine was a second flat, the one that Julien kept for his work, which involved art installations. He represented artists, and the loft was full of oversized masks and paintings in vivid Caribbean colors or bold abstract images. Julien told her that he kept it for his work, but she never saw him actually work there. Sometimes he arrived, out of breath from the one-hundred-step climb, carrying a canvas. Sometimes he left with a piece of the art from the apartment. But he never spoke on the phone or looked at papers or brought artists inside. Once, he went out on the small balcony and called down to someone standing near the Saint-Paul Métro stop across the street. "He could come up," she'd offered. And Julien had laughed and tousled her hair and said, "Impossible."

She decided she loved him more than she'd ever loved anyone before.

She lay on the hot pink sofa that formed a large U in the center of the loft, stoned, watching him want her, watching his desire grow, become fierce. His wife must be older, like him. Of course he couldn't get enough of Maggie, who never refused him, who let him do anything he wanted to her. He brought her such good-quality drugs that sometimes they knocked her flat for days. When that happened, everything turned soft and gauzy. His voice sounded as if he were at the other end of a tunnel, his body moving on her felt like they were underwater. One afternoon, whatever he gave her to smoke, cooking it so carefully in a tiny pipe for her, holding it so gently to her lips, cupping her chin in his large callused hand as she inhaled, whatever it was, it produced a halo around him, a golden light so beautiful that she believed he was truly sent from heaven.

That was when she knew for certain she loved him.

She told him so too.

She said, "I love you I love you I love you," and he grinned, showing all of his adorable crooked teeth.

"Ma petite chatte," he murmured, nuzzling her neck. "Tell me again."

"Je t'aime," she whispered, holding onto him as tight as she could, as if he was an anchor, holding her in place.

"More of that," she'd told him as he left. *"J'en reprends."*

He did bring her more of that, and she began to lose track of time.

"You've been gone so long," she'd say to him, and he would laugh and say, "But I was just here last night."

"What day is it?" she asked him one morning in the big white bed.

"Sunday," he said. "And I can stay all day today."

"Which Sunday?" she asked him.

"What does it matter, *mon petit pamplemousse*?" he said, tenderly stroking her cheek. "Everything you need is right here."

When he left to go to the bakery for fresh croissants, Maggie tried to think, tried to make her brain land on something concrete. She remembered that he'd cooked a baked pasta. Yesterday? Last week? She'd watched him as he boiled the tiny shells in milk and garlic. Her mother had just boiled them in water, but not Julien. She remembered how sometimes he looked like he was under a strobe light when he moved, how she'd watched from the hot pink sofa as he moved around the kitchen leaving those streaks of light as he did. She remembered that one afternoon, alone, she'd written a very good sentence in her notebook. A brilliant one. She'd used green ink.

Julien was climbing back up the ladder, a tray with café au laits and the chocolate croissants she liked so much in his hands.

"I'm writing a wonderful story," she told him.

He fed her a croissant, wiped the flakes of pastry from her collarbone.

"Like Hemingway?" he asked her.

Her heart sped up. He was taking that pipe from the tray; she hadn't even seen it there, and now he was holding a match to it.

"In the minimalist style," she said, feeling her body tremble ever so slightly.

"Sit up, *coccinelle,*" he said.

Grapefruit. Ladybug. He called her so many pet names.

"I love you," she said, lifting her face up, opening her mouth, eager.

He bought her clothes too. Even though she told him that her father had put enough money in a bank account for her to live for a year abroad, he insisted. He arrived, huffing from the one hundred steps, with shopping bags from Agnès B. filled with striped shirts and soft V-neck t-shirts, high-waisted black bell-bottoms in a fluid jersey material, Mary Janes with little straps and chunky heels. If he decided to take her out to dinner, he chose her outfit. The snug black dress with the flowered Peter Pan collar or the navy blue and white checked.

He called her his little artichoke, his plum, his tulip. He brought *macarons* from Pierre Hermé, and bread from Poilâne, and cheese from Laurent Dubois.

"This Roquefort," he said, opening the wax paper on the cheese and releasing a pungent stink, "is a very old cheese, dating from before the Roman conquest of Gaul. It ripens for three months in the Combalou caves below Roquefort-sur-Soulzon."

She nibbled the cracker smeared with it that he handed her.

"I'll take you there sometime," Julien said. "Would you like that? To go to the Combalou caves with me?"

She put down the cracker, one tiny corner eaten.

"Yes," she told him. "Take me there. When can we go?"

He held the cracker to her lips. "Eat," he

said softly. "You're too thin."

She forced herself to eat it, but the taste made her gag.

"And the ocean," she said, after she drank some wine. "Take me to the ocean. To Nice."

"Yes, yes," he said. "We should go to Nice and you will lie in the sun and turn golden brown."

"I'll lie in the sun topless," she said. She closed her eyes, as if she could feel the warm sun beating down on her.

Julien opened another package, broke off a piece of hard cheese.

"This is from Monbéliarde cows. They are known for their sweet milk."

He told her to taste it.

"What does it remind you of?" he asked her.

"Butterscotch," she said, and he smiled and kissed her, his hands stinking from cheese grabbing her face and holding it hard.

"My brilliant *pomme de terre,*" he whispered.

She didn't know when his visits became less frequent. When the weather turned colder? When the hard rain began to fall almost daily? Maggie lay on the hot pink sofa, waiting, staring out at the gray sky, the rain on the tiled rooftops of the Marais. She realized then that although he could call her any time, she had no number for him. On her phone, it showed up as blocked. One day, she noticed that Christmas lights had been strung up on the buildings opposite. She went out onto the balcony and watched people with large bouquets of flowers and fresh baguettes moving quickly through the rain. She wrapped her arms around her thin body, shivering out there, watching everyone pass by.

Back inside, she pulled on the black bell-bottoms and a long-sleeved striped top, not even bothering to put on underwear first. She poured a big glass of wine, and drank it down with a handful of pills. Then she grabbed a trench coat, the tags still hanging from it, and an umbrella, and went quietly down the one hundred steps. Julien had warned her that she must never make noise outside the apartment, in the stairs or hallways of the building. He said a cantankerous old woman lived in one of the apartments, and reported noise to the landlord. Later, Maggie realized there was probably no neighbor; Julien wanted her to remain unnoticed.

Outside, the rain fell as heavily as it had

that first night she'd met Julien. A cold horizontal siege. Despite the expensive coat, the large umbrella, she was soon drenched. Maggie closed the umbrella and dropped it into a trashcan. She was already wet, what did it matter? Besides, the pills had kicked in and she felt like she was skimming the sidewalk, not really walking on it, even though her shoes were quickly wet and water sloshed inside them as she moved.

She walked down the rue de Rivoli, through crowds coming or going from important places. She walked and she walked, but she felt like she was swimming now. Her hands made small motions, as if they were helping part the water. Deep inside her, there was a constant roller coaster feeling, as if she were poised at the top of a hill, about to go flying down. She crossed streets, walked along the Seine, lost track of time. Lost track of place for a while, too.

The rain slowed to a steady drizzle. Maggie found herself shivering in front of the Musée d'Orsay, the high that had propelled her outside now faded, leaving a dull headache in its place. All these months in Paris and she'd never been inside this museum. The former railway station was itself considered a work of art, and inside were three hundred paintings and sculptures, mostly by the Impressionists. Maggie patted her wet hair. Where was her umbrella? She remembered taking it with her when she walked out. But somehow it was gone.

"C'est combien, l'admission?" she asked at the entrance.

Despite Maggie's near perfect accent, the woman replied in English, "You're in luck. It's the first Sunday of the month. Admission is free."

Maggie frowned. "The first Sunday?" she repeated.

The woman did not hide her disdain. "*Oui, mademoiselle.* Today is the first Sunday of January."

"But that's impossible!" Maggie said.

She stood, struggling to remember the past weeks. The cheese that tasted like butterscotch. The tender way he'd lifted the pipe to her lips. Vaguely, she could remember speaking to her mother on the telephone. She could remember that golden halo around Julien.

"You going in or what?" a gruff voice said behind Maggie.

She nodded, frightened. Her head throbbed.

Even the vast beauty of the museum, with its large windows and row after row of paintings that seemed familiar, even that could not calm the fear rising in her. How could she have forgotten Christmas? Had there been a present from Julien? A special dinner? She could remember the baked pasta, how carefully he'd measured the milk, how thinly he'd cut the garlic. Had that been their Christmas dinner? He called her his *coccinelle,* his *pamplemousse.* She chewed her lip hard enough to make it bleed, and sucked back the metallic taste.

In a gallery of Monets, Maggie paused. They cast a soothing light across the room, and she remembered how much her mother loved Monet. When Maggie was young, her mother had taken her to the Museum of Fine Arts in Boston to see a special Monet exhibition. She'd tried to explain the beauty of his work, but Maggie had refused to listen to her, or to be kind. She'd discovered boys by then, and drinking and smoking pot in the backseats of their cars. It was what had consumed her, those boys. Sex and drugs, shoplifting gum and candy bars, drinking warm Pabst Blue Ribbons and gobbling pills stolen from parents' medicine cabinets. Standing in front of those Monets, though, her mother hadn't known yet what Maggie was up to.

And now, standing here in front of these

Monets, she missed her mother with a sharp pain in her gut that made her hurry out of the room. She considered calling her, and telling her that she was here, at the Musée d'Orsay, that the Monets were lovely.

But she didn't. She couldn't. She was supposed to be in Florence, studying Renaissance art.

In front of a Degas — it had to be a Degas, she knew, it was ballet dancers rehearsing — she stopped. Her breath caught. Unlike the way she imagined Degas's dancers in her mind, up close Maggie saw that they looked tired, their faces hard and set, weary. They slumped and stretched and held their aching backs. She wondered if she looked that way too?

She hadn't noticed the family standing beside her. They were American. A blonde mother in a navy blue sweater set; a father and son both dressed in khakis and V-neck sweaters, the father's lemon yellow, the son's baby blue; the little girl, maybe only six or seven years old, wore an improbably frilly dress, and imitated the poses of the dancers in the painting. The mother eyed Maggie, and herded the family away from her slightly.

She hadn't noticed the tour guide either, until he spoke.

"As Paul Valéry said, 'Degas is one of the very few painters who gave the ground its true importance. He has some admirable floors.' "

The family laughed.

"Of course," the tour guide continued, "this is all the more appropriate for dancers in that the parquet is their main work tool."

The mother nodded, clearly the one in charge of her little brood.

"Who's the man there?" she asked, pointing to the sole male in the painting.

"The ballet master," the tour guide told her. "He's beating time on the floor with his baton."

The tour guide glanced at Maggie and winked, as if they were in cahoots. He was American too, with a slight hint of a New England accent and an unruly shock of brown hair that kept falling into his eyes, which were a startling blue. He looked as if he were in prep school.

She pretended she hadn't been eavesdropping and focused on a vague point in the painting, *The Ballet Class.*

"The girls look . . . well . . ." the mother stammered. "Streetwise?"

"They are," the tour guide said. "Some of the city's poorest young girls struggled to become the fairies, nymphs, and queens of the stage. At the ballet, you see, Degas found a world that excited both his taste for classical beauty and his eye for modern realism."

"Stop twirling," the father said sternly to the little girl, who kept twirling.

"Sophie, you'll like this bronze sculpture over here," the tour guide said, taking the little girl's hand and leading her to *Small Dancer at Fourteen.*

Maggie followed too, trying to keep a safe distance. But the tour guide was on to her. He grinned in her direction, flashing one deep dimple.

"Originally, she had real hair, a real tutu and real dancing slippers," he explained.

"I have to peepee," the little girl said.

After some negotiating — "Can't you hold it? We're almost done, aren't we, Noah?" — the mother took the little girl to the bathroom. Relieved, the father and brother plopped onto a bench, both of them pulling out their phones.

The tour guide — Noah — walked over to Maggie.

"You got caught in the rain," he said.

"Brilliant deduction," she said.

"And I'm guessing you're not a tourist? You live here?"

"More brilliant still."

"I'm always happy to hang with fellow ex-pats," he said. He took a card from his shirt pocket. "I live over near the Pompidou," he added.

She shoved the card into her coat pocket.

"Near the doll hospital? And that little bookstore?" he said.

Maggie wished she could smoke in here. Her body needed something — nicotine, caffeine, anything.

"There's a café in that same alley. It's the only one there," he said. "If you want to have a coffee, trade expat secrets."

"Maybe," Maggie said, knowing she would lose the card, or throw it away.

"I go there every morning," he said.

In her pocket, her phone buzzed. She took it out, saw the blocked number light up.

"I have to go," she said, turning, already answering the telephone.

"I'm at the apartment," Julien said. "I want you."

"Maybe I'll see you there tomorrow," Noah called to her.

"Did you know it's January?" she asked Julien, her voice trembling. "I mean, how can it be January?"

"Ah! Ma petite camée," he said. "I shall remind you of December."

Maggie didn't know the word *camée.*

Some exotic fruit, no doubt. She thought of kumquats and rambutans and mangosteens. Perhaps he had brought her some. She loved biting into the tart skins of kumquats.

The same woman was at the desk, looking officious.

"Qu'est-ce que c'est une camée?" Maggie asked her.

The woman looked her up and down slowly.

"Mademoiselle," she said, "I would think you would know the word. In English, it is junkie."

■ ■ ■ ■

Part Three: February

■ ■ ■ ■

"You see I usually find myself among strangers because I drift here and there trying to forget the sad things that happened to me."
— *The Great Gatsby* by F. Scott Fitzgerald

Ava

After the monthly faculty meeting, all of the teachers went to the Ground Round for burgers and beer, and to complain about whatever new rules or policies had been discussed at the meeting. Ava used to enjoy these evenings, lost in the bureaucracy of the French department. She liked coming home and telling Jim who was sleeping with whom, who wasn't getting tenure, who was secretly applying for jobs elsewhere. Her colleagues had taken on the stock roles of the characters in commedia dell'arte, the traditional Italian theater. She'd met Jim when she was in graduate school studying French at NYU and he was performing in a commedia troupe on the Lower East Side of New York. Through the years, they'd used the characters from it as a secret code. Even Jim referred to Xavier Plouff, her department chair, as Brighella, the coarse, scheming, low-level merchant who was mean-spirited and occasionally violent to characters whose station was lower than his.

She should join them at the Ground Round tonight, Ava knew. But as they filed out of Plouff's stuffy conference room, she hesitated. As yet another form of torture for the faculty, Plouff insisted on meeting in the smaller room adjacent to his office instead of the larger department one, forcing them to sit shoulder to shoulder at odd angles to fit into the tight space.

"How are your classes this semester?" Plouff asked her.

"Great!" Ava said, because that was what you always said to Plouff. He didn't take criticism or complaints well.

"One more thing," he continued, even though Ava was halfway out the door. "I saw your husband on television the other night."

It wasn't unusual for Jim to show up on TV, talking about high school dropout rates or highlighting one of his success stories.

Ava murmured something noncommittal.

"Yes, yes," Plouff was saying, "something about putting a coat on the Independent Man?"

The Independent Man, an eleven-foot-tall gilded bronze statue, stood on top of the dome of the statehouse in Providence, a symbol of freedom.

"Excuse me?" Ava asked, confused, although she shouldn't have been.

"I guess he didn't mention to you that some friend of his climbed two hundred and seventy-eight feet to the dome and actually placed a knitted coat on the Independent Man?"

Ava groaned.

Plouff was grinning at her. "Do you know her? The friend? Delia somebody?"

"Lindstrom," Ava said.

"Apparently they think he assisted her in this prank," Plouff went on, still grinning. "I never saw Jim as the criminal type."

"He's full of surprises," Ava said.

Plouff nodded. "Indeed. Well, *à demain.*"

With that, he shut the door, satisfied no doubt that he'd embarrassed her.

With relief, Ava saw that Monique was waiting for her at the end of the hall.

"Coming?" Monique asked, holding the door open for her.

Ava nodded. A burger and beer and gossip sounded like just what she needed after all.

A light snow fell as Ava made her way up Benefit Street to the Athenaeum for the book group. She had done it again. She'd started the book, read the first three or four pages, and put it down. There didn't seem to be any plot or setting or character yet, which made Ava think *The Great Gatsby* was going to be a very slow read, just as when she'd had to read it in college years ago. And of course she hadn't picked it up until the day before the book group, her plan being to spend the entire night reading. To her relief, there were actually two movies of *The Great Gatsby,* and she watched them both. She preferred the older one, with Robert Redford and Mia Farrow, but of course she had to keep her opinions on the movies to herself.

Instead, she copied her favorite lines into her own Moleskine notebook, bought to show the others how serious she was about being part of the book group. Daisy said, *All the bright precious things fade so fast . . . and they don't come back.* This seemed to Ava one of the wisest things she'd ever heard. But she couldn't find the quote in the book, so she also jotted down *that's the best thing a girl can be in this world, a beautiful little fool,* from page 21. It seemed like a provocative thing to say. Otherwise, Ava intended to keep quiet.

At Williams Street, Ava stopped. There, again, sat Jim's Prius, the bumper wrapped in pink yarn but this time with red hearts knit into it.

Ava glanced around her. The streets were empty, quiet.

She turned the corner onto Williams Street and walked over to Jim's car. How she wished she could do something, something awful, like scrape her key across the door or smash a window. But she felt as impotent standing there as she had the night she'd woken him, thrusting that phone with the text message — *miss u babe* — in his face. He'd admitted everything that night, and even as Ava saw her life begin to unravel, she'd heard herself saying that if he stopped the affair, they could work this out, stay together, do better. As a younger woman, she had believed that such a betrayal would destroy a marriage. But standing squarely in middle age, faced with her husband's infidelity, she saw things differently. Couples rebuilt from such wreckage, didn't they? Jim had held her hand then, as if they were on a first date, light and careful. "Just end it and we'll get back on track," she told him. "Oh God, Ava," he'd said, "I love her. I'm in love with her."

Remembering that night now, Ava felt tears well up. She saw, in the glow of the streetlight, a short tail of pink yarn at the end of the bumper. Glancing around again, finding the streets still empty, Ava reached down and took that soft strand in her hand, tugging and tugging until the knitting unraveled, the yarn falling in a pink tangle to the snow. When the bumper was bare again, Ava collected the yarn and shoved it into her bag. There was so much of it that she couldn't close the zipper.

"Take that," she muttered, and then kicked the nearest tire, twice. "Babe."

Her unraveling had taken her long enough to make her late. Cate was already talking when Ava walked in, her coat and hair dusted with snow.

"Sorry," Ava said.

Luke smiled and tapped the empty seat beside him. Ava scurried over to it and sat.

By the time Ava got her coat off and opened her Moleskine notebook — hoping the others saw it — Penny was standing.

"We all know the wonderful Twain quote, 'A classic is a book everyone's heard of but no one reads,' " she said. "But in the case of *The Great Gatsby,* I would offer the Italo Calvino quote, 'A classic is a book that has never finished saying what it has to say.' For I have read *The Great Gatsby* numerous times, and always discover new things in each reading."

"I couldn't agree more," Cate said. "I was delighted when Luke chose it, and I wonder if he might tell us why this is the book that matters most to him?"

Luke not only got up, but he walked with his long-legged stride to the front of the circle, where Cate stood. He adjusted his hat, then began to speak.

"I remember the first time I read *The Great Gatsby,*" he said. "Eleventh-grade English. I was that kid who spent all his time in the art room, an okay student, but mostly unremarkable. I was secretly in love with Molly Jenkins, who was not only totally hot, but she practically ran the school. Editor of the newspaper and the yearbook, you know the type. I even contributed drawings to the newspaper just so I could see her more. I spent an awful lot of energy trying to figure out a way to ask her out. But she had this boyfriend, and this aura, you know? Then I read *The Great Gatsby* and I felt like the book was talking to me. The unattainable woman. The green light. The first time we see that light, it's described as 'minute and far away,' which makes it appear impossible to reach. But then Nick says at the end, 'It eluded us then, but that's no matter — tomorrow we will run faster, stretch out our arms farther.' And that gave me this crazy hope, this decision to run faster and stretch out my arms farther. It gave me this belief or this confidence that anything is possible."

Luke looked at each of them in turn.

"It changed my life," he said quietly.

Everyone, including Ava, burst into applause.

It took a few minutes to get back to discussing the book, but then Honor brought up the same quote Ava had decided to mention — *that's the best thing a girl can be in this world, a beautiful little fool* — which led to a lively discussion of women in the 1920s and now.

John brought up the theme of the American dream in *The Great Gatsby.*

"All those shirts," John said, holding the book close to his chest like a precious thing.

Jennifer nodded. "Such excess."

"I wonder if Gatsby would have even loved Daisy if she wasn't so rich," Kiki said. "Remember when he says, 'Her voice is full of money'?"

"Fitzgerald once said that you don't write because you want to say something," Penny said. "You write because you have something to say."

Ava smiled, warming to Penny's propensity for quoting writers.

"So what do you think he had to say that made him write *The Great Gatsby*?" Cate asked.

"That the American dream is illusory," Jennifer offered.

"At the end," Honor said, "everybody's life goes on as if there never was a Jay Gatsby."

"A Jay Gatsby reaching for that green light," Luke added.

"It's a masterpiece," Ruth said. "That's good enough for me."

This time, Ava stayed for the wine and snacks and conversation that followed.

"How come the wine is in teacups?" Ava asked Cate.

"The book takes place during Prohibition," Cate said with a smile. "It was Emma's idea."

"You know," Ava said softly, "I had forgotten how a book can affect you."

The cover of *From Clare to Here* popped into her mind, the thick paper with muted greens and grays and browns.

"I had forgotten," she said again.

John came over and put a big hand on Ava's shoulder.

"How are you holding up?" he asked her.

He looked so sincere, so earnest, that she

couldn't bring herself to explain. Instead, she just nodded vaguely and asked how he was doing.

"I have my moments," he said. "It's lonely. That's for sure."

"It is lonely," Ava agreed. She hesitated, then said, "John, at the last meeting, I gave the wrong —"

"But reading makes the time go by, doesn't it?" John said, as if he hadn't heard anything she'd said. "I look up and an hour or two has passed."

"Absolutely," Ava said. "But John . . ."

Ava swallowed hard as John stared at her, waiting.

"My husband didn't exactly die. I mean, he isn't dead," she said, feeling her cheeks burning with embarrassment.

"I don't understand," John said.

"He left me. For another woman. I didn't mean to mislead everyone. You especially."

John cocked his head, as if he was trying to see her better.

To her surprise, he nodded. "After my wife died," he said, "I went to this grief counselor. I'd never even thought about something like that before, but she helped me. She did. And she told me that there's all kinds of grief. Not just when people die, but all kinds."

"Thank you," Ava said, her embarrassment fading into gratitude.

Penny interrupted, grabbing John's arm.

"John, you and I need to make a date. I'd like to buy you dinner at the Hope Club one night this week," she said, leading him away from Ava.

Immediately, Luke stepped into the space John had left empty.

"What do you say we go for a real drink?" Luke asked.

Ava looked around to see who he was talking to.

"Me?" she asked, since no one else was around.

"I'm thinking of bourbon, maybe even a Manhattan. Some real food."

Both sounded good to Ava, even though the idea of spending more time with Luke and his porkpie hat didn't.

"Okay then," he said, surprising her by already having her coat and bag in his hands. "Let's go."

Luke seemed to know everyone at the Eddy, the small bar downtown where they walked through the snow, which fell steadier and heavier now.

He ordered two drinks called Appalachian Trails from the bartender, Louie, who high-fived and fist-bumped Luke as soon as they arrived. Ava and Luke sat at the corner table near the window, and before they even had their coats off the drinks arrived, followed by deviled eggs, oysters, and salmon crostini.

"Pathetic 1920s' snacks tonight," Luke said, popping a deviled egg in his mouth, whole.

Uncomfortable — what was she doing with this guy? — Ava sipped her drink, which was strong with bourbon and the faint taste of apple.

"I was hoping for caviar, right?" Luke said, eating another in one bite. "Very Gatsby."

She nibbled on a crostini as Luke slurped down two oysters in rapid succession. He polished off his drink and motioned to Louie for two more.

"How old are you anyway?" Ava asked him.

"Thirty-one."

Ava grimaced. But she quickly reminded herself that they were just having a drink together. Jim was actually in a relationship! Wasn't she allowed to have a drink with someone? Even if he was slightly — all right, a lot — younger?

"You're . . ." Luke began. He swallowed

down another oyster. "Enigmatic," he finished finally.

"I've been called worse," Ava said.

The second round arrived just as she finished her first drink. There was an awkwardness to the night that suited her. At least she was out somewhere, and not alone.

"Where's your wife?" she asked.

This was later, after two more Appalachian Trails each and pretzels with maple butter. Ava was pleasantly drunk. The snow was accumulating.

"Wife?" Luke said, surprised.

"Roxy."

He laughed, showing perfect teeth. His parents must have gone broke on his orthodontia bills.

"She's my on-again off-again girlfriend. Presently off."

"Not your Daisy Buchanan?"

"No," Luke said, shaking his head wistfully. "But that girl? Molly?"

"In high school?"

"Yup. That's who took my virginity."

"Really?" Ava said, surprised.

"I told you, the book changed me."

The cover of *From Clare to Here* drifted through her mind again, the drawing of stones, the girl peeking out.

"I understand," she said softly.

"See? An enigma! Not telling me what you mean."

"I mean, I understand," Ava said.

Luke grinned. "One more? Then we'll mush back up the hill."

Two Appalachian Trails later, they emerged into a full-blown blizzard.

The streets were deserted. Several inches of snow already on the ground and more falling fast.

Luke skated down Eddy Street on his shoes, sliding along the slick snow and falling at the end.

Before Ava could make her way to him, he was up, laughing, shaking snow off. He'd told her he was a metal sculptor, and he'd explained his projects — gates and trashcans and benches. To be thirty-one, Ava thought. With an on-again off-again lover. With confidence and nothing holding you back.

At the corner, he grabbed her arm and pulled her through the snow.

"Peggy Fleming's mother used to sew all of her costumes, you know," he said.

"I know."

"My mom loved Peggy Fleming," he said, shaking his head.

"Is this a mother complex or something?"

Ava asked. She pointed to him and then to herself.

"Today's her birthday," he said. "She would have been sixty-six."

"Oh!" Ava said. She stopped walking and looked him in the eye. "I'm sorry, Luke."

"God! I hate when people say that."

"So do I! I can't believe I just said it."

Luke cocked his head.

"I'm going to kiss you," he said.

"Oh no you're not," Ava said. Was she actually flirting with this guy? This kid, she reminded herself.

But then he leaned down and kissed her full on the mouth.

"Wahoo!" he screamed into the snowy night, embarrassing her.

"Mine," he said, pointing to a metal trash-can with an intricate geometric pattern.

"Prettiest trashcan I've ever seen," Ava said.

"Yes!" Luke said happily.

"So, you make trashcans? For a job?"

"I'm a metal sculptor. Went to RISD and never left."

They slipped and slid some more in silence.

"I have the most awesome idea," Luke said.

"Awesome?" Ava said, groaning.

"Let's go ice skating," he said.

"Now?"

"No time like the present. Carpe diem and all that."

"But the rink will be closed," Ava said, even as he pulled her in the opposite direction.

"So?" Luke said, with the confidence of a thirty-one-year-old.

Of course it was closed, but he lifted her over the railing and onto the ice. The snow obliterated everything around them.

"We need skates," Luke said. "Size?"

"Eight. But everything's locked up," Ava said, pointing to the little building that housed all the skates.

Luke walked off, leaving her alone in the swirling snow. Then he reappeared, on skates, another pair dangling from his hand and a lopsided grin on his face.

"How in the world —"

"My criminal past," he said, bending to take off her boots and slowly tie up her skates.

He put his arm around her waist, and kicked off with his skate. Like that, the two of them glided, side by side, around the snowy rink. Ava found herself wishing he would kiss her again, then chastised herself for being ridiculous. Too soon, the snow made it impossible to skate, and Luke released her.

"I feel like we're the only people in the world," Ava said.

"We are!"

Then he did it. He kissed her again, quick and hard, before he left her to put the skates back.

They struggled up steep College Hill, each of them slipping half a dozen times before they reached Benefit Street. The wind blew harder, making it even more difficult to see.

At Williams Street, she tugged him around the corner. Jim's car still sat there, covered in snow. Ava pulled the heap of tangled yarn from her bag and placed it on the hood.

"I borrowed that from somebody," she explained.

"It's going to get wet."

"I know," Ava said.

At her door, she paused.

"Wait. Where's your car?" she asked Luke.

He was leaning against her doorframe, looking down at her.

"I don't own a car."

Before she could ask him if the buses were still running, he was kissing her. He was finishing turning the key she'd placed in the lock. He was inside her house. He was inside her bed. This man — this boy — whom she didn't even like. But she had not been kissed in a year; not kissed like this, with passion and yearning and desire, for longer than she could remember. She was embarrassed by her body, her thickened middle-aged waist, her breasts that sagged. She wanted to tell him that she would read *The Great Gatsby,* that she would . . . what was the phrase? Run faster and stretch out her arms farther.

Instead she said, "Oh my God, I cannot believe I'm having sex with you."

Ava had forgotten.

She had forgotten how younger men, men who are not your husband, do not finish making love, roll over, and go to sleep. Making love invigorates younger men.

By the time he walked out her door into the still, white morning, they had made love three times. Her thighs still quivered. She considered calling Cate and telling her what had happened, but would Cate be angry at her? At least he'd removed that dumb hat, Ava thought with a smile.

She poured herself a cup of coffee, and the phone rang. Early for a phone call. And in a blizzard. And on the landline, which no one even used anymore.

"Hello?" she asked into the receiver.

"Is this Ava North?"

Ava frowned. Who would be using her maiden name, which she'd abandoned so happily, so foolishly, when she married Jim.

"Who is this?" she asked sharply.

"My name is Detective Hank Bingham," a man's gravelly voice said. "I'm sure you remember me?"

Ava did. Of course. Which was why she couldn't speak.

"I'm retired now," Hank continued into the silence. "And I want to put it to rest."

She thought she might faint. Her heart was beating too fast, she couldn't catch her breath.

"I . . . I don't," Ava said.

"Ava," Detective Hank Bingham said gently, "you and I both know that you do."

CHARLOTTE

That Morning
1970

She wore a lavender dress that morning. Soft and sheer. She wore a nude-colored slip underneath it and put the silver necklace with the odd-shaped chunk of turquoise around her neck. She smoothed the thyme mint oil on her bare arms and legs, rubbing it into her elbows, callused from too much time spent leaning on counters and desks. Barely eight o'clock and already the day was hot and humid, the sun a hazy white ball in the sky. When she looked at it she thought of fire, heat. She thought of sin. Of sins. Of *sinning.* Despite the heat, a shiver ran up her back. And she smiled, running a pale lipstick across her full lips.

From the kitchen: sounds of breakfast getting made. The gas flame catching. A fork beating batter in a ceramic bowl. The hiss of butter on the griddle. Her husband's voice, steady, firm — "It's coming" — then her daughters' high-pitched little-girl voices: "I want mine with blueberries!" "I want mine plain!"

She pulled a comb through her wavy, still wet hair, and as she lifted her arm to do it she smiled at the soft hair under her arm. How he liked that she didn't shave there! He would press his nose to it and breathe her in.

The smell of pancakes and bacon filled the air, the sounds of plates slammed onto the counter, of juice being poured. "I hate blueberries in mine! Daddy, I told you!"

Her hand hesitated over the can of deodorant. She wouldn't use any today, she decided.

"Hon?" her husband called to her. "Breakfast is ready."

She slipped on her white Dr. Scholl's, and made her noisy way out of the bathroom to her family already sitting at the kitchen table, waiting.

"Sorry," she said, "I'm going to pass today. I have to meet with a sales rep first thing."

Her older daughter, Ava, frowned over her juice glass. It was always unnerving how that girl seemed to see through her, even at just ten years old.

But Lily's face contorted. "Breakfast is the most important meal of the day, Mama. They told us that at school."

Absently, she tousled Lily's hair.

"That seagull book," Charlotte said, deliberately meeting her husband's gaze and holding it. "Full of wisdom like, 'Find out what you already know and you will see the way to fly.' "

"What does that even mean?" he asked.

She shrugged, shook a Valium from its bottle, and swallowed it with a gulp of juice. She was aware that her husband was watching her take the pill. He didn't believe in taking drugs to feel better — one of their many petty disagreements. "You don't need to get stoned to be happy," he'd told her more times than she cared to remember. "No," she'd correct him, "*you* don't need to get stoned to be happy." As if to score a point, she took a second pill, and gave him a small smile.

"Mama, what will we do all day without you?" Lily asked, obviously on the verge of tears.

"Aunt Beatrice is coming to take care of you!" She said it like they'd won a prize. *Aunt Beatrice!*

"No!" Ava groaned. "She doesn't pay attention to us."

From the corner of her eye she saw her husband frowning. She sighed. It was true, her sister wasn't the best babysitter. She didn't even like children very much. But Charlotte had been so distracted that she hadn't yet lined up any babysitters for the summer and until she did Beatrice would have to suffice.

"Mama, don't leave. Please please please," Lily was whining, and Ava was saying, "She's so boring!"

But the Valium had already started to kick in, and the noise of her life didn't make her tense or angry or depressed like it did without the pills. Instead, there was a low hum somewhere deep in her brain and her limbs felt loose and rubbery.

"They want end caps and window displays," she told her husband. "I've got to set everything up so we're good to go for pub date next week."

"It sounds like a terrible book," he said.

"It's all right," she said.

Ted didn't like books very much. *Any* books, never mind one about a philosophical seagull. Over a decade ago, when they lived in Manhattan and she was working at the Strand bookstore on Broadway and Twelfth, she would come home excited, a bag full of review copies and hard-to-find used books. She would lay them out on their enamel-topped kitchen table as if they were precious things. They *were* precious things, she reminded herself now. How she'd hated the way he shoved them aside to make room for his own textbooks; he was getting his MBA then, poring over facts and figures at that table long into the night.

The memory of it made her pause to tenderly touch his arm, and he looked up at her almost gratefully. This was the time when she should feel guilty for lying, wasn't it? For falling in love with another man? But she didn't. Instead, Charlotte scooped up the rotten avocado pit suspended in water and tossed it in the trash.

"Does this ever really work?" she asked no one in particular.

"Susan's mom grew one this big," Ava said, holding out her hands to show Charlotte.

"Susan's mother doesn't work," Charlotte said. She slung her macramé hobo bag over one shoulder. "She has time to grow avocados."

"Off I go," she added.

When she bent and kissed the sweaty top of Lily's head, Lily grabbed her arm and began to wail.

"Don't go! Don't go!"

She had to pry away Lily's fingers, and then hurry out the door before Lily blocked it; the child had done that before.

It wasn't until she was outside that she realized in her haste to escape that she hadn't kissed Ava goodbye. She stared at the front door, the muffled sounds of Lily crying inside coming through the open window. No, she couldn't go back inside. She'd bring Ava something special this afternoon, a shell or a shiny beach stone. An apology.

His dark green Valiant was already in the motel parking lot, waiting. The sight of it always made her smile. A Plymouth Valiant! An old-man car, she liked to tease him. He liked when she teased him. Not like Teddy, who looked wounded if she ribbed him, even gently. Sometimes she had to tell him, "That was a joke," and even then he had to force a smile. Across the street from the motel lay the ocean, sparkling blue in the bright sunlight. A line of cars already waited to enter the beach's lot, inching slowly forward.

She pulled over just outside the motel parking lot to reapply lipstick and smooth her still damp hair. In the mirror she caught sight of her heavy-lidded eyes and flushed cheeks. The extra Valium had made her slightly woozy and sleepy, in a good way. God, it was hot today! The smell of her sweat filled her car. She dabbed at her chest and neck with some crumpled Burger Chef napkins, then tossed them on the floor and continued into the parking lot, sliding her beat-up Citroën into the spot right beside him. She didn't move until he realized she was there, his face lighting up at the sight of her. Before he could get out of the car, she got out of hers, and entered the Valiant on the passenger side.

"Good morning," he said.

Charlotte grinned at him. "Good morning, you," she said.

The crackling sounded faraway at first, but then grew louder and more persistent. Someone was shouting too, and for a moment she thought she was home and her daughters were calling to her, or crying. But no, the voice was a woman's and what she was saying, over and over, was, "Do you read me? Do you read me?"

He jumped from the bed and grabbed his pants from the floor.

It was still morning, but late, and the sun streamed in through the crack where the drapes didn't meet. The air conditioner chugged noisily, and from the radio came

"Brandy, you're a fine girl . . ." and now he had a walkie talkie pressed to his ear and he was saying, "Roger."

She couldn't focus on what the voice on the other end was saying. Her head throbbed and her mouth was so dry that even licking her lips didn't help. Pulling the thin sheet from the bed and wrapping it around her shoulders, she went to the bathroom and filled the plastic cup with water, drinking it straight down. She was on her second glass when he appeared in the doorway, already dressed.

"I'm sorry," he said, "but some kid died and it looks like maybe she was pushed or something."

"I thought Lee was covering for you," she said, hating how needy she sounded. Jesus, a kid had died.

"He was. But not for something like this."

She nodded.

He wrapped her in a hug. "I know," he said softly.

He released her and was heading out of the bathroom already.

"I love you," he said. "You know that, right?"

She shook her head. "No," she said, "I don't."

He grinned. "Well, now you do," he said.

She watched him walk out of the door. This was what it would be like to be married to a cop, she thought, and as soon as she thought it she chastised herself. Married? She hardly knew him. They'd met a few months ago when he came into the bookstore to buy a present for his wife. *The Stepford Wives.* He'd had it gift-wrapped with the paper that looked tie-dyed and orange ribbon. "Have you read it?" he asked her, and she told him she had and that it was a strange gift for a man to give his wife. He came in again the next week, and this time he bought *The Winds of War.* "Do you think I'll like it?" he asked her, and she said, "I have no idea what you would like." And just like that he was lingering until the store closed and she was locking up and then bringing him into the back room and they were making love, right there.

Marrying? That was ridiculous. But the idea had somehow taken hold. The whole way home that hot hot morning, she was imagining it: how she would tell Teddy and how she would even give him custody of the girls and be the one to have them on weekends and how she would sleep next to this man she hardly knew every night feeling safer and more herself, finally.

By the time she turned onto her street,

she felt like she was already, in her imagination, halfway to this new better life.

But then she saw him standing by a squad car with the light on the roof slowly turning, and an ambulance with the back doors gaping open, and Ava alone on the sidewalk and a small still figure on a stretcher.

She slammed on the brakes and got out of the car without even turning it off, and ran toward him.

Hank looked at her emotionless, blank.

"Ma'am," he said. "I'm afraid I have some very bad news."

Maggie

Maggie wanted to tell Julien to lay off the drugs. Not completely, of course. But every time she decided it was time to tell him, he filled the little pipe, and heated it, and she couldn't ask him to stop. Instead, she climbed on his lap to get it sooner. She parted her lips and inhaled deeply. One day, she smoked it and her brain felt like it exploded, knocking her right off the bed, onto the floor.

"Too much," Julien said. "Forgive me."

He picked her up in his arms and laid her back on the bed and rolled onto her. She hardly felt him make love to her. Her heart beat so fast she felt like a hummingbird. She tried to think of the word for hummingbird, but couldn't. Letters floated through her mind: *c, b, i, i . . .* She struggled to connect them, to make them form a word, as Julien's movements grew faster, his breath heavier.

The next time he came to her, after they ate the boeuf bourguignon he made for her, standing by the stove stirring and tasting it while she drank wine and smoked a joint, waiting, when he brought the little pipe to her, she said, "Make it like you did last time."

"That was too much," Julien said gently, kissing her on the neck and the collarbone. "I'm making sure you are safe, *mon petit radis.*"

She eyed the pipe, now on the table so that he could caress her breasts, kiss them.

"I'm keeping you safe," he murmured.

"All right," she said. "Thank you, for protecting me."

Julien smiled up at her.

"But now look what you've done," he said, pointing to his erection. "You will have your pipe when we finish, yes?"

Panic rose in her. She could taste it, the panic. The pipe seemed to gleam in the winter sunlight.

"Like last time then," she whispered.

"No, no. It was too much," he said.

"Please," she begged. "Please."

"Tell me you love me," he said. "You haven't told me you love me in too many minutes."

She licked her lips.

"I love you," she said. "I love you so much it hurts."

"In French," he said. He picked up the pipe, put it back down.

"Je t'aime," she said, trying not to sound as desperate as she felt.

Julien clucked his tongue. "You sound like you love the little pipe more than you love me."

"No!" she said, too quickly.

"But you want it."

She licked her lips again. Sweat trickled between her breasts and under her arms. She could smell it. The smell of desperation.

"Beg for it," Julien said, smiling.

"Please —" she began.

But he was already shaking his head.

"That's not begging, *ma petite chatte,*" he said.

She climbed onto the floor, onto her knees. She looked up at him, grabbed his hands in hers.

"Please," she said, her body trembling, her voice trembling. "Please, Julien. Please. Please. Please."

"Shh," he said, bending her over the back of the pink sofa so that she could see the pipe, waiting for her. She stretched her hand out but couldn't reach it.

She felt like she might burst out of her skin. She felt like she might scream.

But then he finished, slumping over her, murmuring to her.

Finally, finally, he was lighting the match under the bowl of the pipe. Her eyes burned, eager, desperate. She could feel them shining. He patted his lap, and she crawled across the sofa and rested her head there. It smelled like sex and sweat. She parted her lips, and he taunted her, moving the pipe close, then jerking it away.

"Please," she begged again. "Please."

Finally, finally he put it to her lips and she bit it so he couldn't pull it away.

"Like last time," he said.

"I love you," she said before she inhaled.

Her eyes rolled back in her head. Her body jerked. But he was there, holding her tight.

She got an email from her brother in Uganda. He was there protecting the last remaining mountain gorillas in the world. It was sometimes very hard for Maggie to be the sister of such a person.

She stared at the screen.

Dear Maggot,

I'm staring at a bowl of obusera (don't

ask) and dreaming of the drunken spaghetti we had in Florence when Mom and He Who Will Not Be Mentioned dragged us around Italy. In August. You lost your retainer. I practically lost my mind. But we had that spaghetti. Insert orgasmic emoticon here. And of course thinking of Florence makes me think of you. Have you gone back to that place? I looked it up for you (because that's what big brothers are for!) and it's called Osteria de' Benci, in case you get a hankering. Mwirima, my favorite silverback, wandered into the souvenir shop today, scaring the shit out of the family from Michigan. Definitely the highlight of my day. If you actually wrote me back for a change, that would trump Mwirima's appearance.

Love, Wills

Maggie smiled. She could picture Will checking for typos and punctuation errors before he hit Send. She had tried to explain to him that you don't write an email the same way you write a letter, reminding him that salutations and signoffs aren't necessary. She would tease him about this, if she answered him, which she probably wouldn't because what could she possibly say to him?

That oh by the way, I left school and I'm being kept by an old dude in Paris? And also, I've developed quite a taste for heroin? How are your gorillas?

How could such opposite people come from the same gene pool? Will was cursed with being overly responsible, too neat, too cautious, a worrier. Maggie lost things, all the time — keys, cell phones, her passport, her wallet. She courted trouble, always falling for the wrong guys, taking too many risks, experimenting with things Will, three years older, still hadn't tried. Maggie had bungee jumped and hitchhiked and dropped acid. She'd most definitely had sex with more people than he had, which wasn't hard since he'd only been with Sally Greer, his college girlfriend.

He was worried about her, she knew that. Worried about how she was taking it, the way their family fell apart so fast. She exasperated him, but Maggie knew she was his favorite person on earth.

Another email popped up.

PS I'm not sure exactly where in Florence you are staying, but Osteria de' Benci is conveniently located on the eponymously named Via de' Benci!

"Will," Maggie said to the screen. "Stop trying so hard."

Ever since their parents separated, Will had grown even more protective of her, as if his love and concern could fill in for the gaping hole in their lives. Her brother had always loved their last name — Tucker. It had made him feel safe, Tucker, like being tucked in. Now, she knew, he felt the opposite, tossed about, turned upside down. So did she.

She thought she heard Julien's key in the lock, and quickly turned off the computer.

If Julien didn't come to the apartment for several days, she could only think of how much she wanted to get high. One evening, her nerves grew so edgy that she left the apartment and went to Les Deux Magots in Saint-Germain. She had not been there since she'd met Julien, and this time she had on a beautiful black knit dress from Agnès B. and textured hose and her chunky-heeled Mary Janes. This time she had money in her purse, because Julien always left her euros, thick stacks of them.

She ordered oysters and a carafe of *vin maison.* She opened her little notebook and wrote a Hemingway quote that she half-remembered: *As soon as I ate the oysters, I lost the empty feeling and began to be happy and make plans.* Just writing those words settled her somewhat. She turned the page and wrote the number 1. She would make plans, like Hemingway. Beside the number 1, she wrote: *Write every day.* This was a good start. Writers wrote every day, she knew that. Hemingway wrote every morning. Her oysters arrived, and her wine. She stared at the number 2 she'd written. Then she wrote: *Tell Julien to stop bringing the little pipe.*

Instead of going home, Maggie walked past the apartment, past the Bastille, up rue du Faubourg-du-Temple, to the scruffy part of Canal Saint-Martin. Maybe she would see a cozy bar and she would step inside, have a brandy, make more plans. But her gaze as she walked did not settle on any of the little bars ahead. Instead, she searched for someone who might be standing in the shadows, someone who might help her. It didn't take long. She saw a man, tall, lean, in a leather jacket, dark hair over the collar, eyes narrowed, watching.

She slowed.

He saw her slow. He said something low, under his breath.

Maggie turned to him. He beckoned her with his hand, as if to say, quick, quick.

She stepped into the shadows with him.

His French was terrible and he smelled like fried food. He pressed something into her hand, a ziplock bag with white powder inside. But Maggie shook her head, her body tingling with anticipation.

"I don't know how to do it," she said.

"It will cost you more," he said.

She was nodding, that feeling of bursting through her skin building.

He walked away and she followed him, down that dark alley, down another. "Be careful," her mother had told her at the airport when she left. "Don't do anything dumb. Please." A maze of rights and lefts, garbage in the street, the smell of urine, until finally they went through a door, up a dimly lit stairway, into a dimly lit room. Maggie laughed to herself, thinking of the Hemingway title *A Clean, Well-Lighted Place.* She had arrived at the very opposite of such a place. The room stank of unwashed bodies and garbage. She thought of home, not the loft on the rue Saint-Antoine, but home, where her mother cooked elaborate meals, like coq au vin or risotto, sending the warm smells of spices throughout the house. She heard her mother — *Did you wash your hands before you sat down to dinner?*

A boy smiled at her. "Welcome to hell," he said in an American accent.

"Oh no," she said. "I'm just getting a little something here. I live in the Marais. With my boyfriend."

The boy's eyes were glassy. He said, "I'm from New Hampshire. Junior year abroad."

"I used to go skiing in New Hampshire," she said politely.

The man reappeared. He had a length of rubber hose and a needle and syringe. Gruffly he picked up her arm and began tapping her vein.

"No!" Maggie said. "I don't do that."

The boy from New Hampshire laughed. "Then why are you here?"

The man's fingers pressed into her flesh.

"To get high," Maggie said, suddenly feeling frightened. She'd heard of these places, shooting galleries. This was where drug addicts came. *Ma petite camée,* he'd said.

"To smoke it," she finally managed to say.

"Alors," the man said, dropping her arm.

"It's so much better the other way," the American told her. "You have no idea."

Maggie licked her lips.

"I snorted it, back at school," he said. "This is like a whole new level of great."

"You sound so American," she said.

"You know what?" the boy said. "We can go back to my apartment and I'll do it with you. That will be better than here."

"This place is pretty bad," she said.

"I live nearby. On the Place Sainte-Marthe."

"Okay," she said hesitantly. *Don't do anything dumb. Please.*

The boy stood. He wasn't very tall, and he was thin, his jeans sagging at his butt. He spoke to the dark-haired man who had brought her here, and gave him a pile of money. The man went into another room, then came back with a paper bag that the boy took from him.

"Let's go," he said, taking Maggie's hand like they were on their first date.

"God," she said, "I'm glad to be out of there. Thanks."

The night air was surprisingly warm and pleasant, and walking like this, holding the boy's hand and strolling past boutiques and cafés, she almost felt normal. Except that hunger gnawing at her, aching for what he had in that paper bag.

He told her his name was Gavin, and that he went to Dartmouth. He told her he was majoring in French.

"The word for hummingbird," she said. "Is it *colibri*?"

He laughed. "I have no idea."

"I'm a writer," Maggie said.

"Cool," Gavin said, unlocking a big

wooden door.

His apartment building smelled so good, like lemon cleanser and home-cooked dinner. Up two flights of steps, another door that he unlocked and politely let her enter first.

"Home sweet home," he said.

It was neat and pretty, all blues and greens and wood.

Gavin rubbed his hands together. "Let's have some fun, shall we?"

Maggie watched him prepare the heroin.

"I know this sounds weird," she said, her voice dry, "but I'm worried about shooting up."

"You won't die or anything," he said.

"No, no. I don't want to be addicted to it. I just like getting high, you know."

He was nodding. "I do know. The thing is, you can use for eight hours, and then as long as you take sixty-four hours off, you can go another eight hours without being addicted. It's like a scientific formula."

"Really?" she said. Was that why Julien made her wait? Was that why he didn't come every day? He had said he was protecting her, and he was. She felt a sudden pang for him. She did love him.

Gavin said, "We should do this in the bathtub."

"What?" she said.

"You might pass out. It can happen. I don't want you to get hurt."

She thought of the times the drug had knocked her down.

"Okay," she said.

In the small bathroom, he said shyly, "Take off your clothes."

"I have a boyfriend," she told him.

But he wasn't listening to her. She recognized the look on his face. All he wanted was what was in that baggie, not her.

She undressed quickly and climbed into the clawfoot tub. Gavin climbed in too. She could see his ribs, and the sight of them made her miss Julien's soft, doughy body.

Gavin scooted close to her, wrapping his legs around her waist, his semi-hard penis on her thigh.

"Ready?" he asked her.

She stretched out her arm and closed her eyes.

Maggie found the café in the alley beside the doll hospital and the bookstore. The bookstore looked familiar, like a black and white picture she'd seen in a guidebook, or maybe at one of the kiosks along the Seine. No, she realized. It was Ganymede's, the one she'd tried to find when she first came to Paris. It hadn't gone out of business after all. Even though it was cold, she sat outside. Her hand trembled as she lit a cigarette. The sun was bright but did not warm the cold February air. She ordered a large café au lait and eggs on toast.

She would have taken out her notebook, but she'd lost it. So she just sat, smoking her cigarette and watching the people who came and went. She didn't know if Julien had called, because she'd lost her phone too. Somewhere, between the man in the alley and the time with Gavin, she'd lost everything. She shuddered thinking about the weekend. How she puked for what seemed forever after he put the needle in her arm. How she'd loved the high anyway, and lay there in that tub in her own puke, so happily stoned she didn't even care.

At some point, Gavin turned on the shower and washed everything away, but he didn't remember to put the shower curtain in the tub and the bathroom flooded and they slipped when they tried to walk across the wet floor. At some point, they had sex. Then they were back in the tub, and she heard herself asking if the eight hours was up and Gavin telling her it was. At some point he left for class, and she got up on trembling legs, and dressed, and walked home, and changed her clothes and decided she had to make a plan. A new plan. A better plan. One she could stick to.

The doll hospital had a window of dolls' heads, stacked one on top of the other.

Maggie lit another cigarette, ate her eggs even though they made her queasy. Part of her new plan was to eat three meals a day.

She watched the people coming and going but none of them were the tour guide Noah from the Musée d'Orsay.

A gray-haired woman walked down the cobblestone alley, to the bookstore. She bent and lifted the heavy iron gate, revealing two narrow windows of books. She unlocked the door, turned the "Closed" sign around so that it read "Open," and disappeared inside. When Maggie finished her coffee, she gave up on Noah appearing and made her way across the cobblestones to the bookstore. Above the door, a sign read GANYMEDE'S in purple ink.

"Bonjour," Maggie said as she entered.

The bookstore smelled musty, like old books and yesterday's coffee and ink. Maggie stood in the doorway, inhaling, taking it in — the long narrow store, the crowded shelves, the owner with long silver hair in a braid down her back.

"I'm just looking around," Maggie added

when the woman didn't answer, forgetting to speak French.

The woman did not even glance at her.

"So look," she said gruffly.

Maggie ran her hands over the spines of books that lined one wall. Signs handwritten with different-colored Sharpies marked the sections: "Big Fat Books." "Banned Books." "Written for Children But You'll Like Them Too" "Read These Again!"

Maggie took *The Lion, the Witch, and the Wardrobe* from the "Written for Children But You'll Like Them Too" shelf, and sank onto a beat-up leopard beanbag chair. From time to time, the little bell above the door tinkled, and Maggie heard voices and footsteps and the sound of the old-fashioned cash register. But she didn't look up from the book. Not once.

■ ■ ■ ■

Part Four: March

■ ■ ■ ■

"All the variety, all the charm, all the beauty of life is made up of light and shadow."

— *Anna Karenina* by Leo Tolstoy

Ava

Detective Hank Bingham sat at Ava's kitchen table, his navy blue jacket unbuttoned, a lighter blue button-down shirt beneath. For an older man — seventy? seventy-five? — he'd stayed fit. His waist was narrow above a worn brown belt with a monogrammed buckle. Ava didn't offer to take the jacket from him. She didn't offer him a cup of coffee either, though she held one in her hands. All she wanted was for him to go away.

"I'm not trying to upset you —" he began.

"Really? Walking back into my life after all this time? Bringing this up again?"

He looked sad, Ava thought. Maybe it was the job. Maybe dealing with death all the time did this to a person. She didn't feel any sympathy for him, even as she took in the mostly bald head with gray bristles, the dark heavy-lidded eyes. A general air of sadness, or maybe defeat, emanated from him.

Ava could almost smell it.

"Do you remember that case back in the eighties —" he tried.

But Ava interrupted him.

"I didn't live here then," she said.

He nodded. "Okay. Well, there was this girl named Chloe Doon. A nice kid. Worked as a lifeguard and swimming instructor at the Y. She always went early, to set up for her Tadpoles class. The little ones."

"And?" Ava said.

"It was just a summer job. She was only sixteen. She left early, to set up for her Tadpoles, like she always did, and she got there, to the Y. Her car was in the lot. Her clothes were in her locker. The noodles or whatever you call them were lined up at the edge of the pool, ready for the kids. But no Chloe. She was gone. Just like that."

"Look, Detective Bingham —"

"Hank," he said. "You're an adult now. You can call me Hank."

Ava sighed. She didn't want him in her kitchen, in her life. She didn't want to go back where he was determined to take her. For years she'd been able to put it behind her. Why did he have to show up now?

Detective Bingham leaned closer to Ava.

"I have to find out what happened to your sister that morning," he said softly.

■ ■ ■ ■

The first person she wanted to talk to after Detective Bingham left was Jim. Who didn't know anything except that her sister had died long ago. Who didn't know that Ava herself had been questioned that morning, right at the kitchen table. So had their mother and Aunt Beatrice. Jim only knew that the year had been marked by tragedy, the double deaths, first Lily, then their mom jumping off the Jamestown Bridge the next summer. So close together that Ava's father never really recovered.

Ava called Jim's office. As the phone rang she could picture him there, in the yellow Victorian on Parade Street where Pathways to Success was located on the ground floor. Above them was a yoga studio; above that, an acupuncturist. At this time of day, he was probably at his desk with takeout pho from the nearby Vietnamese place, helping a kid with his college essay, or arranging a school visit to reach out to more students who, without Jim, would never go to college.

After half a dozen rings, Jim picked up with a hurried, "Pathways to Success."

"Jim," Ava said. Was he wearing his usual

black turtleneck over worn jeans? Had he remembered to shave today, something he often forgot to do? "It's me. Ava," she added, as if he might have forgotten the sound of her voice.

"I know who it is," he said warmly. "It's not a good time, I'm afraid. I've got an entire Hmong family in the next room up in arms about me helping their kid get in to Mount Holyoke. I've got a guidance counselor in the other room with a stack of profiles of high school freshmen and I can only fit three of them into the program next year. And college decisions have started coming in so I've got sixty anxious seniors emailing me every three minutes. Sorry."

She had always felt like an intrusion into Jim's more important world, guilty about bothering him with the small details of the household: a tooth falling out, a missing electric bill, needing to know when to expect him home for dinner, and then him always late because something important came up. Even then, guidance counselors and high school seniors and anxious parents had taken precedence over Ava's domestic and personal worries. So did shoes that needed to get shipped to Honduras, dinner with the woman who was helping tsunami victims, a meeting to improve education or health care or small business loans. How many times had she and the kids sat waiting for him, dinner on the table, only to discover he'd been with a family trying to convince them their child could get into college? How many weekends had he opted to go to college fairs or take a stranger on a college tour instead of spending time with her, with the family? It felt wrong to be angry at someone for helping people, even if she was sad or lonely or overwhelmed sometimes.

But she'd grown used to it, which was why she heard herself saying, "I completely understand. But something's come up and I hoped we could discuss it. Maybe after work?"

How easily she fell back into accommodating him, she realized even as she spoke.

"I've got a meeting over at Hope High School at five, and then a social with the juniors at seven. Damn. Maybe tomorrow morning?" She heard papers shuffling and then Jim said, "No, I have to be in Central Falls all day. How about the day after tomorrow?"

She heard him slurp. Pho, she thought.

"Look," she said, "it's not important. Go help your families."

"The kids are okay?" he asked.

"As far as I know. Will keeps posting pictures of his gorillas and Maggie is having too much fun to call very often. But she must have gone to Barcelona last weekend because her Instagram is full of Gaudí lizards."

"Good, good," he said, distracted suddenly. "I'm sorry, a student just showed up. Great kid. I don't want to make him wait."

"No problem," Ava said, wondering if he had to squeeze in Delia Lindstrom, or if she somehow had managed what Ava had not — to become more important than Jim's desire to save the world.

The first thing Ava noticed about *Anna Karenina* was that it had a thousand pages. One thousand and eight, to be exact.

She opened the book.

She read the first line: *All happy families are alike; each unhappy family is unhappy in its own way.*

"Each unhappy family is unhappy in its own way," she read out loud.

Such a simple idea, but Ava wondered if she'd ever read anything more true.

"I brought you glazed doughnuts," Ava told her father, offering the bag to him.

He took it eagerly. "A real treat," he said.

"And a coffee, two sugars, extra cream," she said, opening the tricky spout on the lid for him.

Ava's father looked at her, suspicious. His wiry white eyebrows crinkled above his milky brown eyes.

"What's wrong?" he asked, dribbling coffee as he sipped.

"Can't I buy you coffee and doughnuts without something being wrong?"

He didn't answer. He didn't have to.

"I had a visitor yesterday," Ava said.

Her father's studio apartment at Aged Oaks looked down on the parking lot. Sunlight reflected off the handful of cars there. Ava didn't like sunny days, even in the midst of a harsh winter. She turned from the window toward her father's waiting face.

"Was it your mother?" he asked her hopefully.

"No, Dad," Ava said, trying to stay patient. "Mom died. Remember?"

He shook his head, sending the sugary crumbs from his chin onto his plaid shirt. Ava reached over and wiped them off.

"She was here," he said, brushing Ava's hands away. "At Christmas."

"My visitor was Detective Hank Bingham. Name ring a bell?"

"He's the guy who couldn't figure out what happened to Lily," her father said.

"Right. And now he's decided he can't live with himself if he doesn't solve the case."

Her father looked surprised. "It was an accident, wasn't it? He said so himself."

The image of Detective Bingham that rose in Ava's mind wasn't of the older balding man sitting at her kitchen table. Instead, she saw that youthful face, set hard. She saw the dark hair peeking out from beneath his cap, his broad shoulders and trim uniform and shiny black shoes. The light on the police car spun, red and white in the bright sun. Detective Bingham had stared down his full length, all six feet four inches of him, and said, "Ava? You're coming with me." As he led her into the kitchen, she could still hear her mother howling, like a wounded animal. When she glanced over her shoulder, Ava saw the ambulance doors gaping open, and her mother being pulled off Lily's body.

"I don't want to talk about it," her father said. "And I'll tell Hank Bingham that too if he has the balls to show up here."

Ava nodded, but she wasn't sure that she agreed. What if Hank Bingham could figure out what had happened that day? Maybe it would free her. Of course, she understood it could also ruin her.

"Maggie!" Ava said into the telephone. "I'm so glad you called —"

"I know, I know," Maggie said. "I've been sick. I didn't want to worry you."

"Sick?" Ava said, trying to tamp down the worry that threatened to take over.

"Some flu," Maggie said. "Everybody got it."

"Did you get antibiotics?" Ava asked.

"Mom," Maggie said, "I'm fine. You know how the flu can knock you down for a while."

That was true, Ava reminded herself. She sighed.

"Tell me about you," Maggie said.

"I joined Cate's book group," she said. "Did I mention that? We're reading *Anna Karenina.*"

"Count Vronsky!"

"Have you talked to your father?" Ava asked.

"Please," Maggie said. "I don't even want to talk *about* him. Never mind *to* him."

Ever since Jim moved out, Maggie had refused to speak to him. Sometimes Ava had to admit this delighted her. He should pay for the mess he'd made. But mostly she knew it was important that Maggie forgive him, or try to anyway.

"Maggie," Ava began, but Maggie cut her off.

"He sends me emails all the time. I suppose I could answer one. But I'm not going to talk to him."

"That's a start," Ava said.

Someone knocked on the back door and she began to make her way through the living room and dining room toward the kitchen.

"You're sure you're all better now?" she asked Maggie.

"Positive! Did you see the Gaudí pictures?"

"Yes," Ava said. "But next time have someone take a picture of you. Okay? I miss your face."

By the time Ava reached the door, Maggie had hung up, promising to do that.

"Oh dear," Ava said when she saw Luke standing there, porkpie hat low over his forehead.

"I was in the neighborhood," he said.

Luke was already inside, not waiting for an invitation. He had a bag of food in his hand, and the smell of curry filled the kitchen.

Ava held up *Anna Karenina.*

"I'm only in part two," she explained.

Luke took containers from the bag and set them on the kitchen table.

"Saag paneer, dal, raita, chicken biryani." He glanced up, worried. "Sorry," he said. "Are you a vegetarian?"

"No," Ava said, amused. Roxy was probably a vegetarian. Half the people Maggie's age were vegetarians. Not so much middle-aged women.

"A six-pack of PBR," he said.

Before Ava could ask what PBR was, six cans of Pabst Blue Ribbon beer landed on the table. *Why not?* she thought, and went to get the plates and silverware.

"You know this is ridiculous," Ava told him later in bed. "Wonderful, but ridiculous."

"How so?" he asked.

"I'm old enough to be your mother."

"If you had me when you were super young, I guess," he said. "And anyway, it's nice."

"Yes, it is," she said. "Very nice."

Suddenly Luke sat up.

"It's late! I've got to go," he said, pulling his t-shirt on, and over it a green sweater covered with pills.

"My friend's band is playing at Lupo's. They go on at midnight," Luke explained as he yanked his jeans on. "Want to come?"

Ava glanced at the clock. 11:40. "Not tonight," she said.

Luke leaned in and kissed her lightly on the lips. He tasted of Indian food, stale beer.

"See you," he said. He paused at the door. "Sure?"

"I'm sure," she said.

Ava sat a few minutes in the dark. Thinking about Luke and what she was doing, she closed her eyes, but knew right away that sleep was impossible. Turning on the light beside her bed, she picked up *Anna Karenina.* And before she knew it, wrapped up in Anna's affair, she'd forgotten about him.

Cate, dressed in some vaguely Russian period dress, complete with an enormous fake white fur coat, sat across from Ava at a window table in New Rivers, looking worried. Between them lay the shells of grilled Plum Point oysters and Rhode Island littlenecks. Ava had suggested they meet here for dinner before the book group, and as they ate and talked about their kids and what to do now that their Pilates instructor had left, she tried to build up her courage to confess about Luke.

When Cate glanced at her watch, Ava

knew it was now or never.

"I've done something kind of interesting," Ava said.

"That's what I was afraid of when you said you had something to tell me," Cate admitted, looking even more worried.

Ava cleared her throat.

"You know Luke? From the book group?"

"Of course I know Luke," Cate said.

"We . . . uh . . ." Ava struggled to find the right word or phrase.

"For heaven's sake," Cate said. "You what?"

"Had sex."

"You *what*?"

Ava's cheeks burned with embarrassment. "I know. It's crazy."

Cate started to laugh.

"Did he take off his hat?" she managed.

Ava covered her face with her hands. "Thankfully, yes."

"Don't be so embarrassed," Cate said. "I think it's good. A step forward."

Ava dropped her hands and smiled at her friend. "That's kind of you, but he's way too young for me, and he dredged up too many feelings I'm way too old to have."

"Such as?"

"Does he like me? Will he call again? Stuff I thought I'd never have to deal with at this point of life."

"You are too old to worry about that nonsense," Cate agreed. "There's something I have to tell you. I saw Jim."

Despite herself, Ava asked, "You saw Jim? Where?"

Cate winced. "At one of those neighborhood parties. I figured you didn't go so that you could avoid him?"

"I didn't get invited," Ava said, hurt. Lines had been drawn, and other than Cate it appeared people had taken Jim's side.

"Probably so you wouldn't have to interact with him and Delia," Cate said, thrusting her credit card at the waiter as he passed.

"He brought Delia? To a neighborhood party? He doesn't even live in the neighborhood anymore."

"I thought you knew," Cate said, that worried expression returning. "He does live in the neighborhood. On Williams Street."

Ava thought of his reliable blue Prius parked there with its bumper yarn bombed.

"With Delia Lindstrom?" Ava asked, needing to know.

"So what?" Cate said in her good friend voice. "You've got a new young lover. Right?"

As if on cue, Luke walked past the restaurant, his arm casually flung across Roxy's shoulders.

Penny approached Ava as soon as she walked into the Athenaeum, as if she'd been waiting for her. Ava noticed immediately that two plastic tubes snaked into her nose, pumping oxygen from a small portable tank. Her face was a map of lines and wrinkles, but her blue eyes twinkled and her hair in its neat silver bob was shiny and thick.

"A touch of emphysema," Penny said when she saw Ava's eyes follow the path of that tubing.

The heavy gold charm bracelet laden with charms clanged as Penny put her hand on Ava's arm.

"Come sit near me."

"I'd love to," Ava said.

From across the room, John gave her a sad smile. Ava took the chair beside Penny's.

"I was struck by the first sentence of the novel," Cate began.

From memory, she recited it. "All happy families are alike; each unhappy family is unhappy in its own way."

The words pierced Ava, so much so that she placed a hand on her chest. She had read the line, of course. But hearing it out loud in this quiet musty room made it sound true. Hadn't she believed that together with Jim they'd created a happy family? Hadn't she believed as a child that her parents had created a happy family too? Yet both of those fell apart, proved themselves to be unhappy after all.

"Arguably," Cate was saying, "that's one of the best first sentences in literature."

"I'm afraid I have to respectfully disagree," Ruth interrupted. "My selection holds that honor, doesn't it?"

"That's why I said arguably," Cate said. "The first line of *One Hundred Years of Solitude* is often cited as one of the best too. But to me, Tolstoy hits on something so human and real, while Márquez creates a beautifully written sentence."

"Tolstoy is exactly right," Ava surprised herself by saying, with great passion. "We fool ourselves into believing we're happy, don't we? That our family is as happy as all the other ones we see every day? But honestly, we're all uniquely unhappy. If we'd just admit it."

Beside her, Penny looked bewildered.

"But the novel's all about the importance of family," Honor said in her professorial voice.

"Yes," Diana agreed, standing. She'd chosen *Anna Karenina,* and seemed ready to have her say. "But Tolstoy recognizes the difficulties too."

"Exactly!" Ava said.

Diana said, "Tolstoy says that if you look for perfection, you'll never be content. Yet isn't that what we do? I sure as hell did," she added softly. "And then one day your doctor calls with the news you've dreaded your whole life and you wonder why you gave up so much, why you worked so hard, why you needed that idea of perfection."

"That's what I did," Ava said. "I did it right here."

"What do you mean?" Penny asked her.

"I gave you the wrong impression and I should have corrected it. My husband didn't die. He left me. For someone else. And I'm so hurt, yes, but also humiliated, and it seemed better somehow to be a widow than an ex-wife."

"Why do you think I moved back to Providence? My husband left me and I couldn't bear to stay anywhere near him," Monique said.

"It's another kind of grief," John said.

"Yes, it is," Monique agreed.

"Adultery," Ava said. "I've given a good segue to that theme."

Everyone laughed.

"It occurred to me as I reread this novel, that mid-nineteenth-century literature explored adultery quite a bit. *The Scarlet Letter. Madame Bovary,*" Honor said.

John cleared his throat. "I didn't get it," he said. "I mean, Karenin didn't really seem to care that Anna was cheating on him with Vronsky. He cared more how they looked to everyone else. He was like, as long as the neighbors think you're a good wife and we don't get divorced, this is fine with me. And I just can't imagine that. If my wife fell in love with someone else, it would destroy me."

"That's why I see the novel as social criticism," Honor said. "It's not a love story, per se. Instead, it illuminates the restrictions of society on women."

Diana opened the book and read, " 'Respect was invented to cover the empty place where love should be. But if you don't love me, it would be better and more honest to say so.' "

"But respect isn't the opposite of love," Ava said. "Or a substitute for it."

Diana nodded. "Then what is it that covers that empty place where love should be?"

"That's what I'm trying to figure out," Ava said.

As the discussion turned to Anna as she got off at the station in Obrazovka, deciding to throw herself in front of the approaching train, Ava found herself thinking again of that long-ago summer day when her sister died. And of her mother jumping off that bridge a year later. Like everyone after a loss, life seemed divided into Before and After. Her family had been happy Before, hadn't they? Or had they? Ava wondered. Could a happy family fall apart that fast?

Everyone started to move toward the snack table, where the smoked salmon with sour cream and dill lay on cucumber rounds beside small red new potato halves topped with caviar.

Awkwardly, Ava stood and cleared her throat, hoping to get the group's attention.

Honor and Kiki paused, and Monique looked up at her.

"Excuse me?" Ava said.

She paused until the room grew quiet.

"I just want to say," Ava said, "thank you all for letting me into the book group. I haven't read, I mean, really read, in such a long time."

A sharp memory of her mother's small bookstore came to her. She could see the little girl she was, sitting in a worn easy chair, happily reading.

"It used to bring me such pleasure," Ava said softly. "And then things happened in my life, and books lost the magic they once held for me. I feel like I'm rediscovering that."

Penny nodded knowingly.

"You've added a lot to the group," Luke said.

"And you're bringing Rosalind Arden," Kiki said. "Which is awesome."

"How did you find her?" Jennifer asked, excited.

Ava swallowed hard. A perfunctory search on Google had turned up nothing on Rosalind Arden, and Ava hadn't yet made a plan B.

They were all looking at her now, waiting.

"It wasn't easy," Ava said.

Hank

Hank Bingham stared at the green chile tamales spinning in the microwave. Dinner. He tried not to think about the dinners he and Nadine used to have, just six months ago, the two of them sitting at the table overlooking the patio, containers overflowing with purple flowers. Nadine loved her purple flowers. She grew herbs too, thick branches of rosemary and sweet basil and parsley and cilantro, their scent filling the warm air. She'd be standing at the stove cooking and say, "Hank, stir this," and she'd hand him the long wooden spoon so that she could go outside and pluck a sprig of this, a handful of that.

He tried not to think of Nadine in her funny aprons. She had the one with sparkly skulls on it from her friend Amy in New Mexico; the one with the bottom half of the famous painting of Venus standing in an open oyster shell from Amy's trip to Italy;

the frilly one with lemons on it that she sewed in a class she took with her lady friends. But the more Hank tried to not think about Nadine, the more all he could do was think about her.

Nadine.

He had not always been a good husband. He liked to go out with the guys for a few beers after work. And some Jameson's, neat, when the bars were closing. He liked reviewing clues, tips, theories, with his pals. He liked the feel of the wood of a well-worn bar. The smell of beer from the tap, of whiskey, of night.

He had fooled around on her too. Hank wasn't proud of that, but he'd done it. Women liked men in uniform. Clichéd but true. More than one woman had asked him to keep his uniform jacket on, the shiny silver badge, the gleaming buttons, all a turn-on. Quickies during his lunch break. Or back at someone's house after the bars closed, the woman as hammered as Hank. Mostly, it was meaningless. Mostly. There had been one that mattered, one that was wrong for every possible reason. At first, she was just married. With little kids. And then later, he was investigating the death of her daughter. He should have stopped seeing her, of course. Or recused himself from the case. But he couldn't do either. He couldn't stop seeing her because he was crazy in love with her. And he couldn't resign because he had to help her, to figure out what had happened that morning. And he failed.

That summer, after her kid died, she told him she was writing a book. He'd arrive to find her in the back office, at her messy desk, pounding on an old manual typewriter. "This book is going to matter, Hank," she'd tell him. It was summer, hot, no air conditioning. Hell, no air at all back there. He'd wait until she finished the page or the paragraph or the chapter, watching her type, watching the way her front teeth worried her bottom lip as she wrote. He could sit there and watch her forever. Even like that, ravaged with grief, her eyes flat and glassy.

Finally she would look up and say his name, say *Hank* like no one had ever said it before. She'd unbutton her dress, slowly. She had what seemed like a million of the same kind of dresses, longish, sheer, buttons down the front. She had them in floral prints and checks and plain soft colors like rose and moss green. Beneath them, an old-fashioned ivory silk slip. Beneath that, just beautiful her.

The microwave beeped.

Hank opened the door, touched the tamales. Still not hot. He punched in another minute.

Nadine would be so mad at him for living on microwaved food. She'd be angry that her plants were brown and shriveled in their terra cotta containers. Angry that he'd grown so old and sad in these past six months without her. "Well," she'd said when the doctor gave them her diagnosis, "this is a surprise. I thought Hank would die first." That's how it usually happened, wasn't it? The hard-drinking, hard-living husband dropped dead, leaving the spry wife who took spinning classes and morning walks and ate grilled fish instead of steak. Nadine allowed herself only one drink a day, a martini before dinner, vodka, with a twist.

The cat moved in and out of his legs, purring.

Nadine would really be angry that he'd gone to Petco on adoption day and brought home this cat. She hated cats. She thought they were not to be trusted. But he was so damn lonely, and he saw that big sign — CATS! TODAY! — and went in and immediately fell for this one. She would be good company, he'd decided, and he was right. She slept on the bed with him, putting her orange face right on Nadine's pillow and blinking at him. She sat on his lap while he watched TV. He hadn't known what to name her, having never had to name anything before, so he called her Miss Kitty, after the character in *Gunsmoke.*

The microwave beeped again. Now the tamales were too hot. But Hank took the plate and another cold beer and followed Miss Kitty to the den. The TV was already on; he never remembered to turn it off. Or maybe he left it that way on purpose, just to have some noise in the house. Nadine would not approve. Together, they sat at the table and ate dinner. She used linen napkins. She lit candles. He'd stopped playing around a long time ago. Most nights he came straight home. If you wait long enough, someone had told him once, you settle into being married.

Miss Kitty played with a ball of yarn. Nadine would kill him if she knew he'd taken all of her yarn and given it to the cat. But, Hank thought, she'd never know. Just as the doctor predicted, she died, swiftly and horribly.

Nadine.

Hank opened a tamale, steam burning his fingertips.

He'd loved two women, and they'd both died.

Maggie

Maggie paced the loft, nervous energy building in her with every step. Back and forth, across the cold cement floor, until she heard the sound of Julien's key in the door. She stopped pacing and stood, her back to the tall window that overlooked the street below. The silvery late afternoon light would soften her face, she hoped. The window was open to let in the cool almost-spring air and the smell of the hyacinths that had burst into bloom just that morning. She wore long sleeves to hide the light bruises on the insides of her arms, but a short black skirt, flared and pleated like a schoolgirl's, with no stockings and her Mary Janes, hoping the sight of her long bare legs would turn him on, make him so eager that she could leave the lacy white blouse on and keep her secret.

When she returned from the bookstore yesterday, she'd found a note from Julien waiting for her, hastily scrawled on the back of the electric bill. *Where are you? Why aren't you answering the phone? I am very very upset with you. J.* Beneath that he'd added in a different pen, *Be here tomorrow at noon.* She'd been waiting since then, pacing and smoking and worrying about what he might do if he knew where she had been, what she'd been doing. And now, at half past four, the key in the lock turned and the heavy door swung open.

Julien stepped in, sweaty and out of breath. He looked fatter, Maggie thought. Or was the memory of Gavin's too-skinny body still so strong that Julien seemed enormous in comparison? How had she ever thought he looked like Gérard Depardieu? He looked nothing like him. Nothing at all.

He was carrying his reusable mesh grocery bag, and he placed it on the stainless steel island, pulling out the breakfast radishes she liked so much, and butter and sea salt — her favorite snack. Maybe he wasn't angry? He hadn't looked at her yet, and she hadn't moved from the window. Julien took a bottle of champagne from the bag, and deftly wrapped a towel around the cork, twisting it in such a way that it opened with just a small sigh. He arranged the radishes, the butter, the salt, on a tray. He poured two glasses of champagne, and placed the bottle in the ceramic ice bucket.

Was he humming? Maggie cocked her head. Yes. He was humming.

"Julien," she said, "I lost my phone. I didn't know how to reach you —"

He turned toward her, the tray in front of him.

"I worried," he said matter-of-factly.

"I didn't know how to reach you," she said again, less confidently this time.

He watched her closely as she spoke, as if he were looking for something.

Slowly, he walked toward her. He placed the tray on the big square table in front of one side of the hot pink sofa.

"My favorite," she said, smiling, feeling the pulse in her throat quicken.

"Mais bien sûr," he said without any kindness in his voice.

She went to him and leaned in to kiss him, but he turned his face.

"Maybe we should make a plan," Maggie said, speaking fast. "So that I can let you know if something like this happens again. Or if anything at all happens."

"Yes," he said, "we need a plan."

Maggie gave him a nervous smile and sat down across from him, leaving her legs parted so that he could see she was not wearing any underwear. He did see, but pretended not to.

"Hemingway always made a plan," she said. "He was a planner."

She took the glass of champagne he offered her, and sipped it.

Julien came and sat beside her. Without warning, he took her face in his hands, roughly, pressing his thumbs into the soft flesh below her jaw, his fingers into the hollow of her cheeks.

"The next time you lose your phone," he said in a way that let her know he didn't believe her, pressing his fingers into her face harder still, "you sit here and wait for me. You don't go out. You don't move until I show up. Do you understand?"

His grip on her was so tight that she couldn't open her mouth, so she nodded.

When he released her, it was with a shove hard enough to send her head reeling backward. Maggie moved her sore jaw up and down a few times, trying not to cry. She didn't want him to see her cry. All she wanted was to be out of here, away from him. She thought of her morning yesterday in the bookstore, how calm she'd felt there. For the first time since she'd come to Paris, she hadn't felt alone, even though no one spoke to her, or even noticed her.

Julien's fingers grabbed her hair, yanking, and he pushed her down onto the sofa. He was unzipping his trousers, unbuttoning his shirt.

Then he paused above her.

"Next time it will be worse," he said.

Maggie needed to get out of here, away from him, she thought, as he rolled each small pink radish first in sweet butter, then in salt, and tenderly gave it to her. He brought her ice wrapped in a towel for her cheek, which stung and ached. He smoothed her hair, and explained that she had broken their deal, he had to make her pay for that, didn't he? She nodded, said, "Of course, I am stupid," tried to think of where she could go. The only other person she knew in the entire city was Gavin, and that would be a mistake. A terrible mistake. Hadn't she promised herself yesterday to change her life? To stop making bad decisions?

Julien kissed her on the lips.

Then he walked away, but she didn't hear him leave. Instead, he was busying himself in the kitchen. Maggie closed her eyes, as if she could shut him out. But his movements echoed, assaulting her.

"Ma coccinelle," Julien said softly. "Open your eyes. Look. Look what I brought you,

my love."

Maggie looked, and saw the little pipe in his hand.

"They say that it's possible to inject it without becoming addicted," Maggie said to him the next day, or the day after that.

They were in the white bed at the top of the stairs. Julien was heating the pipe for her. He frowned.

"No, I don't think so," he said.

She wanted to grab his hand and tear the pipe from him. She wanted to swallow it whole. Somewhere, he had a baggie of junk, and he carefully doled it out to her and she wanted to find that baggie and pour it into herself, to lick every bit of the powder from it.

"I saw on television something about an eight-hour rule," she said, trying not to sound desperate. Trying not to shout at him to hurry up, goddamn it!

"Shh," Julien said, lifting the pipe, finally, to her quivering lips. "I gave you more this time. I see how much you like it, and how sweet it makes you. You won't go away again like that, will you?"

Maggie inhaled so deeply that she thought her lungs would burst, that her brain would explode. Her body twitched.

"Maggie?" Julien said anxiously.

She wanted him to know she'd heard him, but she couldn't speak.

"Maggie!"

With a struggle, she opened one eye. She gave him a lopsided smile. She slurred, "I love you."

"You scared me," he said.

But she had stopped listening. She was in that big, empty, glorious place.

With her new phone in her purse, Maggie stepped into the day. She thought about calling her mother, how the sound of her voice would help Maggie keep moving forward. But what if it didn't? What if her mother only sounded worried? Or grilled her about the art classes she was supposed to be taking in Florence? Quickly, Maggie found an image of the *David* and texted it to her mother. *My new boyfriend,* she wrote. Almost immediately her mother texted back *Cute!* Maggie smiled. She had made a mistake but today was a new day. No more Julien. No more drugs. She had bought a new notebook and written two sentences in it. Then, afraid Julien would find and read it, she'd torn the page from the notebook and thrown it away in the trashcan on the corner, ripping it first into tiny pieces in case he looked through the trash and found it.

Where the street turned into rue de Rivoli, Maggie paused. Her plan had been to go to the bookstore again and spend the day there, safe. But standing here, the air that peculiar blend of warm and cold at the same time, she thought perhaps it would be better to be outside, to get fresh air and feel the sun. Yes, she could take a walk first. Hadn't Julien said she was too pale?

She stood, deciding.

The bookstore would bring her that sense of comfort that had soothed her. Maybe while she was there she would hear people talking, hear someone looking for a roommate, meet someone who could be a friend.

But.

She looked in the direction of the bookstore. It had been there seemingly forever, she thought. It would be there later. Or tomorrow. Or the day after tomorrow.

Maggie turned and walked away, in the direction of the Bastille.

"I know you."

Maggie lifted her head in the direction of the voice. It was hard to keep her head up, so she peeked from beneath her heavy eyelids. A boy stood there.

"From the Musée d'Orsay, right?" he said, pulling up a chair beside her.

She sat at a table at the café across from the bookstore, waiting for the store to open. She had never been so stoned in her life. Every now and then, she had to remind herself to breathe.

The boy ordered two espressos and croissants.

"You okay?" he was asking her.

Maggie nodded.

"Whoa," he said in a low voice. "You're wasted."

It was too much, sitting there, listening, trying to keep her eyes open, her head up. Maggie leaned over and rested her head on the boy's shoulder. He had on the softest sweater she'd ever felt. Cashmere. And he smelled so good, so clean, like soap and toothpaste.

"What did you take?" he asked her. "You have to be careful."

He let her keep her head on his shoulder, and for this Maggie was grateful.

"Here," he was saying, and she realized some time had passed because she was just a little less high. "Drink this."

He held the small cup of espresso for her because her hands were shaking so much. It was hot and bitter.

"Good," she mumbled.

"Jam?" he was asking her. He slid a plate with a croissant covered with gobs of strawberry jam in front of her.

Some more time had passed. She could sit up now.

"Yes," she said. "Lots. Please."

"I'd like to think you came here to find me," he said. "But I think you just got stoned and maybe lost."

She didn't answer him. She just chewed the croissant. When she could hold a pen, she would write in her notebook that she must never ever go to Gavin's again. Even as a small electric thrill raced through her body remembering the last twenty-four hours. When she'd explained she had a boyfriend who couldn't see the marks on her arm, he'd shot her up near her ankle. How many times? she wondered now. And when had she left? And how had she gotten here?

"My name is Noah," the boy was saying.

Maggie sighed. This was too much. The last time, she decided, already wanting one more hit. Then that would be the real last time.

"You dropped this," the boy said, holding up a cell phone.

"Shit!" Maggie said, grabbing it out of his hand.

No calls. The sight of that made her weep.

"Whoa," he said again. "Hey."

"I need to go," she said.

Why had she left Gavin's in the first place? Slowly it came back to her. He'd given her a final hit and gone out to get more. She was supposed to wait for him right there.

"Do you live nearby?" Noah was asking her. "Will you come back tomorrow?"

There were so many people clogging Gavin's street that Maggie couldn't get through. In the distance, she saw police cars, an ambulance.

She stopped pushing.

"What happened?" she asked no one in particular.

"Some stupid American kid," a man said, turning to walk away. "OD'ed."

The door to Gavin's apartment building opened and two men emerged, carrying a gurney. The shape on the gurney was covered with a blue and green blanket. She knew that blanket.

Maggie tried to hold it back, but she couldn't. She bent over and threw up into the street. Someone handed her a handkerchief with a scalloped edge, and she wiped her mouth with it. When she turned to give it back, the person was gone. In fact, the crowd was parting to make way for the ambulance, which moved slowly past them. No siren. No lights.

■ ■ ■ ■

Part Five: April

■ ■ ■ ■

"Things have a life of their own," the gypsy proclaimed with a harsh accent. "It's simply a matter of waking up their souls."

— *One Hundred Years of Solitude* by Gabriel García Márquez

Ava

Ava did not have the slightest idea how to find someone. But she supposed the best way to start was at her computer with a Google search. As she typed in Rosalind Arden's name, she hoped that an obituary would not pop up on the screen. How would she ever explain that to the book group?

Did you mean Rosaline Arden? Google asked her.

Apparently, Rosaline Arden was somebody. An Olympic speed skater back in the 1960s, she had a Wikipedia page and newspaper links, videos, and interviews. She was even on LinkedIn.

But Rosalind Arden had nothing.

Ava typed in the name again, adding *From Clare to Here* after it. This time she got pages and pages of information, all of it about the song and none of it about the book.

Now what?

Maybe if Rosaline Arden was on LinkedIn, so was Rosalind Arden. But she wasn't. She wasn't on Facebook or Twitter either. Was it possible for a person to disappear this completely?

Ava got up from her desk and made a cup of tea. Will or Maggie would probably know some way to find a person who seemed unfindable. When she was a kid, she used to spend hours in the library looking up famous people and obscure facts. She loved pulling out the drawer in the card catalogue, fingering the cards with their secret code typed across the top, then jotting down the code on a scrap of paper with the tiny pencils put there for just that use. She loved sitting at the long wooden tables and poring through information, taking notes, discovering. Ava could almost smell the mildew and new carpet smells of that library, could see the cat glasses hanging on the fake pearl chain around the librarian's neck.

Of course, she thought, reaching for her phone. Librarians know how to find anything.

She stared out the window as she listened to Cate's phone ringing. It had been a cold spring, but this afternoon the sun had unexpectedly come out and warmed the city. Ava could see the purple of crocuses around the base of the trees on the street, the yellow tips of daffodils in her neighbor's yard.

A woman cut across Ava's line of vision. A woman in a leopard coat that was too warm for this spring afternoon. She was walking a very large dog.

Ava squinted against the bright sunlight.

That wasn't any woman. It was Delia Lindstrom.

"Hello?" a voice in Ava's ear said. "Ava?"

Ava had forgotten she'd dialed Cate's number, forgotten the phone pressed hard to her ear.

"I can't believe this," Ava said, her gaze following Delia Lindstrom's long-legged stride down her street. *Her* street.

"Delia Lindstrom is walking a dog right in front of my house," Ava said, her voice rising. "I think it's the kind that rescues people stranded on mountains."

"St. Bernard?" Cate asked, as if it mattered.

"I don't know. Maybe."

The dog paused to pee on the crocuses, and Ava shouted, "Stop that!"

"Ava?"

She had to keep herself from tapping on the window. Did Delia know this was her house? The house where she and Jim had raised their children? Did she know their Christmas tree had stood right here, in front of this very window, every year? Jim used to wrap the railing on the front stoop with boughs of evergreen, the kind that had the little blue berries on them. Did Delia know that?

The dog's big square head turned toward Ava, as if it knew she was standing there watching.

"It might be the other kind," she said. "The ones raised by monks?"

"Ava," Cate said, "walk away from the window. Go in the kitchen. Or upstairs."

But Ava seemed stuck in place, her eyes glued to the woman and the dog trespassing on the sidewalk in front of her house.

"He hates dogs," Ava said softly.

"Maybe she came with a dog," Cate said. "Gray doesn't like cats, but when we met I had two of them. Package deal."

Package deal, Ava thought. Jim was a package deal too: he came with a wife, two kids, a twenty-five-year history. Delia smoothed a strand of hair out of her face, stood with the bright red leash in her hand, and looked around. The dog sniffed the crocuses, the base of the tree.

"Is she gone?" Cate asked.

Ava had forgotten about the phone again, and Cate's voice startled her.

"She's standing there like the Queen of England," Ava said.

Did Delia Lindstrom know that Jim had planted those crocuses? That every fall, after the first frost, he planted bulbs? Tulips mostly, because those were Ava's favorite.

"Hang up," Cate said. "Get away from the window."

The dog moved suddenly, jerking Delia forward. Ava watched as Delia regained her balance, laughing and talking to the dog as she did. She didn't look back as she walked down the street.

Ava waited until she was out of sight before she said anything more.

"Is this going to happen every day?" she said to Cate. "I can't even look out my own window or step outside for fear I'm going to walk right into her and Cujo?"

"She's gone?"

"Jim hates dogs," Ava said again.

"Maybe you should talk to him," Cate said in her problem-solving voice. "Tell him that it's too upsetting for you to worry about running into her. Tell him they need to respect your space."

"You can't tell someone not to walk down a street," Ava said, sounding cross. Then she remembered why she had called Cate in the first place. But she couldn't ask her how to find Rosalind Arden. Then her friend would know she'd made up that she was coming.

Ava put *One Hundred Years of Solitude,* a beach blanket, and a peanut butter and jelly sandwich in her big straw bag and drove to Elephant Rock Beach. Jim didn't like peanut butter and jelly sandwiches. And he didn't much like the beach either. Or at least, he didn't enjoy sitting on the beach and watching the waves. If Jim went somewhere, he needed to do something, to keep moving.

The ocean appeared before her, reflecting the brilliant blue of the April sky. Ava parked in the nearly empty lot, and made her way onto the wide stretch of smooth sand. A young couple tossed a Frisbee to their puppy. Two women walked along the water's edge, heads bent close as they talked together. Ava inhaled the salty air, spread her blanket, ate her sandwich, and fell into the magical world of Colonel Aureliano Buendía as he recollected the years in Macondo, when a band of gypsies brought technological marvels to the dreamy, isolated village.

When she looked up from the book, the

couple with the puppy was gone and the two women were in the distance, walking back toward her. The sun had dropped lower in the sky, and Ava shivered in the cool air. For the first time since Jim left, she'd passed a few hours without thinking about him. In fact, she'd enjoyed the time alone, immersed in the novel. With a sharp ache, she thought of her mother and the bookstore she'd owned. Ava could almost smell the shop, a crowded, seemingly disorganized store with books stacked on tables in her mother's and aunt's own peculiar system. Over the years since Lily died, Ava worked hard not to think of her mother, or Lily, or her childhood. But sitting here on the beach alone with the sun starting to set and a book in her lap, Ava couldn't stop.

Lily's small sticky hand in hers.

Their mother, perched in the rocking chair between their twin beds, reading to them at night, her deep raspy voice lulling Ava to sleep.

Afternoons after school in the bookstore, flopped in a beanbag chair, that smell — patchouli and dampness and books — all around her.

Family dinners. Her mother's thick rich soups and homemade bread.

But those memories always, *always,* got

shoved aside by the other ones. The sirens. The police. Lily's lifeless body. Her mother's screams.

And later, her mother's retreat from them. At first, she just stayed in bed. Family dinners became makeshift efforts by her father. Hot dogs and canned beans. Hamburger Helper. Scrambled eggs. Later, she stayed at the store. She went in early and sometimes didn't come home at night, sleeping on a cot in the back office. Ava stopped going there after school. The once comforting smells, the way the beanbag chair would mold itself into the contours of her body, her mother's happy chatter, all of it was gone.

And then, the next summer, her mother left. No note. No goodbye. One morning she got into her car and drove away. By then, Aunt Beatrice had left too, leaving Ava's mother to run the store alone, unable to cope with Lily's loss and how it had affected all of them.

Then came the call telling them she was dead. Her car had been found on the Jamestown Bridge, the engine still running, the driver's door open. Workmen standing below saw something drop into the water.

That was the summer Ava read *From Clare to Here.* It was about a family in England who lost their young daughter, Clare. The parents' relationship is strained, and the remaining daughter tries desperately to comfort her mother. On a weekend trip to Stonehenge, they get lost and end up at another stone circle. The mother and daughter wait while the father goes to park the car. It begins to rain, and the wind picks up. Frustrated, the mother decides to enter without her husband. The girl, Jane, follows her mother around the massive stones, the wind howling around them. They seek shelter in what appears to be a clearing beneath some of the stones, but once there they find stairs leading down. Jane urges her mother not to go, but she doesn't listen. Frightened, Jane follows. They walk along a descending sloping corridor, giant stones all around them, the light growing dimmer, Jane pleading for her mother to stop, until they reach the bottom. There, they find the souls of the dead, blurry images of people, bursts of light. And from this, Clare emerges, holding her arms out to them. The mother, overjoyed and relieved, takes her dead daughter into her arms.

Ava closed her eyes as she remembered the story.

So many details she thought she'd forgotten came back to her. The way those souls looked. The mother's joy. And then the realization that they can't take Clare back with them. If they want to be with her, they have to stay there.

From far above, they hear the father calling to them.

Jane and her mother's eyes meet over Clare, who has nestled onto her mother's lap.

"Go," the mother tells Jane.

Jane shakes her head. Her father's voice calls her name, desperate.

"Go."

"Not without you," Jane says, crying, frightened.

"Jane," her mother said evenly, "you deserve to live a beautiful life. I deserve to give mine up."

Her mother is holding on so tight to Clare that Jane understands her mother will never leave. And she runs. She runs up the long stone corridors, the sounds of all those souls echoing behind her. She runs and runs until she bursts through the clearing. The rain has stopped and the sun is bright and sharp. Her father sees her. He turns his tear-stained face toward her, and now he opens his arms, and Jane runs into them, rests her head on his chest, and listens to the steady, comforting beat of his heart.

Somehow, Ava had stood as she remembered all of this. *One Hundred Years of Solitude* had dropped to the sand, and her own heart was beating hard against her ribs. A different young couple with a different puppy ran across the sand in front of her. Slowly, Ava collected her things and walked back to her car.

MAGGIE

Julien held up what looked to Maggie like a handful of blue and green strings.

"For you, *ma mure,*" he said.

He pressed it against her naked bony hips, pulling the strings across her concave stomach, smiling as he did.

"So pretty," he murmured.

Maggie was too stoned to respond. You would think a person who saw her friend's dead body wheeled out in a body bag would stop taking drugs immediately. You would think that person would be scared into sobriety. But the opposite had happened. Last night she had finally convinced Julien to shoot her up instead of having her smoke it. He had pushed the needle into the inside of her ankle. When she'd opened her eyes after the initial surge of the drug through her body, he kissed her on the mouth.

Maggie struggled to remember what he was talking about. They were going somewhere. But where? Soon enough, her head would start to clear, but for now, she was happily wasted. She didn't have to think. No. She didn't want to think. Because if she started to think, she'd see that body bag with Gavin inside it. She'd see the small bruises from shooting up. She'd see the unanswered emails from her brother, the missed calls from her mother.

For now, she stayed on the pink sofa and let his words float around her, the pile of strings against her pasty skin, a bright hot sun streaming in the tall windows.

Where he was taking her was the south of France. A small town on a bay. A stone house with no refrigeration so that everything that had to be kept cold was kept in the well. A long walk past almond trees and olive trees led to a steep cliff, and at the bottom of that cliff was a rocky beach that looked across the water to Marseille.

Maggie watched Julien as he walked into the crashing waves, ridiculous in his tiny Speedo. A thought flashed through her mind: maybe he would drown. Maybe there was an undertow and he would be swept away. The thought should have frightened her, but instead, she felt relief at the idea. Her next thought: I have to get away from him. Her next thought: But how?

Down the beach three boys around her own age sat on a blanket, smoking and drinking wine and playing cards. They looked so normal, so ordinary. She wanted to be like that again. Her eyes drifted back to Julien, splashing in the waves. Maggie pulled on the white crocheted top she'd brought and walked over to the boys.

How beautiful they were! In their ordinariness, they seemed more appealing than someone extraordinary. One had curly brown hair, a long face, green eyes. One had short cropped blond hair and pale blue eyes. The other was dark, and hairy, and pudgy.

"Bonjour," Maggie said.

The curly-haired one smiled up at her.

"We need a fourth," he said in heavily accented English. "Do you want to play?"

She glanced toward Julien again.

"Your father's entertaining himself," the hairy one said, patting the blanket. "Don't worry."

"He's . . ." she began, but couldn't bring herself to finish. Instead, she sat beside him, and picked up the cards they dealt her. She took the cigarette the blond offered her, and a glass of wine too. The next time she looked up, Julien was gone. Not drowned, as she'd fantasized, but gone from the beach, with their blanket and the small cooler of fruit and cheese and Chablis.

She knew she should get up and follow him. But she didn't. She sat and played cards and smoked cigarettes with these boys, whose names were also ordinary and beautiful. The blond one, Henri, kept smiling at her in a way that made her feel pretty and interesting. Maggie smiled back at him. When they decided to go for a swim, she joined them, lifting the crocheted top over her head, noticing Henri noticing her breasts. As they walked to the water, she slipped her hand in his. She needed to escape. Maybe Henri, with his clear blue eyes and his long lean body, could help her get away.

"Je t'aime bien," Henri told her.

They had walked alone together down the beach to where the rocks formed caves and grottos. The sky had darkened to violet and orange, and the tide swirled water around their ankles.

Maggie knew that *Je t'aime bien* literally meant *I love you well.* But in French there was no way to say *I like you. Je t'aime bien* came the closest.

"Je t'aime bien aussi," she said.

"Puis-je t'embrasser?"

Maggie nodded, and he leaned his long frame down until his lips met hers.

In the distance, his friends called to him.

"À demain?" he asked her.

Maggie nodded, although she had no idea how she would be able to meet him tomorrow. What would she do with Julien? Already she worried about how angry he was going to be at her for staying away all afternoon.

"We'll meet here? On the beach?" he was asking her.

Maggie realized her legs were trembling. Was it fear? Or the need for a fix that had started in her gut?

"Oui," she said. *"Ici."*

Henri said something to her, but all of a sudden she could only think of the long way back. The climb up the steep rocks. The walk past the almond and olive trees. And the sun was starting to set.

With her legs shaking it was harder to climb up the rocks. Henri stood below her, calling something that she couldn't hear through the whooshing sound in her head. The rocks loomed sharp and jagged above her. Maggie looked beyond them, then down at Henri and the beach. She took a breath. She knew she could never go back to Julien. Never. Slowly, she began to make her way down the rocks.

Hank

Hank Bingham stood in Nadine's garden, a brand new garden hose stiff in his hand. At Benny's, the local store that sold everything from tires to Barbie dolls to coffee pots to . . . well, to garden hoses, he'd stood staring at the hoses like he'd never watered anything before. They sat, coiled like bright green snakes, waiting for him to choose one. Honestly, Hank couldn't remember ever buying one in the first place. Maybe the old one had come with the house? The people they'd bought it from, an old retired couple, had left things behind. A hummingbird feeder that Nadine dutifully filled with sugary water. A box of old postcards that Hank had tried to return to them because they seemed special, full of memories and signed with love. Except the old guy had told him to throw them out. They weren't special at all. His wife had bought them at a junk shop on Wickenden Street, thinking she might use them in one of her craft projects. But she never did. Remnants of those craft projects had been left behind too. Scissors that left whatever they cut with a scalloped edge, scraps of felt and bits of embroidery thread. Nadine had used some of the stuff, like the scissors. But not those postcards. He'd finally thrown them out after she died. So maybe the old couple had left the hose behind too.

This morning Hank decided to water Nadine's garden.

Hank looked at all the dead plants. He owed it to Nadine to keep her plants alive. It was too late to save the tulips. Those, apparently, had to be planted in fall, before the first frost. Somehow a few had appeared anyway, standing tall and yellow among the brown leaves in the corner. Hank pointed the hose at them, turned the nozzle, and felt the water gurgle and then shoot through the hose. He adjusted the nozzle to a spray, and lifted it high so that it rained down on all the dead things.

Years ago, Hank had a Korean partner. A nice guy named Lee who came and went from the precinct so fast that no one even noticed he'd been there. Every afternoon, Lee made a big bowl of those instant ramen noodles, the kind that Nadine wouldn't let

Hank eat because they had too much sodium. But Lee added an egg to his, and thin strips of American cheese, and chopped scallions. He would sit happily slurping the soup while Hank ate his tuna salad sandwich — one slice white bread, the other wheat — and carrot sticks and an apple. That ramen smelled so damn good, and Lee looked so happy eating it that Hank sometimes had to walk away.

Tonight, dirt under his fingernails from planting and his back aching from kneeling so much, Hank made himself that soup.

"Sorry, Nadine," he said out loud as he stirred the flavor packet into the boiling water and noodles.

He wondered what had happened to Lee, why he had come and gone so quickly, where he'd ended up. They weren't close, but they'd had some fun together. Hank got the crazy idea to track Lee down and tell him what he was having for dinner. But then he realized he wasn't even sure if Lee had been the guy's first name or the last name.

Miss Kitty, smelling the cheese Hank was ripping into orange ribbons, moved in and out of his legs, purring. Funny how he'd never known a cat's purr before, how satisfying a sound it was.

"Sorry, Nadine," he said again, dropping

half the cheese onto the kitchen floor for the cat.

Hank picked up the bowl of soup and took it to his usual spot in front of the TV to watch *Wheel of Fortune,* Miss Kitty at his heels. The soup was good; Lee had been right to slurp it with such joy.

Hank glanced up. The wheel of fortune was spinning. His soup had cooled. He got to his feet heavily — the sore back, the shot knees — and went into the bedroom. He opened the bottom drawer, lifted the neatly folded row of his summer shirts. Nadine had washed and folded them and put them away when the weather cooled and summer turned to autumn, just before she got sick. Or before they knew how sick she was, anyway.

His hand slid along the bottom of the drawer until he found what he'd come for: *From Clare to Here.* He carried it back to the sofa, and for the first time in months he turned off the television. A loud silence filled the room. The cat stretched out on his chest and immediately began to purr. Hank stroked its short fur, opened the book, and read: *Jane's parents had not talked since her sister died last summer. Oh, they talked —* please pass the salt, *and* can you get Jane at school at four — *but they didn't talk talk. Instead, her father went to work and her mother stayed home and cried. But today, for reasons Jane didn't understand, they were going on a holiday. The three of them . . .*

Hank

That Morning
1970

Hank Bingham loved being a cop. He loved the stale coffee, the satisfying snap of blank paper inserted onto the clipboard, the weight of his gun against his hip. He loved the long hours, the way the sky turned silver just before sunrise, the way it turned violet at dusk. The only thing Hank Bingham hated about being a cop: a dead kid. Blood and gunshot wounds and heads cracked open didn't make him flinch. He'd watched the jaws of life free twisted broken bodies from wrecked cars without even flinching. But a kid . . .

He saw her as soon as he turned the corner, a small patch of pink against ridiculously green grass under an almost too bright sun. A woman paced with the nervous energy some people get in catastrophes. Another little girl stood so still she didn't seem to be real. An ambulance with the red light on top spinning was parked on the side of the road, two men stood over the body. Hank took it all in as he parked, and walked toward them.

The woman ran to greet him. Her cheeks were tear-stained.

"She's dead!" the woman screamed.

Hank's partner Lee arrived, and he stepped from his car. He'd let Lee handle the hysterical woman, Hank decided, and continued to the scene.

The little girl in pink on the green grass had a broken neck. Hank saw that right away. And a bruise on her cheek. He looked at her, and then away, swallowing hard. His gaze lifted upward, to a tall tree covered with white blossoms.

"She fell," he said.

He went over to the girl standing frozen in place. Someone so young, and in shock, wasn't going to be helpful, he knew. Still, he had to try.

Hank kneeled so that he was eye to eye with her. Her eyes were hazel, that color you don't see much, kind of brown and green and gold all at the same time. They were hazel and flat with shock.

"Sweetie," he said, "I know this is hard, but I need you to talk to me."

Nothing.

"I'm Hank," he said. "And you're . . . ?"

Her mouth opened and closed a couple times.

"I can't hear you, sweetie," he said. "What's your name?"

She licked her lips, whispered something.

"I'm going to write it down," he said, holding up the notebook. "Can you say it nice and loud so I get it right?"

"Ava," she said. Then she added, helpfully, "A–V–A."

She started to cry, the tears falling fast and hard.

"Is Lily okay?"

"Lily's your sister?"

Ava nodded.

"And she was what? Climbing that tree?"

"I told her she was up too high," Ava said, trembling.

"And so she was coming down?"

"No! She wouldn't come down."

"So you went up for her?"

"I don't like heights," Ava said. "I'm afraid to be too high up."

Lee was questioning the mother.

"Did your mother go up after her?" Hank asked.

"My mother's at work," she said.

"That's not your mother over there, talking to Officer Lee?"

"My mother's at work," Ava said again.

"So who's that then?"

"Aunt Beatrice. She's babysitting us today. Is Lily okay?" she asked him again.

Hank wrote down that the mother was at work and that the aunt was babysitting.

"Did Aunt . . . what did you say her name is? Beatrice?"

"Aunt Beatrice," Ava repeated.

"Did she go up to help Lily?" Hank asked.

Ava shook her head. "She was inside."

"You stay right here," Hank told her. "Don't move. I'm going to talk to Officer Lee."

The sound of a car taking the corner too fast and screeching to a halt made them turn.

Hank frowned.

"What the hell?" he said out loud.

Did she follow him here? he thought, ridiculously, because if she'd followed him she wouldn't be arriving now.

But it was her, most definitely. No one else drove a beat-up lime green Citroën. And now she was getting out of the car in her lavender dress and she hadn't brushed her hair so it was snarled like it always got after sex and she was running toward him, yelling something. Yelling, he realized, *"Lily Lily Lily Lily Lily."*

Ava

"García Márquez said that nothing happened in his life after he was eight years old," Cate began. "And he went on to say that the atmosphere in his books reflects the atmosphere of his childhood in Aracataca, Colombia —"

"Cate?" Ruth said. "May I take it from here? I mean, I chose the book and although I really really love you as a facilitator, I just have a few things I'd like to say, right off the bat, you know?"

"Oh sure," Cate said, stepping aside.

"She's got her index cards," Honor said, and everyone laughed.

Penny leaned toward Ava. "She's very organized," she said. "She makes outlines and puts everything on those cards. I suppose if I had six children I'd do the same."

Ruth glanced at the first card, then looked at her audience.

"The things I'd like to discuss are, one:

the provincial experience in Márquez's life and his fiction," she said. "Two: the political ideas in the book and in Latin America. Three . . ."

As she spoke, Ruth counted off her points on her fingers, holding them nice and high.

Luke casually placed his hand on Ava's knee. She stiffened, and swatted at it, but Luke didn't seem to notice.

"Five: how his descriptions reflect Colombian history, and Latin America's struggles with colonialism and modernity," Ruth continued. "And six: what the book says about human nature."

"Bravo!" Honor said, looking absolutely delighted with Ruth's presentation.

"That's exactly what makes the novel so great," Luke said.

When everyone turned toward him, Ava wondered if they could see his hand on her knee. Was John staring at them? Or did he just look confused, as usual?

"It's political and historical," Luke said. "But in the end, isn't it mostly about the possibility of love? And the sadness of solitude?"

"The book does speak to all that, Luke," Ava said. "And so beautifully. I was surprised how moved I was by this novel."

Out of the corner of her eye, she saw John

nodding.

"The burden of memory," Diana said. "The characters consider forgetfulness dangerous, yet ironically they speak of the burden, the weight, of memories."

"Look at Rebeca," John said. "After her husband died her memories force her to lock herself in her house."

"She would rather live alone with her memories than deal with the world around her," Kiki added.

Ruth flipped through her cards.

"Colonel Buendía is kind of the opposite of Rebeca, isn't he?" John said. "He doesn't have any memories at all."

"We're kind of jumping ahead," Ruth said. "Aren't we?"

Cate smiled. "You know this always happens, Ruth. Do you ever get through your outline in order?"

"What did all those little gold fish he made mean?" Kiki asked.

"That comes under symbolism," Ruth said. "Number four."

"Yes," Diana was saying, "but when he realizes that the little gold fishes represent a mistaken ideal, he stops making them."

"Stops making them," Honor agreed, "but melts down the old ones, again and again. A perfect symbol of . . ."

Ava glanced around the room, at John wearing his befuddled expression; and Monique nodding enthusiastically; and Ruth standing there gripping her index cards, flustered; and Honor lecturing them; and Diana with her dramatically made up eyes and dark red lips; and Kiki taking notes in her Moleskine; and Cate, such a good friend for letting her come here in the first place, sitting back and listening to their voices rise in their love of books. The sight of them all filled Ava with a warmth and comfort she had not felt in a long time.

■ ■ ■ ■

Part Six: May

■ ■ ■ ■

"Until I feared I would lose it, I never loved to read. One does not love breathing."
— *To Kill a Mockingbird* by Harper Lee

Ava

Ava's father looked especially blank when she walked in to his apartment at Aged Oaks.

A plate of food sat on the table, untouched.

She cut the meat into small pieces and placed a napkin around her father's neck like a bib. But he stared at her, defiant.

"Come on," Ava urged, spooning some applesauce and holding it to his mouth. "You have to eat."

Reluctantly, he parted his lips enough to let a little applesauce find its way in.

"She called me last night," he said after he swallowed.

"Who?" Ava asked him as she put a small piece of meat and some mashed potatoes on the fork.

"Your mother."

"Dad —"

"I couldn't make sense of what she was

telling me. It sounded important."

Ava held the fork to his lips but he pressed them closed.

"I called last night," Ava reminded him. "Remember? I asked you about the book?"

Her father looked puzzled. "You called?" he said.

"I wanted to know if you have a copy of that book I loved when I was a kid. For some reason, I think you have a copy too."

"Your mother called after that," he said, nodding. "That's right. I was already asleep when she called. She explained why she was calling so late, but I can't remember what she said."

He pressed his fists into his forehead.

"That's okay," Ava said gently. "I'm glad she called."

Her father looked at her, his eyes suddenly bright.

"Someone's in trouble," he said.

She lifted the fork to his mouth again. This time he opened wide.

"This food is terrible," he said after he swallowed.

Ava smiled at him. Somehow, he was back again. For now.

Every day of her childhood, her father left the house early in a suit and tie and shiny polished wingtips, his black briefcase in his hand. He sold life insurance, sitting at a desk in a small office downtown phoning potential clients in the morning and getting in his car after lunch to call on customers. He ate cold cereal with a banana for breakfast and brought a lunch of two bologna sandwiches with ketchup on white bread to eat at his desk. Her father was solid, predictable, and grateful for the tempestuous, erratic, unpredictable woman who was her mother and his wife.

Sometimes, Ava's mother frightened her with her passion. She screamed about the war in Vietnam and chemicals in food and why the government didn't admit that Lee Harvey Oswald had not acted alone. Even her fierce love of Ava and her sister Lily sometimes frightened Ava. She hugged them tightly, and worried when they were sick, so much that Ava feared that such a love could destroy her somehow. True, there were the tea parties and the fairy costumes and the performances of plays, all led by her mother in the woods behind their house. And there were homemade waffles with fresh strawberries and whipped cream for dinner, perfect hollandaise sauce, golden madeleines dusted with powdered sugar. But there was also the crying, the long hard sobbing that none of them could stop. *How can any of you love me?* she'd ask. They all did, of course. Perhaps Lily most of all.

After Lily died, and then her mother, the magic went out of the household. As predictable as her father's breakfasts and lunches had been, their dinners became predictable too. He made a spreadsheet and hung it on a bulletin board in the kitchen where her mother used to hang three pairs of gossamer fairy wings spraypainted gold. *Monday: American Chopped Suey. Tuesday: Spaghetti. Wednesday: Hot Dogs and Beans. Thursday: Hamburger Helper. Friday: Minute Steaks with Rice A Roni.* Beneath the list was another list, this one of all the ingredients needed for these meals. Ava had to start cooking them by four o'clock so they could eat dinner at six. On weekends they went out to eat at The Chicken Coop or The Hong Kong, silently eating their broasted chicken or chow mein while around them families chattered. To her, everyone else looked bright and happy; she and her father, on the other hand, seemed to be fading with every passing minute.

Her father was kind, gentle, dull. He asked her about school and her friends, and dutifully attended every parent-teacher night. But as she sat across from him over her plate of American chop suey or hot dogs and beans, she would miss her mother's magic with such an intensity that sometimes she would actually lose her breath. High school became almost a relief from the routines at home. She stayed late attending club meetings — just not to be home. French club and women's lib club and Future Teachers of America. She got boyfriends, as bland and loyal as her father.

Foolishly, she thought now, she'd believed that she and Jim were the perfect mixture of predictable and unpredictable. Hadn't he been an actor? Doing commedia, no less? And hadn't they traveled to offbeat, far-flung places, like Cambodia and Tibet? She had taken comfort in finally being neither of her parents, but her own self. And, like with so many things in life, she'd been wrong.

"Hey!" Luke said. "My mom used to make that!"

Ava stared down at the pan of chicken Marbella, her go-to dinner party recipe. Its page in *The Silver Palate Cookbook* had so many splashes of red wine vinegar and olive juice on it that the words were blurred in places. But it didn't matter; Ava knew how to make it by heart. Now, she just wanted to toss the whole thing in the garbage.

"She didn't use prunes, though," Luke added, frowning.

Prunes were Ava's personal touch. With the dried apricots and green olives, the prunes made the dish look even prettier.

She tried to think of something to say, but Luke's eager face and the chicken Marbella in her pot-holdered hands made her mind go blank. Except one thought: *What am I doing with someone young enough to have a mother who cooks from* The Silver Palate?

"Cool," Luke said with even more enthusiasm. "Mom made it with couscous too."

"You need . . ." Ava began.

Suddenly her brain was too full. *To go home? To grow up? To stop comparing me to your mother?*

She looked at him, grinning, wearing nothing but boxer shorts and his dumb hat.

"To get dressed," she said. "You need to get dressed. They'll be here any minute."

With the words barely out of her mouth, the doorbell rang. Luke bent down and gave her a big wet kiss. Ava tried not to think about how thirty minutes ago, as she was setting the table with her Fiestaware and the napkins she'd bought at a market in Lyon, he'd walked in, tossed a bouquet of daffodils on the table, lifted her onto the table, and made love to her. She tried not to think about how much she'd liked it.

"Go," she whispered.

The doorbell rang again.

Ava scooped up the Lysol wipes she'd used to clean up after the sex, and the daffodils, and went to answer the door.

Gray and Cate stood soldier straight, he clutching a bottle of wine and Cate clutching, coincidentally, daffodils. They hugged Ava stiffly, and frowned at the balled up wet naps and the profusion of daffodils she now held in one hand. Why had she thought having Gray and Cate for a dinner party was a good idea?

"Where's the kid?" Gray asked as soon as they were inside, martinis in hand.

"Be nice," Cate said.

"Luke," Ava said. "He's getting dressed."

Gray lifted one eyebrow.

Ava had given dozens, maybe even hundreds, of dinner parties in this house, and they were always the same. Hors d'oeuvres in the front living room: a soft cheese and a hard cheese on the Bennington Potters platter with grapes and water crackers. A bowl of cashews. Martinis. After an hour they'd move into the dining room for dinner, and then back in here for dessert. Maybe she should have done it differently, Ava thought uncomfortably. Everything was in place, except that Jim was around the corner with Delia Lindstrom instead of refilling Gray's martini glass and worrying loudly about the state of education or the economy or the environment.

"Ah!" Cate said in her change-the-subject voice. "*To Kill a Mockingbird.* How do you like it?" She picked the book up from the chair where Ava had left it.

"I kind of love it," Ava admitted.

"She wanted to name Nat 'Atticus'," Gray said. "Did you know that?"

"I did," Cate said, nodding.

"With this new Harper Lee book, he'd be doomed, right?" Gray said, shaking his head. "Atticus as a racist would send the poor kid to therapy."

"They're going to end up in therapy anyway," Ava said, intending to sound ironic.

Instead, she thought of Maggie with a sharp pang. Her daughter's angry eyes as she sat, sullen and belligerent, in the family therapy sessions that had seemed at the time to go nowhere. But Maggie was fine now, Ava reminded herself. So maybe they had helped after all. And she was fine, wasn't she? Ava thought, feeling unsettled.

"I have two friends with daughters named

Scout," Luke said, surprising them all.

He strode into the room and popped a handful of cashews in his mouth. Gray raised that eyebrow again.

"How about a martini, guy?" Gray said.

"If you're buying," Luke said.

Ava cringed. Had he really just said that?

"Luke, this is Gray, Cate's husband," she said, getting to her feet. "And obviously you know Cate."

Luke shook Gray's hand and gave Cate a peck on the cheek.

"Marian the Librarian," he said.

Ava wondered if everything he said had always sounded so inane. Had she never noticed before?

"So Scout's a popular name with your generation?" Cate asked politely.

"I guess we'll have a granddaughter named Scout then," Gray complained.

"I think it's nice," Luke said. "Literary."

Cate rolled her eyes. "Should we start naming kids Lolita then? Or Macbeth?"

Luke drained his martini. "That's not the same," he said.

"I for one would welcome a Scout in my class," Ava said. "I have so many Carolines I can't keep them straight."

Gray refilled everyone's glasses. "I think the young people should bring back the name Debbie. Or Kathy. When's the last time you met a little girl named Kathy?"

"That was my mom's name," Luke said.

"Maybe then you'll name your daughter Kathy," Gray said. "Start a trend."

"Maybe," Luke said.

Ava knew this conversation — no, this dinner party — was not going well. But she couldn't think how to save it. Who cared if people were naming their kids Scout? Or Macbeth, for that matter? How had all those countless dinner parties run so smoothly? Was the missing ingredient — Jim — the answer? She could picture him introducing topics for discussion, navigating all the different personalities in the room, making more martinis.

The conversation had somehow turned to student loans. Not in general, but Luke's in particular. Why did every topic have to do with his age? Luke glanced at her. He didn't look happy. But why should he? Gray was being a boor and Cate was egging him on. Ava reached for the empty pitcher, but stopped. Why prolong the agony?

"Dinner's ready," she announced.

As they ate their chicken Marbella, Ava decided this was maybe the worst idea she'd had in a long time. Gray was pontificating about the apathy of Luke's generation, Cate was picking the capers out of her meal — since when didn't she like capers? — and Luke had got up and moved his chair beside Ava's, like they were two teenagers sitting on the same side of the booth in an ice cream shop, instead of staying put across from her.

When Gray paused to take another bite, Cate said, "Isn't tomorrow night *Le Fin*?"

Ava cringed. She had purposely not told Luke about *Le Fin,* because he would surely want to go with her. Which was out of the question.

"The End?" Luke asked, baffled.

"Ava's big end-of-the-year party," Cate said. "Plouff throws it."

"Like, at work?" Luke asked Ava.

She pretended to fluff the couscous. She pretended he hadn't started his sentence with *like.*

Ava could feel him staring at her. The couscous was definitely fluffed, but she kept lightly tossing it with the serving spoon. Until Luke put his hand over hers to stop her. "Plouff?" he asked.

"Ava's boss," Cate explained. "The head of the department."

Plouff went all out for this party, transforming the biggest conference room into a French bistro. His wife made a giant papier mâché Eiffel Tower and vats of boeuf bourgignon. There was plenty of wine and Edith Piaf crooning on Plouff's Bose. Even Jim had liked *Le Fin.* In past years, he'd danced with Mrs. Plouff and the ancient Madame Levesque, the department secretary. He'd once baked profiteroles for dessert, an effort so grand and noble that the whole department had fallen in love with him.

This year, there would be no profiteroles, no Jim. But Ava had no choice but to go.

"It's just a lot of French teachers swaying to Edith Piaf," Ava said dismissively.

"I love Edith Piaf," Luke said. "So it's tomorrow?"

"It is, but it's totally boring," Ava said. "I don't even want to go."

"What?" Cate said, choking on her wine. "You love *Le Fin*!"

"Love would be too strong a word," Ava said.

"Is that the thing Jim made all those profiteroles for?" Gray asked. "How many did he make? A hundred?"

Even though Ava was staring hard at the chicken remnants on her plate, she could feel Luke's eyes boring into her.

Abruptly, she stood.

"That reminds me," she said. "I made that peach cake for dessert."

"Isn't there salad?" Gray asked, confused.

Ava always served salad after the main course, a mix of greens with herbs and a mustardy vinaigrette. In fact, a salad sat in her big wooden salad bowl on the kitchen counter, waiting to be tossed and served.

"Not tonight," she said. "The lettuce looked wilty."

She ignored Luke's frown. Of course he had seen the salad on the counter. She didn't care. She just picked up the dinner plates and went into the kitchen. Cate followed.

"Is this the salad of wilty lettuce?" Cate asked, standing close behind her.

"This is a disaster," Ava moaned, scraping chicken bones and Cate's capers and someone's prunes into the trash. Was it Luke who hadn't eaten the prunes?

Cate picked lettuce from the bowl with her fingers and nibbled. "You make the best dressing. I've even tried your recipe and it doesn't come out this good."

"I can't take Luke to work," Ava whispered. "With Plouff and Monique and Greg and the rest? I'd never live it down."

"But if you care about him —"

"I do!" Ava said. "I think," she added.

Cate's eyes met hers.

"You will never be able to give him a

daughter named Scout," Cate said.

Ava laughed. "True."

Cate ate another fingerful of salad. Her lips glistened with dressing.

"It's okay to just have sex with the guy —" she began.

"He thinks I'm his girlfriend," Ava said.

Cate's eyes widened. "Why would he think that?"

"Because he asked me and I kind of said yes."

Cate's lips twitched the way they did when she was trying to stay serious.

"You mean, you're going steady?"

Ava picked up the tongs and put salad on two plates. She handed one to Cate.

"I am," Ava said.

"Babe?" Luke called.

Ava looked at Cate. "Don't say a word."

"What?" Cate said, eating her salad.

"Babe?" he called again.

Ava picked up the salad bowl and scraped all of the beautiful lettuce into the trash.

As she stood beneath the twinkling lights of a fake Eiffel Tower, Ava couldn't help but wonder if her new role in her own life was to destroy things. Of course Luke had left hurt this morning (true, he'd stayed the night and managed to not be angry as he bent her into shapes her body had forgotten it could make). Of course Gray was also angry with her, even though he was the one who had acted like an ass last night. No, Ava corrected herself. Gray wasn't angry. Worse: he was disappointed in her. She'd let Jim get away and now she was involved with someone only slightly older than her son. No, Ava corrected herself again, taking a big swallow of Plouff's very good burgundy. Gray wasn't disappointed. He thought she was pathetic. So did Monique, who was glaring at her from beneath the fake Arc de Triomphe, a new addition to this year's party.

Madame Levesque pushed her walker to a halt beside Ava and frowned up at her. The woman got smaller and more hunchbacked every year. Still, she wore two spots of rouge, one smack in the middle of each cheek, dark red lipstick, and enough perfume to last a week.

"Where's Jim?" Madame Levesque shouted up at Ava.

Ava took a deep breath. "He couldn't come," she said.

"Why not?" Madame Levesque asked, sounding more like a spoiled child than an octogenarian.

"Because he left me, Madame Levesque,"

Ava blurted. "He ran off with someone he knew years ago when they had a fling on Mykonos."

"The Greek island?" Madame Levesque asked, as if that was the detail that mattered.

"She's a yarn bomber," Ava said. "She takes over things that aren't hers."

Madame Levesque shrugged. *"C'est la vie,"* she said. "I left my first two husbands. Number one for number two, and number two for number three. They survived."

"Thanks for understanding," Ava said.

Greg sidled up to her on the other side, red-faced and smelling garlicky. He loosened his tie, a garish one with multicolored Mona Lisas smiling out from it.

"Came to drag you into the hot debate," he said, linking an arm through hers.

Ava glanced back to find Madame Levesque dancing with Pierre, one of the adjuncts. Pierre wore his hair like Tintin's, and as he twirled Madame Levesque in his arms, his hair seemed to bow to her.

"I'm sure I'll be able to piss someone off," Ava said, relaxing into his side. "Topic?"

"Should they get rid of the locks of love on the Pont des Arts?"

People from around the world sealed their love these days by attaching locks to the railing on the Pont des Arts in Paris, and then throwing the keys into the Seine. Two Americans living in Paris had a petition calling for the locks to be removed, turning the fate of the locks into a hot debate.

"Should I be for or against?" Ava whispered as they approached the small but loud group.

"Definitely for," Greg whispered back with a warm puff of garlic breath.

"I'll try," Ava said. "But as one who does not believe love can be sealed, even with heavy ugly locks attached to a bridge, I can't make any promises."

"L'amour, c'est impossible," Greg agreed, steering her toward the debaters.

For a French professor, Ava thought, his accent was terrible.

"What do you think, Ava?" Plouff asked as soon as he saw her. "Surely that bridge is going to drop into the Seine at any moment."

"Not to mention how ugly all those ridiculous locks are!" Monique added. She was so worked up her eyes bulged slightly and the veins in her neck popped.

"What can I say? I like them. I like the *idea* of them," Ava said.

Greg beamed at her.

"How can any of you not be for love?" Ava asked them. "Because that's what those locks stand for? Love." Saying it, it almost seemed true, and she heard her voice catch.

"Love?" Monique practically spit. "Bondage maybe."

"Hey," Greg said, "don't put down bondage till you've tried it."

Everyone, even those against the locks, laughed.

Monique was shouting about locks and love and bridges, and Marie, another adjunct, was shouting the opposite side.

Greg linked his arm through Ava's again and escorted her onto the dance floor. Soon, Plouff's wife would play the can-can and make the entire department stand in line and kick their legs. It was that time of night. But for now, Ava danced with Greg to a few songs she didn't recognize, and to a surprise non-French song — Frank Sinatra singing "Strangers in the Night." That one was a slow dance, and Greg, with his hand on the small of her back, led her expertly through a foxtrot.

But after "Strangers in the Night," Greg said, "That's it for me, I'm afraid. *Je suis fatigué.*"

She grimaced at the way he said it, but Greg didn't seem to notice.

"To locks on bridges," Greg said, tilting an imaginary glass in her direction. "May they never crash into the Seine."

He said *Seine* like *sane.* The French professor who couldn't even pronounce *Seine* correctly.

Even after he left, Ava stood at the edge of the dance floor watching as Pierre and his Tintin hair twisted wildly with Madame Plouff. Soon enough, the faculty was corralled into the can-can line. Ava joined in half-heartedly. Everything was covered with Jim's fingerprints it seemed, even *Le Fin.* That's when the idea struck her. The semester was over. She had nothing keeping her here. Instead of feeling sorry for herself, she should do something fun, something crazy. Like what? she thought as she kicked her legs into the air. And she answered herself: Visit Maggie in Italy. The music sped up. Legs flew higher. And Ava smiled.

Maggie

"Want to party?" Maggie asked Henri.

They were on a chaise, wrapped together beneath a striped blanket. Mouths sour from wine and sore from kissing. Hair damp from swimming. The smell of chlorine and grilled meat in the air. It was that time just before night became morning, the sky beginning to lighten, the moon still bright.

He looked at her, confused. As if she could read his mind, she knew what he was thinking: *Isn't that what we've been doing?*

After they'd left the beach, Henri took Maggie back to the house where he and his friends were staying. It had a big pool and many bedrooms and a refrigerator full of food. She told him that her father was a horrible person and that she needed to get away from him. "You can stay with us, of course," Henri said.

It was the hairy friend's family's country house, and Henri opened one of the bedroom doors and told Maggie she could stay there. He went back to the beach, promising to return soon.

Maggie sat on the white iron bed, her bag in her lap, trying to make a plan. She would go back to the apartment for her things. No. Julien might be there waiting for her. This time, he might actually kill her, she thought. She shivered. She could try to find the boy, Noah. But even if she did, then what? She wished she had a pen and some paper so she could write down her plan. Except, of course, there was no plan. How many times had her mother told her: *It helps to write things down, to see them in black and white.* Panic rose in her gut, sending a sour taste to her mouth. She had no plan, and this terrified her.

On the desk across the room, a computer glowed at her. She thought of all those emails piling up in there. She thought of her brother and his gorillas, how he'd loved them since he was a kid and read some book by a guy who'd discovered them or something. Even in middle school he'd spent summers volunteering at the zoo, and then he'd gone to the Bwindi Impenetrable Forest every summer during college, observing the mountain gorillas in their natural habitat. Will, Maggie thought, always had a plan.

She walked over to the computer and went to Gmail, wincing when she saw her brother's emails there, stacked up one on top of the other.

First she wrote a quick breezy one to her mother, pausing only to choose which city to tell her she'd visited. Amsterdam, she decided. *The van Goghs are crazy cool,* Maggie wrote. *I'll post pictures soonest.* She ended with dozens of Xs and Os.

Next, Maggie thought, and typed:

Dear Wills,

It's impossible to hide anything from you, Bro. Let's just say that I got involved in an intense relationship that maybe is turning out to be a bad idea. (Add emoticon of shocked face here! Maggie? Having a bad idea???) Let's just say I've had an existential crisis (again) about what I'm doing and why and how and generally WTF? (Wills, WTF means What the Fuck, BTW) (BTW means By the Way, BTW) (It's so hard having a brother who lives in the wrong century!!!!!) Also. I've been pretty sick.

But I'm OK! Really!!!!! Please please please don't mention any of this to the madre, who will just freak out. And if you speak to the padre, tell him to go fuck himself. Or his girlfriend. Or himself and his girlfriend. (and did I tell you her stupid art or whatever it is she does with fucking yarn was actually in the International Herald Tribune??? Apparently she bombed a phone booth in London or something. I mean WTF????)

But.

That spaghetti! Sigh. So purple and wine-y and yummy. (and that you were probably saving for breakfast . . . WAIT!!! I'm quoting or should I say misquoting poetry!!! Get the poetry police!!!) Remember when I asked for grated cheese and they practically threw me out? The first of my many crimes. Parmesan on drunken spaghetti. It has been downhill from there, I'm afraid.

I hope your gorillas are swell.

I luv u. Maggie

She clicked out of Gmail, sat back, and stared at the dark screen. Now what? She licked her lips. A humming started, somewhere deep inside. A humming that grew steadily.

Maggie sat back down on the bed, her brain all sharp and jagged.

Her fingers played with the zipper on her bag, sliding it open and shut. Open and shut. Henri had said he'd be back soon, but it seemed like hours and hours had passed. Maggie slid the zipper open and rested her hand inside the bag. Maybe just a little, she thought, to calm her down. To take the edge off.

She pulled the suede pouch from the bag and opened it, her heart quickening at the sight of everything inside: matches, needles, syringe, the white powder.

"Just a little," she said out loud, her voice quavering.

Maggie had never shot herself up. She had convinced herself that if someone else did it, she wasn't a junkie. But now she argued with her own logic. If she did it herself, she was in control of it, wasn't she?

She got off the bed quickly, sending the rest of the contents of her bag onto the floor. The small tube of fennel toothpaste and a pair of delicate silver hoop earrings, pomegranate-flavored lip balm and a pink and green tube of mascara. Without pausing to pick anything up, she went into the adjoining bathroom, locked the door, and climbed into the bathtub, like Gavin had taught her. Gavin! The sight of him under that sheet, on the gurney, flashed through her mind, and she tried to replace it with other images of him. But they were all sad, every one of them. She pressed her fingers to her eyelids, hard, until little starbursts flashed there.

Then, as slowly as she could manage — and it was difficult to go slowly because now that it was so close she realized how much she craved it — she went through the steps, saying each one out loud to steady herself.

"Now," Maggie said, "find a good vein."

She licked her lips. She turned over her left arm, and found only two small bruises.

"Find a good vein," she said out loud again, tapping a pale blue line.

It took a while to respond — forever, Maggie thought — but then she could see it clearly, finally bulging ever so slightly.

"Draw back the syringe," she said, lying back in the tub. "Now insert the needle."

She had a brief memory of herself as a little girl screaming in the pediatrician's office as he prepared to give her a shot. She remembered her mother's lap, how safe it had felt there. She remembered her mother's arms around her, her mother's voice in her ear soothing her. *It will be over so fast, and then you'll get a lollipop!*

Maggie hesitated, the needle just piercing the skin. What was she doing? What the hell was she doing?

Her legs were jumping, her stomach

clenching.

With too much force, she pushed the needle into her vein and released the drug.

She felt her eyes roll back in her head, felt the waves rush over her like an orgasm that doesn't stop. Her body bucked, lifted, and slammed back down, lifted and slammed back down. She'd forgotten that Julien had bought very good heroin so she would forgive him.

"So good," she said.

Or thought she said, because her body was lifting, lifting, going to that place she loved.

When she came down, it was dark. The needle was still in her arm and there was a tight hard purple ball at her vein. Dried blood speckled her flesh. She licked her dry lips and tried to stand up. Too soon. Her knees buckled, and she eased back onto the hard, cold porcelain.

But later, she managed to stand, to pull on her long-sleeved pale blue button-down shirt, and make her way out to the pool where Henri and his friends were eating cubes of meat from long skewers. The sight of it made her stomach roll and for a moment she thought she might throw up.

"I didn't want to wake you," he said politely.

He got up and put a skewer of meat on a plate and handed it to her.

She pretended to eat. She drank a lot of wine. When they brought out the drugs — pot, pills, a little cocaine — she happily joined in. Someone put on music and they all danced, wildly, around the pool. Of course they ended up jumping in, half-dressed, splashing each other and drinking wine straight from the bottle. Henri put his hands around her waist and lifted her so that her legs wrapped around him and they were face to face, kissing.

"You're so light," he told her. "Like a fairy."

Maggie smiled at that. She imagined wings, made of gossamer or, better yet, cotton candy.

"When I was a little girl," she told him, "I was a fairy for Halloween. My mother made me white wings covered in silver glitter."

She watched Henri trying to translate what she said.

"Paillettes," she said.

He laughed, kissed her again.

"Ma fée," he whispered.

"Yes," Maggie whispered back. "I'm your fairy. I can fly."

When they got out of the pool, their skin pruny, it was dark and they lay on the white chaises staring up at the stars, heads throbbing pleasantly from drugs and wine. Maggie lifted her arms, let the spins whoosh through her.

"Don't fly away," Henri whispered.

She didn't remember climbing onto the chaise with him. Maybe she'd done it, half-asleep. Maybe he'd brought her there himself as she slept. But here she was, looking up at him, asking him if he wanted to party. Somewhere, Julien was raging, searching for her. She squeezed her eyes shut hard to block out the thought.

"I think we have used it all up," Henri was explaining.

Each chaise had a lump under a blanket on it. She saw an arm drooped over the side of one, the top of curly dark hair peeking out above another.

Her gaze drifted back to Henri. They hadn't had sex yet, just kissed and kissed. She couldn't remember the last time she'd kissed like that. Somehow, kissing had become almost perfunctory, the quick prelude to sex. But it had been nice, all that kissing, and she slid up his long body to his lips and kissed his sour mouth.

"I have something," she said into his mouth, her tongue lazy on his. "Something good."

"Sure, sure," he said.

She glanced around. The lumps under the blankets didn't stir.

"I need a plan," she said softly.

He didn't answer. Maybe he'd drifted off to sleep again.

This was the time when she should fall back asleep too, in his arms. That's what people did. But her gut was clenching. Her mind felt like broken glass. She thought of her pouch, back inside. She could get it and bring it out here. She could show it to him, share it with him.

No. Not out here.

She would wake him, tug him gently inside the house. Share it with him like a gift.

Maggie licked her lips.

"Hey, sleepyhead," she said.

He opened his eyes, smiled lazily. *"Ma fée,"* he said.

She took his hand. *"Viens avec moi,"* she said, urging him off the chaise.

Henri groaned. "This better be good," he said.

Night had gone, and the sky was pink and pretty with light now.

Maggie's bare feet rushed across the cool dewy grass, into the dark house, Henri close behind. In the room, she closed the door after him, then sat on the bed where the pouch lay waiting.

But he mistook her intention. Grinning he said, “Yes, the bed is better, *n’est-ce pas?*”

“Yes,” she agreed. “But let’s get high first?”

She noticed that his underwear was still wet from the pool.

Henri waited.

Maggie opened the pouch, her throat and mouth dry with wanting it. Her brain felt so jagged, so sharp. She thought again of broken glass.

He was watching her as she pulled out the little bag of white powder, then the syringe. She felt him watching her.

“Qu’est-ce que c’est?” he asked.

Maggie looked at him then, her hands trembling, the syringe and needle and powder in them. He was frowning.

“No, no,” she said quickly. “If you take just a little there’s no problem. Really. Just a little doesn’t change anything.”

That wasn’t what she meant to say, but he was moving away from her, a look of disgust on his face.

“Really,” she said again, “it’s not what you think.”

But of course it was. It was exactly what he thought, and he was repulsed by it. By her. She couldn't let him walk out. He was the one good thing that had happened in a long time.

"It's fun," she said, hearing the desperation in her voice. "That's all. You want to have a little fun, don't you?"

She dropped everything back into the pouch, and patted the bed beside her.

"It's okay," she said. "I thought it might be fun, but it's okay."

He was at the door now, studying her face as if he had just seen her for the first time.

"I don't need to do it," she said. *"Viens ici?"*

He hesitated.

"I liked kissing you so much," Maggie said.

At that he shook his head.

"Je suis désolé," he said.

"You're sorry?"

"I can't," he said.

She was crying again. Her brain, glass against glass. Her stomach hurting.

"Please," she said, feeling the tears and snot on her face.

"I will get you back to Paris," he was saying. "To your father."

Maggie nodded. She had ruined this. She had ruined everything. She heard the door close, and she lay back on the bed, and she thought: Go to Paris and fix your life.

She got up, opened drawers until she found a small notebook with an orange cover and paper covered with grids on it.

Number 1, she wrote. *Go to Paris.*

Maggie took a breath, tried not to think about the fact that she had no place to live there anymore.

From somewhere in her bag, her phone rang.

Julien, she thought.

She wrote, *Number 2.*

The phone rang again. She dug it out, stared at the number. Not Julien. Her mother. Maggie put the phone back in her bag.

Fix your life, she wrote beside Number 2.

Her mother was right. It felt better to see things in black and white. It made them seem possible.

She sat listening to the phone ring. When it finally stopped, she reread what she'd written. Then she tore the paper from the notebook and folded it and put it in the little pouch.

Henri knocked on the door, then said, "There's a train in an hour. I'll drive you to the station."

He didn't come inside, just spoke through the closed door.

She nodded as if he could see her.

"Just a little," she said to herself. "Last time."

As if to make it true, she took the paper out of the pouch, unfolded it, and wrote: *Just a little. Last time.* Then she folded the paper again and put it away.

She didn't bother to go into the bathroom. She just rolled up her sleeve and lay back on the bed again. She took a deep breath full of anticipation and that feeling, that beautiful feeling that came just before the rush of the drug through her body. If she could capture that feeling, if she could feel that all the time, Maggie would be happy. She licked her lips and pressed the needle into her vein. The pieces of glass tinkled softly, fell into place, quieted. By the time she climbed into the car beside Henri, she was stoned enough not to care that he wouldn't even look at her.

Hank

Even when he used to misbehave, even when he was in love with a woman who wasn't his wife, even drunk as hell, Hank Bingham always slept through the night without waking. *Like a log.* That's what Nadine used to say, frustrated or surprised or even angry at him for sleeping so well. *You didn't even roll over once.* Hank used to feel almost proud of this singular achievement. He was, if nothing else, a good sleeper.

But not tonight. Tonight Hank woke up, not in the groggy way that sometimes happened these days when he woke up having to piss and stumbled to the bathroom, only to drop right back to sleep as soon as he got back in bed. No, this time Hank was fully awake. Outside his window, only darkness. The nightlight he'd bought at Home Depot when this nighttime need to piss started was the only light in the house, small and white in the hallway. Ever since Nadine died, Hank had slept on her side of the bed. But in the darkness, that too felt disconcerting, like he was seeing the world from the wrong angle.

What did people do when they had insomnia? Watch television? Call friends in other time zones?

Hank sighed, closed his eyes, waited for sleep.

No luck.

He got out of bed and followed that nightlight down the hall to the bathroom. Something had woken him up. For the first time in his life, something had actually interrupted his sleep, the one thing he did perfectly.

Miss Kitty appeared in the bathroom doorway, looking confused.

"No," he told her. "It is not time for breakfast."

He went into the smallest bedroom, the one that would have been a nursery if they'd ever had kids. Instead, it was an office of sorts, the room where their hulking desktop computer sat and file cabinets held their tax returns and important papers.

When Nadine got her diagnosis, she'd insisted they get passports. Neither of them had ever been out of the country, or wanted to go out of the country as far as Hank knew. But she got it in her head that they were going to Paris. "The City of Light," she'd told him. He had always thought Paris was the city of love, not lights. But what did he know? He didn't want to fly across the Atlantic Ocean, that was for sure. He didn't want to go where people didn't speak English. He didn't want to go to Paris. At all. "Paris," he'd said to her. "What a great idea." "Really?" she'd asked him, her eyes bright. "Why not?" he'd said, trying not to list all the reasons why not.

For their honeymoon they'd driven to Key West. Sometimes they would stop along the road and grab the blanket from the trunk and find a secluded spot and make love. In Key West they watched the sun set every night. Hank had heard about the Green Flash, the sudden appearance of bright green above the horizon at sunset. He'd watched intently, waiting for it, wanting desperately to see it. He never did, though. They never went to Paris either. Nadine got too sick too fast. But they had those stiff blank passports in the file cabinet anyway.

Hank turned on the desk lamp and looked around the room. Nadine always called it his office, but he'd never needed an office. His office was down at the station. The slightly larger third bedroom was Nadine's sewing room. She'd fixed that one up nice. Her sewing machine was in there, sure. But she had a rocking chair and shelves with plastic see-through bins that held her yarn and fabric and whatnot. That's what Nadine called everything else, the buttons and needles and threads and measuring tapes. Her whatnot. She had a nice hooked rug on the floor in there, one she'd made out of fabric scraps. Not scraps, he corrected himself. Remnants. He could almost hear Nadine reminding him. She'd hung a framed poster of irises on the wall too. "Van Gogh's *Irises,*" she'd explained to him in that voice she used when she couldn't believe what a dope he was.

This room, his *office,* had no personality. Just stuff. Cardboard boxes against one wall, filled with the files he'd brought from his real office after he retired. The desk and the file cabinet and a yellow director's chair from Nadine's apartment before they got married. She'd had two of them, this yellow one and a blue one, and she'd used them as her kitchen chairs. The first time he went to her apartment for dinner, he'd been impressed by her eye for style, how creative she was. The chairs stood around a small round bright red table that she'd painted herself. On one wall, a big red capital N hung; across from it, a framed poster of Monet's *Water Lilies.* Of course, he hadn't known they were Monet's *Water Lilies* until she told him that the next morning.

That night, she'd served him chicken Kiev and a salad with mandarin oranges and sugary slivered almonds. He couldn't believe how sophisticated she was, or why someone like her would even go out with a guy like him, a cop with a high school education who had never heard of Monet or chicken Kiev. Later, after they got married, he'd watch her make recipes from that hardcover red Betty Crocker cookbook, her head bent over it, her hair tucked behind her ears, a pencil in her hand. But that night he thought she'd produced that fine dinner by magic, by her special powers. The same special powers that bewitched him and led him to propose before the cherries jubilee appeared, surprising both of them when he dropped on one knee and blurted, "Will you please please marry me, Nadine?"

She said yes, jumping to her feet and clapping her hands together like she'd won a prize. She let him take her to bed then, their first time together. Everything in that room was pale blue and flowery — forget-me-nots on the sheets and dried hydrangeas in a vase by the brass bed and a framed poster from the Museum of Modern Art of van Gogh's *Irises* above it.

Goddamn it, Hank thought as he stood in that depressing half-empty room. His *office.*

That was the same poster she'd hung in her sewing room. The one that used to hang above her bed, the one he'd first glimpsed as he made love to her that long-ago night. After, she'd put on his white button-down shirt and went into the kitchen. He'd followed her, dazed from the terrifying realization that he was going to get married. Just a few nights before, he'd met a girl at Alias Smith and Jones in East Greenwich and scribbled her phone number on a cocktail napkin. He still had that cocktail napkin. Still had an image of the girl's rippled red hair and freckles. Damn, he'd intended to call her, to make a date. But here he was in his boxer shorts watching Nadine open a can of cherries, dump them in a pretty bowl because everything Nadine touched or owned was pretty, pour brandy on top and light the whole damn thing on fire. She'd looked over at him from beneath her eyelids.

"Cherries jubilee," she'd said proudly.

Remembering, Hank swallowed hard, because he remembered too how the first thing he'd done when he got home the next morning was dig out that cocktail napkin and call that red-haired girl. He'd met her again at Alias Smith and Jones and bought her beer and shots called Snake Eyes and danced until they were sweaty and achy. Then they drove to a park and had sex in his car.

Oh Nadine, he thought, his throat tight.

He padded out of the room, Miss Kitty moving in and out of his legs hoping for breakfast. He opened the door to Nadine's sewing room, the smell of the potpourri she kept in bowls assaulting him as soon as he stepped inside. Without pausing, he took that poster off the wall, and carried it to his office where he hung it — too high, he knew — from a hook left over from the old owners.

Hank stepped back and studied it. Van Gogh's *Irises.* Who would have thought, that long-ago night, the night of his engagement, as he glimpsed it above a brass bed with a lean lovely girl naked beneath him, that he would hang it on this wall someday?

Nadine.

Hank opened the file cabinet and took out the box labeled *"Lily North."* He sat at the desk, shoving the behemoth computer to the side. The little girl stared out at him from her school picture. Blond with short bangs and blue eyes and a look of surprise.

Then he took out all of his notes, spread them on the desk, and began.

AVA

That Morning
1970

Ava watched her mother running up the street, screaming the way their dog Butterscotch had when he got hit by a car last winter, and that's when she knew: Lily was dead.

Her mother ran past the policeman, who tried to stop her; past Aunt Beatrice, who tried to stop her; past Ava, who called out to her in a voice growing shrill with the realization that her sister wasn't okay, wasn't even hurt bad, but was dead. *Dead.* The word sounded as hard and cold and final as the thing itself. She'd just learned about onomatopoeia in English class, words that sounded like the thing they were: *rat-a-tat-tat, hiss, thunder.* And *dead,* Ava thought again as her mother finally reached the ambulance just as the two men rolling the stretcher did.

"Stop!" her mother yelled.

They both looked up, surprised.

"Stop!" she yelled again, her voice not sounding like her voice. Instead of gravelly, it was high and shaky. Instead of confident, it was desperate.

The men stopped. One of them kept his hands on the place near where Lily's head was. Ava couldn't see her sister — they'd covered her with a bright white sheet — but she could make out where her head lay and the two points of her feet. The man by Lily's feet stepped back.

So fast that Ava didn't even see her mother do it, the sheet was off and there was Lily, blonde hair somehow blonder — *like dandelions,* Ava thought — tiny on that big adult-sized stretcher. Her skin did not look like her skin. It was like blue and white marble, darker in some places, like her legs sticking out from beneath her favorite purple shorts and her feet, which had somehow lost her sneakers and now poked into the sky, bare and more gray than blue.

The sheet was off and Lily was there, clearly broken, clearly dead, Lily but not Lily.

And her mother was screaming again, calling *"LilyLilyLilyLily."* And then *"My baby! My baby!"*

And then she was on top of Lily, hugging her tight and rocking her and saying, softer now, "Wake up, baby. Wake up."

When the man who had stepped back tried to pull her away, she wouldn't let go of Lily, and lifted Lily with her as the man lifted her. The other policeman, not the one who had talked to Ava but the other one, was gently trying to pry her mother's arms from Lily. But he couldn't.

Aunt Beatrice was shouting, "It's not my fault!"

At first, Ava thought Aunt Beatrice was right — it was *her* fault. She shouldn't have let Lily climb so high in the tree. She'd told her to come down, hadn't she?

Ava frowned and chewed her bottom lip.

She'd been sitting under the tree reading *Five Little Peppers and How They Grew,* not just reading it but lost in it, the way books she loved seemed to take her into them — as if she lived in the pages, in the world of the story. And Lily had been bored, begging Ava to put down her book and play with her. And Ava had said, "Just one more page." But after one more page, she said, "Just one more."

Lily stood up and twirled herself around and around until she grew dizzy and fell, laughing, back down to the grass. She kept twirling like that, Ava relieved her sister had found something to do so she could at least finish the chapter.

But if Lily twirled herself into dizziness so many times, she shouldn't have climbed that tree at all. Ava should have realized that. She should have put her book down and started a game of hide and seek. Or gone inside for a deck of cards and played War until Aunt Beatrice finally showed up.

Her mother wasn't listening to Aunt Beatrice. She was still stretched on top of Lily, rocking slightly, murmuring now, "Come on, baby. Wake up."

The policeman who had talked to Ava came over to her again.

"Sweetheart," he said. Ava narrowed her eyes at him because her mother always said, *Don't trust someone who calls you sweetheart.*

"I need you to come inside," he said.

Ava glanced over at her mother, as if she might somehow intervene. But she was still on top of Lily and now all three men were trying to move her.

"Okay," she said, hesitantly.

"I'm just going to talk to you about what happened today," he said.

Lily died today, Ava thought.

The policeman put one big hand on her shoulder and steered her away from her mother and Lily.

They were sitting inside, at the kitchen table. It was hot and stuffy, the way it always got around lunchtime in the summer. Lunch, Ava thought. Her mother made them chilled melons scooped into perfect little orange and pale green balls. Or egg salad with chopped tarragon served in a hollowed-out tomato. Cool, colorful things for hot days. She immediately felt guilty for thinking about something as normal as egg salad on a day like today.

"Ava?" the policeman said. He'd brought her a bottle of Coke, even though she'd said, "No thank you" when he asked if she wanted one. Ava and Lily weren't allowed to drink soda; their mother said soda rotted your teeth. Coke, their mother told them, could take the rust off metal. Even though she was thirsty, Ava didn't take a sip. The bottle, with a flimsy paper straw sticking out of the top, sat between them.

"Tell me about her," the policeman said, sliding the bottle a little closer to Ava, as if that would make her drink the Coke. "About Lily."

She shrugged.

"Was she smart?" he asked. "Did she like to, um, draw or play ball or read?"

Ava licked her lips, which were suddenly chapped and stinging. She wished her mother were here. Her mother always carried lip balm with her, a little round jar of it. If she were here, she'd open the jar and stick her finger in the waxy stuff inside and gently run it over Ava's lips. "There, kiddo," she'd say, and immediately Ava would feel better.

"Was she a good kid?" the policeman was asking.

Her lips stung. She wished she had some lip balm. And she was so thirsty her throat hurt. When they'd learned similes last week, she'd written, *her throat was as dry as the Sahara Desert,* and Mrs. Gaffney put a check plus next to it.

"My throat is as dry as the Sahara Desert," Ava said.

The policeman glanced up at her. "You need another Coke?"

She shook her head. He didn't even notice that she hadn't touched the soda. She decided he didn't have kids. A father would pay more attention, maybe bring her a glass of water.

Ava picked up the bottle, and put the straw between her lips. It was disgusting, She drank the room-temperature Coke. Her tongue felt all fuzzy from it.

"So Aunt Beatrice shows up late today," he said, looking at Ava.

"Yes."

Ava thought of the time that had stretched empty and dangerous while she and Lily were alone waiting for Aunt Beatrice. If she had known those were the very last hours she'd ever spend with her sister, what would she have done differently?

"Had Lily already climbed the tree when Aunt Beatrice showed up this morning?"

"I already told you," Ava said uncertainly.

He stared at her. His eyes were blue, which was unexpected because his hair was so dark. This time Ava looked away.

"I told her not to climb so high," she said.

The events of the day were starting to crush her. When she thought about Lily, tears sprang to her eyes. How could someone who had been twirling around under a warm sun a few hours ago be dead?

"I . . ." Ava began, but she didn't know what to say.

"Remind me," he said. "Your aunt was where?"

"Inside?" Ava said hesitantly, afraid she was getting Aunt Beatrice in trouble. "Maybe?"

The policeman put his pencil down.

A thought hit Ava. *Like lightning striking.*

"What?" Detective Bingham said.
"It's my fault," Ava said. "It's all my fault."

AVA

To Ava's surprise, when they got to the library, Luke was presiding over the drinks and snacks rather than Emma. He looked so young standing there in his silly hat that Ava actually blushed thinking about their foolish relationship. Was that even the right word? Relationship?

"Southern theme," Cate whispered to Ava.

Ava watched as Kiki glanced up at Luke from beneath lowered eyelids, flirting as she took the metal cup from him. A small pang of jealousy shot through Ava, embarrassing her even more. Kiki *should* flirt with Luke. And go steady with him. It was age-appropriate. So why did she find herself elbowing her way past Monique and Honor to get to the front of the bar? After the dinner party with Cate and Gray she knew she couldn't see him anymore and had ended it.

As a middle-aged woman — an adult! —

she did not glance up at him like Kiki did; she looked him straight in the eye. "I'll have whatever you're making."

"They're *good,*" Kiki gushed.

"It's all in the muddling," Luke said, pushing his hat back on his head.

As Ava stood sipping her mint julep and wondering how to extricate herself gracefully, Kiki leaned her hip against a corner like she intended to stay put. The others were swarming around, tasting the pimento cheese and artichoke dip.

"The secret is mayonnaise," Ruth told Ava, tilting her chin in the direction of the dip. "Lots of it."

Muddling and mayonnaise. So many secrets, Ava thought. Like the one Jim had kept from her, claiming meetings and early-morning coffees when all the while he was courting someone else. Ava glanced at the people swarming around her. What secrets did they each have?

Up close like this, she saw that Kiki wore braces. Hot pink and purple ones on her upper teeth. A metal bolt pierced the space between her chin and lower lip, and her fingernails were covered in chipped dark blue polish. She reminded Ava of Maggie somehow, and with that realization came the sharp stab of worry. Now Diana was asking her if she knew what exactly was in pimento cheese that made it so orange, but Ava needed to sit down and calm herself.

"Are you all right?" Jennifer asked her.

Kiki was looking at her too, and Ava had to fight the urge to take that girl with her braces and her bolt and chipped nail polish and hug her.

"Too much mayonnaise," Ava said, attempting a smile.

"Mayonnaise?" Diana said, and folded her napkin around the cracker.

Thankfully, Cate was taking her place at the front of the room and everyone began to find seats.

"To Kill a Mockingbird," Cate began when the room hushed. "A U.K. survey recently selected it as the book written by a woman that most impacted, shaped, or changed readers' lives."

An impressed murmur spread through the group.

"I just want to add," Jennifer said, getting to her feet, "that with human rights under attack worldwide even more than ever, this is a timely and important book to discuss. It gave me hope that justice will prevail, and I want to thank Honor for choosing it."

Honor put her hands together and bowed her head slightly, the same way Ava's yoga teacher ended every yoga class. Ava half expected Honor to intone "Namaste." Jennifer stood in her white cotton peasant blouse with hand-embroidered colorful figures dancing across the yoke, apparently trying to compose herself.

"Thank you, Jennifer," Cate said. "That's an important observation."

Ruth said, "We don't have to discuss *Go Set a Watchman,* do we?"

"I think that's a conversation for another time," Cate said. "Honor? Do you agree? This is the book that matters the most to you."

Honor strode to the front of the room, her multitude of bracelets clanging noisily together, her layers of scarves and necklaces swaying and billowing around her as she walked.

She let her gaze settle over each of them, which took long enough for Ava to squirm beneath it. Clearly, Honor commanded a classroom. Which was surprising since, as a babysitter, she could never even get the kids to bed at a normal time.

"Actually, Jennifer touched upon the very thing that makes *To Kill a Mockingbird* the book that matters most to me," Honor said after she cleared her throat and straightened her shoulders. "Moral injustice. Good and evil."

Ava flashed back to college-student Honor lazily reading *One Fish, Two Fish, Red Fish, Blue Fish* to Will and Maggie. Her voice had hardly held their attention.

"Imagine me," Honor was saying, "a little girl growing up in New Orleans, Louisiana, surrounded by the very prejudice Harper Lee so acutely portrays. Like Scout and Jem, in my childish innocence, I assumed that people were good because I had never seen evil.

"That perspective changed," Honor continued, "when they had to confront evil, didn't it?" She danced her fingers in the air in front of her. "Childhood to adulthood. Innocence to experience."

"Yes!" Jennifer said. "Hatred and prejudice and ignorance are a threat to innocent people everywhere."

"But you know, *To Kill a Mockingbird* won the Pulitzer Prize in 1961. The criteria for that prize is a distinguished piece of writing about American life by an American author. It's easy to see why Harper Lee won the Pulitzer at that time in our history," Honor said.

"Evil destroys Tom Robinson and Boo Radley, doesn't it?" Ruth said.

Honor nodded, then continued, "Actually, Jem is almost destroyed by evil too. The evil of racism."

"But Scout isn't," Ava pointed out.

"True," Honor said. "However, Atticus Finch is the moral compass. I wrote my dissertation on him."

"That's so cool!" Kiki gushed.

"Yeah, because he never loses his faith in humankind," Luke said. "He understands that people aren't all good or all bad."

"I don't know," John said. "He comes across as almost too good. I don't have kids, so maybe I'm speaking out of turn here. I should ask an expert. What do you think, Ruth?"

Ruth laughed. "Well, I think a moral education is important, and that's what Atticus is trying to give Scout."

"My favorite thing, actually," Diana said, "is how Scout's character grows throughout the course of the novel."

"And Jem," Luke said. "I could really relate to Jem."

"What's the symbolism of the mockingbird?" John asked. "I don't get the title."

"Miss Maudie tells Scout that the only thing mockingbirds do is sing their hearts out for us," Monique said.

"Exactly!" Luke said. "That's why it's a

sin to kill a mockingbird."

"It's a sin to kill innocence," Honor said. "The mockingbird is the symbol of innocence."

Ava saw that summer day, that tree, her sister on that branch. She turned to find Penny, whose calm sure gaze Ava liked. But Penny hadn't come. Ava thought of the plastic tubes and oxygen tank, Penny's dismissive *touch of emphysema,* and hoped she was all right.

When the discussion ended, Ava forced herself to stay and have a piece of the lemon chess pie Honor had made.

Thankfully, John came and stood beside her.

He chewed a piece of pie and shook his head. "I'm learning so much here," he said. "I read *To Kill a Mockingbird* back in middle school and didn't really appreciate it. Now I'm thinking about this idea of a moral education,"

Ava watched a woman with a frosted bob walk in and look around. She had on a black dress and cardigan, and clutched a black bag close to her chest.

"I wrote something down for you," John said.

He reached into his pocket and handed her a piece of paper.

"From the book," he explained.

Cate approached the woman, who tearfully began to talk.

"Thanks," Ava said.

"Go on," John said. "Read it."

"With him, life was routine," Ava read out loud. "Without him, life was unbearable."

"That really got to me," he said. "Except, I substituted *she* for *he.*"

"Of course," Ava said, touching his arm.

"Excuse me," Cate announced in a quavering voice. "I'm afraid I have some very sad news."

The woman in black began to cry, sending small rivulets of mascara down her cheeks.

"Uh oh," John said under his breath. He glanced toward the exit.

"This is Helen Frost," Cate said, putting an arm around the woman's shoulders. "Penny's daughter."

She didn't even have to say the words; everyone knew. But of course, she did say them.

"Penny passed away yesterday."

"I hate that," John said to Ava. "Passed sounds temporary. Like she might come back."

"I know," Ava said, touching his arm again.

The woman was talking quietly to Cate.

"Helen will send me the particulars about the funeral and I'll email everyone," Cate said.

Helen whispered something more to Cate.

"Ava?" Cate said, sounding confused.

Helen Frost nodded.

"Apparently Penny has left you something and Helen would like it if you could go to the house at some point to pick it up," Cate explained.

"There must be some mistake," Ava said.

But there wasn't. Helen handed her a business card with a phone number circled on it and told her to call before she came by.

"Honestly," Ava said apologetically, "I don't want anything."

"I didn't know you two were close," John said to Ava. "I'm so sorry for your loss."

"We weren't close," Ava said.

Her phone vibrated in her purse, and happy to have a reason to leave she pulled it out. The name "Maggie" flashed on the screen.

"It's my daughter," she said, relieved Maggie was calling, relieved to get out of there.

She pressed the phone to her ear as she headed to the exit.

"Hold on, sweetie," she said. "I'm here."

"Madame Tucker?" a man with a thick French accent said.

"Yes?" Ava said, stepping out into the dark night.

He said something in French that she couldn't understand, because he spoke so fast. She thought she heard him say Maggie.

"Maggie?" Ava said. "Where's Maggie?"

The man answered her again in French.

"I can't understand you," Ava said, panic mixing with the sour taste of lemon in her throat. "Please slow down."

"La jeune fille," he said carefully.

"The girl?" Ava said. "Maggie?"

"Oui," he said. "The girl is missing."

■ ■ ■ ■

PART SEVEN: JUNE

■ ■ ■ ■

"We'll leave now, so that this moment will remain a perfect memory . . . let it be our song and think of me every time you hear it."

— *A Tree Grows in Brooklyn*
by Betty Smith

Maggie

Maggie looked at the beautiful boy in bed beside her back at the hostel. He was Swedish or Danish or Norwegian, she couldn't remember, but tall and blond with eyes the blue of icicles. She smiled and sat up, dug her notebook out of the purple net bag, and wrote *His eyes are the blue of icicles.*

"What are you writing there?" he said, his voice thick and syrupy.

"I'm a writer," Maggie said, happy to lie back down because when she sat up she felt a big whoosh run through her body and her heart pounded too hard. She pressed her hand to her chest, over the place where her heart raced. "I get these ideas and I have to write them down so I don't forget them."

"I'm writing a novel," the beautiful boy said.

"You are? That's awesome."

"I'm writing the great Norwegian novel," he said.

"Right," Maggie said. "Norwegian."

"Can you name a great Norwegian novel?"

"Um, Ibsen?"

"Those are plays," he said. He put his hands over his icicle-blue eyes. "I am so fucked up," he said, not unhappily.

"Me too," Maggie said. Her heart kept pounding too hard beneath her hand, like something trying to escape.

The boy began to talk about his novel, but Maggie couldn't concentrate. Men were in a boat and there was a storm and maybe a dog or something went overboard. She closed her eyes, let herself fall into the buzzing that ran through her body. Her brain couldn't really land on any one thing. Instead her thoughts flitted from one thing to the next. How she'd met this boy in a café and he'd bought her wine, lots of wine. Then what? Then what? She tried to put the pieces of the last six or eight or twenty hours together, but that buzzing made it hard to think. There was a party. That's right. And in the bathroom they'd snorted some coke.

"And then we learn exactly how the earth was destroyed, right?" the boy was saying. "It's like this enormous climax of explosions and death and destruction —"

Maggie sat up again. She realized she still

had the pen in her hand.

"That sounds amazing," she said.

She leaned over and wrote on his pale hairless chest: *Once upon a time*

"Yes!" he said. "Let's write a story on each other! That's brilliant!"

Maggie wrote: *there was a lost girl whose mother said she was coming to visit her in Florence. Who emailed her mother back: Oh no! We're doing farm stay! Agritourism. Slow food. Maybe in September?*

"I have a pen somewhere," the boy said, searching through the drawer of the narrow rickety table beside the bed.

She lay down and waited, the pen in the boy's hand hovering above her naked chest.

Once upon a time, he wrote, *a girl and a boy wrote the Great American and Great Norwegian novels in invisible ink.*

She liked the way the pen felt moving across her skin, both sharp and soft.

I don't know what day it is, Maggie wrote.

I'm falling in love, the boy wrote.

Eventually, words covered their chests and stomachs and arms and legs and feet and hands. He wrote sentences inside her thighs.

Afterward they made love and some of the words smeared. Then he said, "Let's get high, eh?"

Maggie didn't know what kind of drugs

he had, but whatever he put in that syringe gave her maybe the best high of her life.

"Come here," he said.

Maggie stared up into his icicle-blue eyes.

Then he stuck the needle in and her body jumped and her brain exploded and her heart seemed for a minute to stop. She felt suspended somehow, in air, in time. She heard the sound of that seashell back home, the ocean in her ear.

She felt a hard slap on her face. "Hey there! Girl!"

Maggie opened her eyes. A man she didn't know was staring down at her.

"You're going to be okay," he said.

She tried to turn her head but couldn't move. She opened her mouth to speak but only a strange gurgling came out.

"Speedball," the man said to someone else, someone she couldn't see.

"We're going to move you now," he said to her. "On the count of three."

Someone counted *"Un! Deux! Trois!"* For a moment she thought maybe she was climbing the stairs to the loft on rue Saint-Antoine. But then she was lifted up and carried out of the room and through a door and down the stairs and down more stairs and then out the door where it was evening and warm and everything was cast in a beautiful lavender light.

"Am I dead?" Maggie managed to ask.

"Almost," the man said. "Luckily someone called for help. You're okay."

She could smell the heavy scent of roses and grass.

"We're going to take you to the hospital, hydrate you, clean you up. Okay?" he said.

Maggie nodded.

"Then we'll let you go home, okay?"

She nodded again.

Home. She thought of her bedroom with the beaded doorway and she started to cry.

"You're lucky someone called," the man said again.

In the hospital they scrubbed the words off her and gave her an IV of sugar water and electrolytes. A doctor with a serious, stern face came in and peered down at Maggie.

"You're in for a week of hell," he said. "Withdrawal is about the worst thing you can go through."

Maggie wanted to argue with him, to tell him that she didn't need to withdraw from anything. But her mouth felt like it was full of sand, so she just stared up at him, silent.

He was right, that doctor. The next week was worse than anything she had ever experienced. First that broken-glass feeling in her head and the cramping in her stomach. Then she began to throw up and shake and beg. "Please," she said to anyone who came in to the room, "please, if you could just get me a little something." She offered them her ATM passcode. "Take all the money," she said, "just bring me a tiny tiny bit of smack." When her teeth began to chatter so much that she bit her tongue, hard, someone came in and tied her to the bed. "We can fix this," she tried to tell the orderly, but all he did was jam a cloth in her mouth. To keep her from hurting herself, he explained.

Miraculously, one afternoon she opened her eyes and realized that although every cell in her body ached, even though she felt hollow, she was not shaking or begging or puking. A nurse came in with a bag of clothes and ordered her to get dressed. It took Maggie a very long time to put on the mauve tracksuit made of shiny polyester that was in the bag. But once she did, the nurse helped her to walk to a room at the end of the hall. Her legs felt like they were made of Jell-O, and she slipped and slid along the pea-green speckled linoleum floor.

"The doctor will be in soon," the nurse told her, gently settling her into a blue plastic chair, an IV still in her arm.

A thin wasted man in the chair beside her told her she could sign up and get drugs at a clinic, free.

"They are weak," he said, "but they'll do." He was missing most of his teeth.

"Oh, I just use them recreationally," Maggie said, which was the same thing she'd told a series of doctors who had come in with clipboards and serious faces.

"We all use them recreationally," the man laughed.

He told her she was on the ward for drug addicts.

"What?" Maggie said. "That's ridiculous."

The man tilted his chin toward her. "You have track marks that would stretch all the way to Marseille. Who are you kidding?"

She turned her face from him and thought instead of the Norwegian boy. Had he been the one who called for help? And where did he go? And what were they going to do with her now? Call the police? Call the American embassy? Call her parents?

A doctor came in, wearing her doctor coat and a stethoscope around her neck. She sat on the edge of Maggie's chair, close enough that Maggie could smell her heavy perfume.

"So Maggie," the doctor said, looking at the papers on her clipboard, "you are

American and you are a drug addict and you almost died. *Alors.* What should we do with you?"

"I'm an American *student,* studying here in Paris. And I am *not* a drug addict. I just like to party and I really need to get a better handle on that. I am always falling for the wrong boys and then doing bad things."

The doctor looked at her, incredulous.

"Well, my dear, you will die if you keep doing these drugs. We've done all we could to make you better." She stood abruptly. "So. Go back to your dormitory and eat a good dinner of steak and salad and drink lots of water and get rest. And resist the drugs. *Oui?*"

"Oui!" Maggie said enthusiastically, because they were letting her walk out of here. No embassy. No parents. No jail.

The doctor brusquely removed the IV, and then made a little clucking sound with her tongue.

"I don't ever want to see you here again," she said, and she walked away.

Maggie stood, her knees weak, and made her slow way outside. It was early morning, and the sky was streaked pink and red. It would be a hot day, she thought. She looked around, searching for something to orient her. A landmark or a street sign. But nothing looked familiar. She walked to the corner, stopped again to look around, still saw nothing familiar, and kept walking, until finally in the distance she saw the green pipes and blue ducts of the Pompidou Center. Relieved, she walked toward it. Nearby was the café where she'd seen Noah, and the bookstore with the beanbag chairs. She would have a big café au lait and an omelet and bread and then she would go into the bookstore and sink down in a beanbag chair, and read.

Ava

Ava called the man back right away, but it just went to voicemail, a robotic taped voice telling her to leave her name and number. She tried it again and again, until it became clear that the man was not going to answer. Why hadn't she asked him where he was? Where Maggie was? The word "missing" rang in her brain. Then she called Jim. "Hi, you've reached Jim Tucker. I'm away for two weeks on a secret mission but I'll get back to you as soon as I return." Yarn bombing somewhere no doubt. She tried to think of who else to call. The school, of course. She did quick math, adding the six-hour time difference between here and Italy. Four a.m. Would anyone answer the phone at four in the morning? Surely they'd been given an emergency number, she thought as she unlocked the door and stepped inside. The house was hot and stuffy. Ava opened the windows near her desk where all the papers for Maggie's program were filed away.

She found them immediately, grateful for Jim's organizational skills. The folder had *"Maggie, Italy"* written across it in Jim's handwriting. The familiarity of his perfect Palmer-method capital *M* with its little hook and that graceful *I* made her heart lurch. But he was away. With another woman, she reminded herself. Ava shuffled through the papers that they had all looked at so enthusiastically just a year ago. The brochure with photographs of students standing happily in front of Renaissance buildings and fountains. The list of items to pack, each carefully checked off by Jim. The welcome letter, the list of fellow students. How relieved Ava had felt as they'd planned all of this. Sending Maggie to this program had been a sign that she had finally — finally! — settled down. The drugs and the drinking, the sex, the reckless behavior, all of it was behind her at last.

Except it wasn't. She'd gone missing and Ava knew that with Maggie that could mean anything. How had she been so naive as to believe that Maggie was really all right?

Slowly she dialed the emergency number. The phone rang right away, and Ava sank into the seat at the desk, waiting.

It seemed to take forever, but at last a

woman answered in a weary voice. "Betty Lewis."

"I'm so sorry to bother you," Ava said, "but I received a frightening call from a man who told me my daughter was missing. Maggie? Maggie Tucker?"

"What man?" Betty Lewis asked.

"I . . . I don't know," Ava admitted. "He was French."

"A French man called you —"

"On Maggie's phone!" Ava said. "He had her phone!" The facts suddenly hit her hard. Why did a French man have Maggie's phone? Why did he know she was missing? Why hadn't he left his name?

"A French man called you from your daughter's phone," Betty Lewis repeated.

"Yes!"

"And your daughter's name is?"

Was this woman listening to anything Ava said?

"Maggie! Maggie Tucker!" Ava said.

"Maggie Tucker, Maggie Tucker," Betty Lewis said under her breath, and Ava could imagine her going through some files of her own.

"She's in the art history program," Ava offered, as if that might move things along.

"Mrs. Tucker?" Betty Lewis said. "Your daughter dropped out of the program in

January."

"That's impossible," Ava said, even though somewhere deep inside her she knew that with Maggie nothing was impossible. "It's a common name. Tucker. This is *Maggie* Tucker."

"Right. Maggie Tucker. Mother Ava? Is that you?"

Betty Lewis didn't wait for Ava to answer. "She withdrew in January, moved out of the dormitory, and as far as I know no one here has heard from her since."

A deep coldness filled Ava. *No one here has heard from her since.* A slideshow of those blurry, distant pictures played through Ava's mind. All the faceless girls on the Ponte Vecchio and in front of the Uffizi. Those pictures were stock photos taken from the Internet, she realized, and posted as if Maggie had taken them herself.

Betty Lewis was talking about calling the American embassy. "Do you want the number?" she asked.

But the number was right there on the contact sheet. Now Ava sighed. "No, I have it."

"In the morning I can ask her roommate if Maggie said anything before she left," Betty Lewis said.

"What's her roommate's name?" Ava

asked. She would call the girl herself. Now.

"I'm afraid I can't tell you that," Betty Lewis said. "I have to protect my students."

"Well you didn't protect my daughter! You let her wander off alone!"

The woman hesitated. "But you signed the withdrawal form. I'm looking at it right now."

Of course, Ava thought. Maggie had learned to forge Ava's name a long time ago.

"I'll talk to the girl," Betty Lewis said.

"That would be helpful. Thanks."

Ava gave Betty Lewis her cell phone number, and then hung up.

Ava stared down at the happy smiling students on the brochure. *Now what?*

After she called the embassy, Ava emailed Will.

> Hey there? Have you heard from your sister lately? Kind of important . . .
>
> She emailed Jim.
>
> Dear Jim, Call me immediately. Apparently Maggie withdrew from the program in January and no one knows where she is.
>
> She emailed Maggie.

Maggie, someone has your phone and called me and said you were missing. I'm a little out of my mind with worry.
CALL!
Please!

Then she sat staring at her phone as if she could make a response from any of them appear just by her sheer will and desperation. She tried not to think of where Maggie might have gone. Of what might have happened to her. Once, when Maggie was fifteen and just back from a wilderness treatment program in Utah, she went missing. Ava and Jim had driven around Providence, looking in all the places where kids went to buy drugs, getting out of the car to show Maggie's picture to stoned teenagers in doorways on Thayer Street. Two days later she showed up back home. "I met a boy," she said as an explanation, as if that was okay.

That's when Ava knew. Maggie had met a boy in Florence and gone off with him. But where?

She got in bed, even though she knew sleep wouldn't come. She kept her phone on the pillow beside her, the one she still thought of as Jim's pillow. From her nightstand, she picked up this month's book club selection, *A Tree Grows in Brooklyn.* It looked like a children's book with an old-fashioned girl sitting on a wall, a bare tree behind her. *Serene was a word you could put to Brooklyn, New York,* Ava read. *Especially in the summer of 1912 . . .*

By the time she heard an email drop into her inbox, Ava was lost in that summer of 1912 and that girl, Francie Nolan. Startled, she dropped the book and grabbed her phone.

Will.

> Not for a while. But she told me she'd been in a bad relationship and was out of it now. I've been worried. Do you know something?

Ava considered whether to tell him the truth. What could he do from remote Uganda? But on the other hand, he was a grown-up, and sensible. Even as a little boy, Will had been full of common sense. The first line of *A Tree Grows in Brooklyn* came back to her. A serene boy, she thought.

As soon as Ava typed the words, *A French man called from her phone,* she realized that Maggie hadn't just left the program. She'd left Italy. And gone to France.

Shit, Will, she typed. *I think she's some-*

where in France.

Will immediately emailed her back: *?????*

She left the program in January, Ava wrote.

Her phone rang and an unknown number flashed on the screen.

Ava answered, surprised to hear Betty Lewis on the other end apologizing for calling so late.

"Her roommate said Maggie met a boy and left for Paris with him," Betty said. "Of course," she added matter-of-factly, "the program has no culpability in this."

A boy. Paris.

"Of course," Ava said.

"I wish I had more concrete information," Betty said before signing off.

She had to go there, Ava thought. To Paris. But how do you find a missing girl in a big city? She went downstairs to make coffee and picked up her to-do list on her notepad. *Find Rosalind Arden,* she'd written. *Go to the library? A used bookstore? Find her publisher???* Even as she wrote these ideas yesterday, the task of finding someone who seemed to have vanished completely felt impossible. Now here she was having to find Maggie.

Ava wrote her daughter's name on the top of the next page. When Maggie was young, her daughter always drew a daisy over the *i* instead of a dot. Sometimes she'd get her colored pencils and make each petal yellow, the center blue. Ava absently drew a daisy over the *i* in Maggie. The phone rang. It was Jim.

"I've called both embassies, Italy and France," she told him after she recounted everything she knew. "I don't know what else to do."

"Haven't you been talking to her all this time?" Jim said. Ava could hear the frustration in his voice. "Didn't you suspect she was maybe not in Florence?"

She thought about all those blurry, distant, generic pictures on Instagram. About the email explaining why she couldn't visit. Agritourism, slow food. Of course she should have suspected something.

"I need to go to Paris," Ava said. "I need to find her."

"Look, I'm in Helsinki. I'll fly to Paris and take pictures of Maggie with me," Jim said. "And go to the police and the embassy. You stay put, in case she tries to call you or, I don't know, come home."

"What if she needs me? What if —" Ava said.

"Sweetheart," Jim said. "One of us needs to stay by the phone."

"But I speak French!" Ava said.

"So do I." Jim reminded her.

"Do you really think she might come home?"

"She always does when things bottom out," Jim said.

"Oh my God," Ava said. "Where the hell is she?"

"I'll call you from Paris," Jim said.

"Thanks. For going there."

"Ava?" Jim said softly.

She waited.

"It's going to be okay," he said.

When Maggie and Will were little, they often climbed in bed with Ava and Jim at sunrise. She could almost smell their sweat-and-powder child smell, almost feel their small legs tangled with hers. Ava always knew when autumn had arrived. Overnight, it seemed, the leaves on the tree outside her bedroom window changed. Once, when Maggie was five or six, she'd pointed to the tree, her eyes wide, and said, "Look, Mama! Someone tie-dyed the leaves!"

Hot tears stung Ava's eyes as she thought of her daughter as a little girl. How had she gone from that sweet child to this reckless young woman?

Her own sister came to mind. Lily had been the sweet one, the bright one. All pale blond hair and light blue eyes. Even now, all these years later, Ava could picture her clearly in her black leotard and pink ballet tights, forming a perfect arabesque. They'd taken those ballet classes together, Ava galumphing across the wooden floor while Lily twirled as light as a fairy. That fall, Lily was going to begin pointe, leaving Ava behind. But of course, Lily didn't live until autumn.

Ava sat upright.

Hank Bingham.

He was a retired police detective.

Still, after a long career in the police force he was respected. Despite what had happened in their family, Hank Bingham was good at his job.

Ava got up and sorted through the ephemera that littered the top of her dresser. Ever since Jim moved out, she'd stopped organizing and filing and tidying up. The dresser was covered in a thin layer of dust, stamps, Post-Its, receipts, scribbled notes, and grocery lists. She searched through all of it until she found the business card Hank Bingham had given her when he showed up in her kitchen.

Ava drove to Hank Bingham's house. Small and painted white, it sat on the end of a street in a 1950s' development surrounded by similar houses. Blue hydrangeas bloomed along the front of the house. A nondescript gray sedan sat parked in the driveway. And Hank himself stood in the yard watering flowers. Ava paused, surprised by this scene of domesticity.

For a moment they stood staring at each other. Hank's plaid short-sleeve shirt had a stain on the front, his tennis shoes were worn, and he needed to shave.

"Have you got something to tell me?" Hank asked her.

When she hesitated, he continued, "About that day?"

Ava shook her head. "That's not why I'm here. I didn't know who to go to for help," she said. "And for some reason, you were the only person who came to mind."

Hank was still frowning at her. He dropped the hose and motioned her forward. "Come on inside then," he said.

Inside had a woman's touch: needlepointed pillows, flowered couch, dried flowers in vases. He led her into the kitchen and asked if she'd like coffee.

"Sure," she said.

Hank took out a jar of instant and said, apologetically, "My wife would kill me for serving this."

Ah. She wanted to tell him never mind about the coffee, but he was already turning on a kettle and spooning crystals into mugs.

"I don't have sugar," he said as he placed a mug in front of her.

"That's okay.

"It's my daughter," she said. "She's missing."

Hank took out an official-looking notebook and wrote down everything she said, nodding from time to time.

"This is what we call a needle in a haystack," he said. He closed the notebook with a finality that Ava didn't like. "She could be anywhere. In the world."

"She could be dead," Ava said. It was the first time she spoke her worst fear out loud. "He wouldn't even pick up when I called back. And I've called back every hour."

"I've got a hunch he's looking for her too."

"But why does he have her phone?"

Hank shook his head again.

"Suppose you were still working," Ava said. "Suppose you got this case. What would you do?"

"I'd question the people she was with last. Her family."

"The administration at the school spoke to her roommate," Ava reminded him. "And I can't talk to her because Maggie never told me her name."

"Here's how I see it," Hank said. "Young girl, bit of a wild child, meets a boy in Italy and follows him to Paris. The relationship goes sour. She's dropped out of the program, left Florence, basically screwed everything up. She's not going to call her parents and she's not going to go home. So she stays in Paris, maybe meets another boy. Maybe meets a guy in a bar and drinks too much and loses her phone there."

"But why call us?" Ava said, frustrated.

"Maybe he's looking for her. Maybe he didn't know he was calling her mother.

"Why won't he answer?"

"Maybe he's busy," Hank said, shrugging.

"All day and all night?" Ava said.

"Dial it again now."

She took her phone from her purse and scrolled to Maggie's number, pressing it, for the forty-eighth time, she saw.

A man answered brusquely.

Ava cleared her throat. "This is Ava Tucker," she said, her eyes on Hank's self-satisfied face. "I'm calling for my daughter Maggie."

"I told you," the man said. "She is missing."

Hank opened his notebook, scribbled something, and held it up for Ava to see.

"Could you please tell me when you saw her last?" Ava read.

"Two days ago," the man said.

"Two days," Ava repeated, relieved.

"I don't know where she is," the man said, "and I don't care." He hung up.

"He hung up," Ava said. "Now what?" Even as she spoke, she was redialling. But the man didn't answer.

"She had a fight with her boyfriend and went to stay with a friend," Hank said. "She'll be back in a day or two. Mark my words."

Although what he said made sense, Ava couldn't shake the feeling that it wasn't that simple. The man sounded older, and more angry than concerned.

"Sometimes," Hank said, looking at her hard, "things line up a certain way and it's still hard to believe it."

Ava met his gaze. He wasn't talking about Maggie anymore, she knew. He was talking about the day her sister died.

"Thanks for your help," she said.

"Let me know when she calls and tells you all about it," Hank said.

He didn't walk her to the door. No wonder his wife left him, Ava thought. Still, she felt better. What he'd said made sense. Any minute now, she would hear from Maggie.

The Bookstore Owner

The American girl came in every morning, and stayed all day. Skinny, pasty skin, straggly hair, a sweatsuit that made her look like she'd been let out of a mental hospital. Sometimes she slept in the leopard beanbag chair, a book open in her lap. Sometimes she read, entire books, without looking up. Sometimes she walked up and down the aisles like an animal pacing in a cage, picking up and discarding books, reading titles.

"Hey! *Jeune fille!*" she called to the girl half-asleep in the beanbag.

The girl looked up.

"If you are going to sit here every day, put yourself to good use."

"Really?" the girl asked hopefully. "Because I really want a job," she added. "Here."

"See these books? Put them back on the shelves."

"Um. Where do they go?" the girl stammered. "I mean, you don't have them alphabetical or anything."

"C'est à toi," the bookstore owner said with a shrug.

"O-kay," the girl said slowly.

The books — the owner thought of them as *her* books — weren't organized in the usual way. When lost children like this found their way here, she always told them the same thing. File them anyway you like. It's up to you.

She gave the girl blank index cards and different colored markers.

"C'est à toi," she said again, and left the girl to it.

Ava

Penny's memorial service was held at the Congregational church. Ava sat with the other members of the book group as Penny's daughter Helen and son James read her favorite poems. The choir sang "Amazing Grace" and, surprisingly, "It Don't Mean A Thing If You Ain't Got That Swing" — apparently Penny's theme song. In no time, it was over, and Ava found herself in the backseat of Ruth's giant SUV, riding with her and Diana to the reception at the Hope Club.

"Funerals have really been getting to me lately," Diana said. "For obvious reasons."

"Oh, sweetie," Ruth said, patting Diana's hand, "you are going to be okay."

"Don't look so glum," Diana said, catching Ava's eye in the rearview mirror. "My kind of breast cancer is very treatable. The treatment, however, sucks."

"Only two more," Ruth said.

Diana sighed. "Two more trips to hell."

"What did Penny leave you, Ava?" Ruth asked.

Ava shrugged. "It feels awkward to show up at their house asking for it. Besides, I have no connection to her other than the book group. I can't imagine why she would leave me anything."

"Well," Ruth said, her eyes on the road, "I'm glad you're in the group."

"So am I," Diana said. "Before long you'll have enough seniority to take me to chemo."

Ava smiled. They turned onto Benefit Street, with its brownstones and gas lamps, passed the library, and turned into the crowded parking lot of the Hope Club. Ava started at the sight of a girl Maggie's age with the same chestnut hair. But of course it wasn't Maggie. Maggie was missing. She fought the urge to jump out of this car and get on a plane to Paris. Jim is there, she reminded herself. Jim is there.

"I can't believe Penny is dead," Diana said softly. "I remember the first time I met her, at Monique's house that very first book club. I was in *A Christmas Carol,* playing Scrooge. Very controversial at the time. Rosie was only about six months old. I had her in one of those Snuglis we all used back then. Penny came up to me and gave me the firmest handshake. And a Manhattan. I fell in love with her immediately."

"Remember when we read *A Passage to India*? She had Kebob and Curry cater a twelve-course meal," Ruth said, wiping her eyes.

By the front door, Ava saw Cate and Monique waiting. No, not just Cate and Monique. Honor and Kiki and Luke were there too.

Then the valet opened her door and Ava was out of the SUV, following Ruth and Diana up the stone steps.

Cate brightened when she saw them. "Good. We're all here."

Ava paused to watch the girl with the chestnut hair, somber but bright-eyed, bow her head, take her mother's hand, and go inside.

Ava shifted the tray of water chestnuts wrapped in bacon that Cate had asked her to carry as they walked to the library, the smell of bacon wafting up from it.

"Are you all right?" Cate asked Ava.

Ava shook her head. "Maggie," she said. "She left school and went to Paris and we haven't heard from her."

Not for the first time, Ava tried to remember why she had thought sending Maggie so far from home had been a good idea. Especially after Jim moved out and Maggie grew so angry at him.

"Does anyone know where she actually is?" Cate asked. "Or with whom?"

Ava shook her head again. "I spoke to a detective. He thought she'd had a lover's quarrel and would surface soon."

Of course, that was over a week ago, and Hank Bingham had predicted Maggie would turn up in a day or two. She hadn't. And fear had gripped Ava again, hard. She had started calling the embassy every morning, as soon as she woke. And every day she got the same answer, *"Nous n'avons pas encore de nouvelles."* The man had stopped answering Maggie's phone.

"There's a boy involved?" Cate asked.

"It's Maggie we're talking about here," Ava said. "What do you think?"

The sound of the voice on the other end of the phone came back to her. Not a boy. A man.

"You know Maggie," Cate said to reassure her, "she's probably having the time of her life and not thinking about you at all. She has no idea you're even worried."

Ava had seen Maggie high too many times, had taken her to the emergency room more than once, had seen the boys she fell for. It was precisely because she did know her daughter that Ava was so worried. There's no news yet, the same woman told her every morning. And Jim's texts confirmed that.

The library appeared in front of them, soft gray in the early evening summer light.

To Ava's surprise, as soon as she walked in, Luke appeared as if he'd been waiting for her, porkpie hat in place.

"Let me get that for you," he said, and took the tray from her. "I've missed you," he said. "Sarcastic, cynical, wonderful you."

He seemed to be waiting. Did he actually think she was going to say "I miss you too"? Jim, she missed. Her kids, she missed. Her old life, her *real* life. But not Luke.

Luke placed the tray on the table, and elbowed her gently. "Come on," he said. "I know you missed me too."

Cate stood at the front of the room and cleared her throat, a signal they were about to begin. Ava took a seat beside John.

"Did you like the book?" John asked, tapping the book on his lap.

"I did," Ava said.

"Not for me, I guess," he said.

"A Tree Grows in Brooklyn," Cate began, "is a perfect example of that writing advice, write what you know."

Everyone laughed. Except John, who frowned and wrote in his notebook in small square letters: *write what you know?????*

"Betty Smith wrote it, and it was published in 1943," Cate said. "But perhaps you didn't know how autobiographical the novel is. Like Francie Nolan, Betty Smith grew up poor in Williamsburg, Brooklyn, in the early twentieth century.

"Although Smith was born five years before Francie, Betty Smith and Francie Nolan share the same birthday," Cate continued. "And like Francie, she went to college without having a high school diploma."

John shook his head. "Why didn't she name it *The Story of Francie Nolan* then? The title confused me. I mean, Francie is the main character, and she's what grew in Brooklyn."

"May I?" Monique asked, standing.

Cate took a seat and let Monique stand in front of the room.

"The title represents the importance of place to the author. This is part of my attraction to the novel. Betty Smith seems most concerned with time and place, and then creating a character out of that setting," Monique said.

"I see," John said, still bewildered.

"That's kind of the opposite of Flannery O'Connor's edict to develop character and then story will follow," Honor said. "Smith seems to be saying develop place, and character — and therefore story — will follow."

"I just don't see why the New York Public Library would pick this book as one of the best books of the twentieth century," John said, shaking his head.

"Hm," Ruth said, "someone did a little research."

John blushed.

"It's because the novel shows us that strong values help us triumph over adversity," Honor said.

Ava glanced at her phone for the hundredth time that day, as if a message from Maggie might magically appear.

Everyone started talking at once, about the themes of class and poverty, gender and sex, perseverance and hardship that ran through the novel. John kept flipping the pages of his book, frowning, as if he were trying to find what everyone else saw in it. Ava forced herself to concentrate.

Luke was saying, almost to himself, "The tin can bank."

"What about it, Luke?" Cate asked him.

"It struck me that Francie and Neeley are

told to put money in the tin can bank so the family can buy land. For fourteen years they put money in there, like when they sell the scrap metal to the junk collector they put the money in the tin can bank," Luke said.

"But they take money out too," Jennifer pointed out. "To pay the ice cream man and to help pay for one of their moves."

"Right, right," Luke said. "And we're always told the amounts too. A dollar for the ice cream, two dollars for the move. We always know how much is in there too. That's what just struck me. When Johnny dies there's $18.62 in the bank, but it's not enough to bury him. Katie has to borrow money to bury him."

"And then she throws the bank away," Monique added.

"That's exactly it!" Luke said, his eyes shining. "Now they own land, so they don't need the bank. But the land is a cemetery plot, not a better home."

"That's sad when you put it like that," John said.

The room grew quiet.

"Actually," Ava said, "I'd like to talk about symbolism."

Monique nodded.

"The tree, in particular," Ava added. "I

think, Luke, the tree is what makes the book hopeful in the end. It's been chopped down and set on fire, but Francie realizes it's not dead."

"There's a new branch," John said.

"The tree survived, just like the Nolan family," Ava said, her voice catching.

Luke smiled at her. In fact, everyone was smiling at her.

"What a lovely note to end on," Cate said. "Thank you, Ava."

Ava moved with the group toward the refreshment table, where Emma stood filling the little wineglasses and fanning cocktail napkins. Her hair was leprechaun green and she had a new tattoo of a small pink Piglet, still slightly swollen and red, right above her left breast.

"That was nice," John said to Ava. "What you said about the tree. It made me appreciate the book a little more."

"I'm glad," Ava said.

"I liked what the grandmother said," John said. He pulled out a folded piece of paper from his pocket and read, "To look at everything always as though you were seeing it either for the first or last time: Thus is your time on earth filled with glory."

When he looked up, his cheeks were wet with tears.

"Oh, John," Ava said, putting a hand on his arm. "What happened to your wife?"

"A brain aneurysm." He snapped his fingers. "Just like that."

Just like that, Ava thought.

In that moment, she saw a tree. A different tree. The large oak that grew in the backyard of her childhood home. The tree she and Lily used to climb, where they built a fort. The tree from which Lily fell that day.

"I think the suddenness is making it harder," John was saying.

"Yes," Ava said.

"In the book," John said, "it says something about how you grieve because you didn't hold it tighter when you had it. That got me."

He folded the paper and handed it to Ava. "I was going to read this tonight, in the discussion."

"You should have," Ava managed to say, even though all she could think of was that other tree, the bright sun coming through its leaves.

Then Cate was standing in front of her with a vaguely familiar woman and John left to fill a plate with deviled eggs.

"You never came," the woman said to Ava.

"This is Penny's daughter Helen," Cate

said. "Remember?"

"I'm so sorry," Ava said. "I meant to come by. My daughter . . ." She stopped herself.

"She specifically said to give this to you," Penny's daughter said, and she held out a package wrapped in soft green tissue paper.

"Honestly, I have no idea why Penny would leave me something," Ava said. "But thank you for bringing it."

Ava put the package in her bag.

It wasn't until much later, back home in bed, redialling Maggie's number and staring at her email in the hope that a message from Maggie would appear, that she remembered the package. She went downstairs to retrieve it, and brought it back to bed with her. She hadn't noticed the small envelope taped to the outside, the kind usually tucked into a floral arrangement. On the card, it said: *I knew your mother. P.* Surprised, Ava tore open the paper. There, in her hands, was a book. Immediately she recognized the cover, but still she read the title out loud.

"From Clare to Here," Ava said into her empty bedroom.

As if those words acted as a magic incantation, an email from Will dropped into her inbox.

Good news! She emailed me that she

was in the hospital with pneumonia but she's better now. She told me not to tell you, of course. Mom, she's fine.

Relief so great swept over Ava that she found herself hugging the book to her chest, the way she had as a young girl. But this time, everyone was alive. Everyone was all right.

■ ■ ■ ■

Part Eight: July/August

■ ■ ■ ■

What really knocks me out is a book that, when you're all done reading it, you wish the author that wrote it was a terrific friend of yours and you could call him up on the phone whenever you felt like it. That doesn't happen much, though.

— *The Catcher in the Rye*
by J. D. Salinger

Maggie

All Maggie wanted to eat was the chocolate she bought at the newsstand. She bought large cheap bars and devoured them. Two or three a day. She had little money left from the funds her father had deposited for her year in Florence. She'd spent too much of it on drugs and bad decisions.

Nights made Maggie homesick. She wanted to be a girl who had a place to go to, a girl with college waiting for her in September, with her own bed somewhere. But she couldn't find her way back to that girl. Instead, she wrote down sentences and descriptions in her little notebook. She went to the bookstore and filed books, and when there were no books to file she sat in a beanbag chair and read. She ate her cheap chocolate bars, and went to the cafés where Hemingway used to go, and slept in her little room in the hostel.

"You like chocolate," a girl said to Maggie

one morning in the bookstore.

The girl, about Maggie's age, had come upon her devouring one of the chocolate bars she bought at the newsstand. Maggie had seen her here before, lots of times. She was the only one Madame let use the cash register, which Maggie understood to mean she was the only one Madame actually trusted.

Maggie was wearing a pale yellow dress. The chocolate had melted in the summer heat, and she'd accidentally smeared some on the front of the dress. Her hair hung down her back in a hot ponytail.

"Today I will take you to Patrick Roger," the girl said. "We will leave here in the afternoon and walk to Saint-Germain-des-Près and there we will gorge ourselves."

The girl was tall and slender with a big toothy smile. Her blond hair was held away from her face with a wide black headband and her dress — knee-skimming, tucked at the waist, flared at the hips — had a pattern of teapots.

"Bon," the girl said, more to herself than to Maggie.

She started to walk away, but came right back.

"Je m'appelle Geneviève," she said, sticking her hand in Maggie's face.

For an instant, Maggie couldn't think what she was supposed to do. Then she took Geneviève's hand and shook it, aware that hers was limp and hot in Geneviève's cool firm grasp.

As soon as Geneviève clomped away in her clogs, Maggie closed her eyes and considered her options. She had taped new postcards on the wall of her room back at the hostel: a rakish Hemingway, a beautiful Scott Fitzgerald, both of them looking young and hopeful. Another one of the Eiffel Tower under construction. Maybe, she thought, she should leave Paris. She opened her little notebook and wrote other futures for herself. *Amsterdam: Canals. Tulips. Windmills. Berlin: Remnants of the Wall. Remnants of WWII. Too depressing??? Prague: What exactly is in Prague??? Wasn't Kafka from Prague???*

"What is this category?" the bookstore owner was asking her.

Maggie looked up to find Madame scowling and pointing to an index card.

" 'My Mother's Books,' " she told her. "My mother joined a book club."

Madame kept scowling.

"I miss her," Maggie said, surprising herself.

■ ■ ■ ■

Maggie picked up a dog-eared paperback of *Anna Karenina* and placed it on the shelf with the other books she'd labeled *"My Mother's Books."* Several copies of *The Great Gatsby* and *Pride and Prejudice* leaned against one another, and she slid *Anna Karenina* in between them. She tried to remember what other books her mother's book club was reading, but even though she'd received the list by email, she couldn't recall the other titles.

"You!" Madame said sharply from her perch behind the cash register. "Don't just stand there!"

Maggie ran her fingers across the few books on this shelf, as if she were reaching for her mother's hand.

"There's soup," the woman said. "In the back room."

When Maggie turned toward her, she was adding up receipts in her big blue ledger, a pair of half-glasses sitting on the tip of her nose.

"Nothing fancy," she said without looking up. "Just soup."

"Merci," Maggie said, suddenly ravenous.

In the back room, the pot of soup warmed

on an old hot plate. Lentil, thick with chunks of carrots and celery and leeks. Beside the hot plate, several chipped bowls sat one inside the other in a crooked pile that made Maggie think of the game Jenga that she and Will used to like to play at the kitchen table as their mother stood at the stove making dinner. *Bowls stacked like Jenga blocks,* she thought. But she was too hungry to pause and get her notebook to write it down. Instead, she took the bright orange bowl on top of the stack and filled it to the brim with soup. There was bread too, a basic bakery baguette already cut into rounds, with a slab of French butter on a plate beside it. Maggie grabbed three pieces, and without even sitting dipped bread in soup and shoved it hot into her mouth, burning her tongue and palate. She finished the first bowl quickly, and took a second one, just as full, and more bread, over to the sofa.

The sofa was old, its springs jutting out, the cushions covered with a quilt, also old and smelling of mothballs and books. Maggie adjusted herself around the sofa's lumps and springs and ate, more slowly now. The quilt, she realized, was made of worn silk, with frayed embroidered birds and flowers on it and small flat mirrored pieces. From here, she could see out a window that needed a good cleaning — "white vinegar and newspaper!" she could hear her mother saying — and beyond to a small yard with dead plants in it, all brown and withered. Still, birds kept dipping in and out of a bird-feeder hung from the bare branch of a tree. A flash of red, and then gold. The flutter of wings. And even in here the distant sounds of their coos. Maggie eyed the old computer glowing on the desk. She would email her mother, she decided. She would tell her she'd come to Paris.

As she tried to navigate the clunky mouse, Geneviève ducked her head inside.

"Oh!" she said out loud to herself. "Lentil!"

She noticed Maggie and smiled, showing all her big horsey teeth.

"There you are!" she said, coming into the room and ladling soup into a turquoise bowl. "Someone came in looking for you."

"For me?" Maggie said. "Are you sure?"

Genevieve nodded. "He asked for Maggie. He said, *'Maggie, la petite fille maigre.'* "

The soup rose in Maggie's throat, and she had to swallow it back to keep from throwing it up.

"Did he say his name?" she managed to ask. "Was it Julien?"

Geneviève shrugged and sat beside Maggie, squealing when a spring poked her thigh.

Maggie shivered. Images of Julien leering at her, hurting her, filled her brain and she squeezed her eyes shut, trying to erase them.

"Best soup, worst sofa," Geneviève said with a chuckle.

Julien slapping her. Julien murmuring to her, calling her his ragdoll, his artichoke, his plum. She squeezed her eyes tighter, tried to forget how it felt when he opened the little suede bag and put the needle in her arm, that feeling of floating, of disappearing.

Maggie's heart was racing. She stood abruptly.

"I have to go," she said. "I have an appointment."

"Maintenant?" Genevieve asked, surprised.

Maggie didn't answer. She just hurried to the door.

"So we will meet back here later and go to Patrick Roger?"

"Sure," Maggie said without stopping.

She didn't say anything to Madame as she walked quickly through the crowded store and out the door into the relentless July heat.

■ ■ ■ ■

For three days Maggie stayed away from the bookstore. If Julien came back, they would tell him they didn't know where she was, they hadn't seen her in days, and maybe he would leave her alone. She stayed in her tiny room in the hostel and tried to pull together her random notes, the descriptions and observations she'd written in her notebook. But she couldn't concentrate. She considered other cities. *Sydney: kangaroos, Opera House (?), southern hemisphere. St. Petersburg: Winter Palace, Nabokov, great art.* She considered the refuge of that needle in her arm, the way it calmed her, made her unafraid, let her float away. She forced herself to not think about that. She wrote: *The girl imagined other cities, cities with icebergs; cities with fjords; cities with castles and bridges; cities with beautiful lights and sparkling rivers and sidewalk cafés.* She reread what she wrote, and smiled. That's here, she thought. That's Paris.

"Where have you been?" Geneviève asked as soon as Maggie walked back into the bookstore a few days later.

"Writing," Maggie said. "I'm working on

a novel."

She picked up a pile of books waiting to be shelved and walked across the crowded store to the far shelves.

"Come on," Geneviève said to Maggie hours later. "Time to go to Patrick Roger."

Geneviève was wearing a dress identical to her teapot one, except the pattern was chickens.

"Patrick Roger?" Maggie said.

"The chocolate shop," Genevieve said. "My mission is to keep you away from those terrible candy bars you eat all the time. I don't even think there's any chocolate at all in them."

She let Geneviève link an arm with hers, and lead her through the store. It was so much more crowded in summer, and with each day the crowds grew. Today, they had to stand sideways to squeeze past all the tourists browsing and exclaiming over the funny categories or the books they discovered.

Geneviève held Maggie's hand and pulled her along the Impasse Berthaud, where the dolls in the window of the Musée de la Poupée stared out at them. Despite the heat, Maggie shivered. She thought of Julien too, calling her his *poupée de chiffon.*

Geneviève paused.

"Ça va?" she asked.

"Poupées," Maggie said with a shrug, because how could she ever explain.

Geneviève grinned. "Yes! They're creepy!"

As they passed the café across from the doll hospital, Maggie searched the crowded outdoor tables for Noah from the Musée d'Orsay. But she didn't find his face among the tourists there, with their oversized beers and carafes of wine.

"Let's have a beer," she suggested.

But Geneviève shook her head and turned down Place Georges-Pompidou.

"Chocolate," she said.

Maggie could feel a hard callus on Geneviève's thumb and another on her forefinger. She tried to imagine what the girl did to get them. Gardening? Guitar? She would try to remember to ask her.

"Who would come to Paris in summer?" Geneviève said as they crossed the Seine. "It's so crowded you can't even breathe."

"Americans," Maggie said.

"You're an American," Geneviève reminded her.

"I don't feel like one," she said.

"Ah! But you are writing the Great American Novel, aren't you? Like every American, you have come to Paris to write it."

Maggie smiled.

At last they were in Saint-Germain-des-Près and walking along boulevard Saint-Germain.

"Voilà!" Genevieve announced, coming to a halt.

Maggie stared at the window in front of them. Small perfect chocolates were neatly arranged in geometric patterns. Some had one perfect pistachio in the center, or a sliver of candied orange. A sculpture of an ape dominated the window, as if it were guarding all the chocolates.

"So tiny," Maggie said, thinking of her big chocolate bars.

"So perfect," Geneviève said, tugging her inside.

The store felt almost cold after the heat outside, and goosebumps rose up Maggie's arms.

"On peut gouter?" Genevieve said to the young woman behind one of the long glass counters.

The woman's hair was in a bun and she wore blue rectangular eyeglasses and very high heels.

She nodded, and began to place chocolates on a small silver tray for them to taste. With each one they tried, she described it in a cool voice.

Praline feuilleté, peppery mint ganache

and citronella, almond paste chocolate walnut, oat ganache, Sichuan peppercorn ganache. Each bite exploded in Maggie's mouth. She tasted vanilla bean, lemon, chestnut, honey. She tasted chocolate like she'd never before tasted.

Geneviève was smiling down at her and nodding.

"See?" she said. "Fifty per cent cocoa, minimum."

"Point taken," Maggie said, letting the last piece melt on her tongue.

"We'll take the nine-piece assortment," Geneviève said to the young woman.

On the way out, she cocked her head at the sculpture in the window.

"Too bad we can't take him home, *n'est-ce pas?*"

Maggie did a double-take. The giant ape was carved completely out of chocolate.

"Patrick Roger is an artist, eh?" Geneviève said, taking Maggie's hand again.

Geneviève lived nearby in a tiny fifth-floor walk-up apartment. On the table in the center was a sewing machine, and piled beside it was fabric and thread in every color.

"Your calluses," Maggie said, noticing scraps of the chicken material.

"Yes! I sew my dresses," Geneviève said from the small kitchen where she was putting cold chicken and grapes and radishes on a platter. "I'll make one for you," she added. "Choose a fabric."

Maggie began to look through the material on the table, all of it covered with funny prints like the chickens and the teapots. She held up one with smiling toasters on it.

"Where do you get this stuff?"

"I don't know the word in English. Leftovers?" Geneviève said.

"Remnants," Maggie said. *"Vestiges."*

Geneviève made room on the crowded table for the food, and pulled out a chair for Maggie.

"How do you know Madame?" Maggie asked.

"I was in trouble and I had nowhere to go. One day I walked into the bookstore and the next thing I knew I had a little job and a bowl of hot soup."

Maggie wondered what kind of trouble she'd been in, but she didn't ask. That would open the way to talk about her own problems, something she did not want to do with Geneviève, or anyone else.

"They say she killed someone," Geneviève said.

"I almost believe it."

Geneviève placed another piece of chicken in front of Maggie.

"Who did she kill?"

Genevieve shrugged. "There are so many rumors about her. They say she is hiding someone upstairs. A lover, maybe."

She rolled a radish in butter and then salt and held it out to Maggie, who took it with a sigh.

"You like the *grille-pains*?"

"They make me laugh," Maggie said, glancing down at the bright blue fabric with the green and orange smiling toasters on it.

"*Grille-pain* it is," Geneviève said.

After dinner they sat on the little balcony smoking cigarettes and drinking brandy and watching the people wandering the streets below. The sky turned lavender and then violet. Geneviève opened the box of chocolates, and they bit each one in half so that they could taste all of them.

"Where do you stay?" Geneviève asked her.

"Like all starving American writers in Paris, I stay in a hovel. I sleep on straw on the floor."

"You don't need to suffer for your art, you could stay here," Geneviève said. "We would have to share the bedroom, but there are two beds in it."

"I don't know," she said. "I'm on a budget. And Madame doesn't actually pay very much."

"Pay me what you pay now," Geneviève said. "It is good to have company."

Sitting out here, the smoke from Geneviève's cigarette curling into the night, Maggie could almost believe she could change everything. Sitting here, she felt almost normal, for the first time in longer than she could remember.

"It is good to have company," she said softly.

Geneviève reached over and took Maggie's hand in her callused one. The two of them sat like that, without speaking, as the night descended on Paris.

Ava

Now that Ava knew Maggie was all right, looking for Rosalind Arden occupied most of Ava's free time. She still called and emailed Maggie every day, and Maggie still didn't answer, but Will was receiving frequent — if cryptic — messages and forwarding them to Ava. This morning's: If the madre finds out I left school, I'm done for. So shhhh, Wills!!!

White Swan Press, the publisher of *From Clare to Here,* had either gone out of business or been swallowed up by a larger publishing house long ago. Ava tried to find information about it on the Internet, but like the author herself, it seemed to have disappeared completely. With summer half over, Ava had just four months before she had to produce Rosalind Arden. How do you find someone who seems to never have existed?

Ava picked up the book, as if studying it

might reveal Rosalind Arden's whereabouts. She had kept herself from reading anything but the copyright page, afraid that those opening pages would pull her back to the summer she'd first read it. She didn't have the strength to relive those weeks when she first learned of her mother's death. Somehow this book was tied up in all of that. When she finished it, she turned right back to the first page and read it straight through again. She read that book over and over all that summer, and when autumn came and she returned to school, Ava put it away, and never found the same pleasure and comfort in reading again.

Hesitantly, Ava turned to the next page. And read the dedication.

To T and A and H.
Je dois.

Ava stared at the shelf of air conditioners, considering BTUs and energy efficiency ratings.

"I've been thinking of you," a man said. She turned to find Hank Bingham standing beside her, a *Consumer Reports* magazine rolled up in his hand. Jim would have consulted *Consumer Reports* too, Ava realized, wishing she had thought to look at one.

"Your daughter show up?" Hank asked.

"Kind of," she said.

"I'm trying to find someone else now." Ava said.

His eyes slid toward her again.

"Other than your kid? People keep hiding from you, huh?"

"Yes," Ava said. "A writer. But she seems to have vanished. Or to never have existed."

"I'd call the publisher," he said.

"They've vanished too."

She watched Hank slide an air conditioner off the shelf and into the oversized cart. Despite his age, he lifted the heavy box easily, his muscles bulging beneath his short sleeves.

"Mine finally died," he explained, as if that was why she was watching him. "Twenty years. Never a problem."

Ava didn't care about his air conditioner, new or old. She smiled politely and went back to comparing BTUs and EERs.

"So if you write down this person, this writer's name," Hank said, "I'll see what I can do. But write it down 'cause I'm a terrible speller and we'll be standing here all night if I have to do it."

He was holding a pen and notebook out

to her. When Ava opened the notebook, she saw the notes he'd taken when she went to him about Maggie. *Left school. Followed boy. Italy/Paris.*

Ava flipped to the next page and printed *Rosalind Arden,* then handed the notebook and pen back to Hank.

He put it in his pocket without even looking at it.

"I'll be in touch," he said, and gave her a little salute.

The problem was how to get the air conditioner out of the car, into the house, and up the steep two-hundred-and-thirty-year-old stairs to the bedroom. The night had become even hotter than the day had been, steamy and humid the way only July nights in New England could be. Ava stood, leaning against her car and sweating as she stared up at her bedroom window.

Long ago, before Jim, she had hauled a VCR to her walk-up on Bleecker Street and installed the thing herself. She'd taken a taxi to Crazy Eddie's somewhere on Fourteenth Street, bought a monstrous desktop computer, and somehow lugged that up all those stairs too. It had taken her almost two weeks to get that computer working, but she'd done it. Why had twenty-five years of marriage rendered her so . . . Ava struggled to come up with the right word. Incompetent? Lazy? Paralyzed?

Goddamn it, she muttered. Ava flung open the door and maneuvered the enormous box out of her car. She dragged it along the side of the house and onto the sidewalk, salty sweat dripping onto her lips. At the front stoop, she paused to wipe it out of her eyes.

"Damn you, Jim," she said.

She imagined him and Delia Lindstrom in cool Helsinki, drinking chilled vodka under the midnight sun.

Wasting her time thinking about Jim, with or without Delia Lindstrom, was not going to get the air conditioner upstairs, Ava decided. She yanked the box first up the three front steps, then half-pushed, half-kicked it into the front door. The steep stairway was in front of her now. Ava took a deep breath, and continued.

Finally in her bed in her cool room, Ava couldn't concentrate on the novel. She decided to send yet another email to Maggie. But when she opened email, there, at last, was a reply:

Guess what??? I'm in Paris. Don't be

mad. Pleeeeeeassse???

Your darling daughter
Maggie

As soon as Ava walked into the library, John came up to her. He held a bottle of beer in his hand, and the tip of his nose was sunburned.

"This one," he said, "I really didn't like."

Ava tried to look sympathetic. She murmured a reassuring sound as she made her way to the table where Emma presided over a rectangular silver trough of bottles of beer sitting in shaved ice. Chips and salsa. Chips and onion dip. Popcorn.

"No wine?" Ava asked Emma.

Emma shook her head, which was the color of cotton candy.

"You know," Emma said in her flat voice, "teenager food."

Ava sighed and took a beer. When she turned, John was standing right behind her looking miserable.

"This book," John said, tapping the red cover of *Catcher in the Rye.* "So cynical."

"Well, lots of teenagers are cynical," Ava said, Maggie's scowling teenager face appearing in her mind.

"I guess," John said. "I wasn't. I was an Eagle Scout, the kid who shoveled the neighbors' driveways when it snowed."

"I'm not surprised," Ava said.

"I didn't like the kid. Holden Caulfield, you know? He says that people who think they're something they're not, and people who won't acknowledge their own weaknesses, are phonies. But isn't lying a kind of phoniness?"

"Yes," she said. "I suppose it is."

"Well, then Holden is a phony, isn't he? He doesn't acknowledge his own shortcomings, and he never thinks about how his behavior affects people around him. And he's a liar! So he's just as guilty of being a phony as anyone else."

"John, that's important to say. You should tell the group," Ava said.

"You think so?" he said, surprised.

"Absolutely."

Cate was calling for everyone to take a seat.

"Thank you," John said, with such sincerity that Ava reached over and patted his arm in a kind of *there there* gesture.

By the time Ava and John sat down, Kiki was already standing nervously beside Cate at the front of the room, holding one of those plastic folders kids used to hand in reports in school.

"I hadn't read *The Catcher in the Rye* in a

long time," Cate began. "Although it was published as an adult novel in 1951, it has become required reading for teenagers and still sells about two hundred and fifty thousand copies a year. One writer said that, along with *Huckleberry Finn* and *The Great Gatsby,* it's one of the three perfect novels of American literature. And the British writer Finlo Rohrer wrote recently that over sixty years after its publication, the book is still the defining work on what it is like to be a teenager."

"It should be required reading for everybody," Ruth said. "Not just adolescents."

"Kiki?" Cate said. "You had something you wanted to say before the discussion got started?"

"Right," Kiki said.

She cleared her throat and fidgeted with the folder, but didn't open it. Ava tried to remember what the girl did for a job. She seemed so inept up there, so young, that Ava couldn't imagine her actually doing something responsible. Kiki looked like someone Ava had met on the other side of a counter. Maybe she worked at the Coffee Exchange, making cappuccino and grinding fair trade beans. Or at Seven Stars, the good bakery on Hope Street. Yes, Ava could picture her there, slicing bread and dishing out scones.

"I wanted to talk about this idea," Kiki was saying.

The room had grown quiet.

"The idea of the book that matters most," Kiki said. "Because I think it's like impossible to pick such a book. When you read a book, and who you are when you read it, makes it matter or not. Like if you're unhappy and you read, I don't know, *On the Road* or *The Three Musketeers,* and that book changes how you feel or how you think, then it matters the most. At that time."

"That's a good point, Kiki," Cate said in her let's-move-on voice.

"When I was a teenager my parents got divorced and it really messed me up," Kiki continued.

Ava sat up a little straighter. She thought of Maggie. "You can't get divorced!" she'd yelled at Ava and Jim. "You can't!"

"I mean, I thought we were, not necessarily the happiest family but, you know, a regular family. A normal family. And then, boom! They sit us down one night after dinner and make this announcement and just fill the air with clichés. How they still loved us, and we had nothing to do with it."

Ava felt her throat tighten. Is that what

she and Jim had done? Filled the air with clichés? They had certainly told Will and Maggie how much they both loved them. She grimaced, remembering Jim saying, "Your mother and I love each other, we just aren't *in* love." When he said it, she'd been surprised. Was it true? They weren't in love anymore? He certainly wasn't; he'd made that clear. But were middle-aged couples who'd been together for over two decades even supposed to be *in* love? Whatever that meant?

She tried to concentrate on what Kiki was saying.

"So when Holden Caulfield calls everyone out on being phonies, I was like, yes! That's right! Every adult I knew at that point was a phony, a liar. Holden Caulfield stated exactly how I felt, and so that book kind of saved me."

"Thank you, Kiki," Cate said firmly. "I think you've perfectly captured why this book is regarded as the defining work on being a teenager. It speaks to the angst and alienation and rebellion of adolescents."

Cate was right, of course. But Ava couldn't stop thinking about how Holden told Mr. Spencer that he was *trapped on the other side of life.* How he kept trying to find his way in a world where he doesn't feel like he belongs. That was why the scene in the Museum of Natural History was so important. Holden was afraid of change, and at the museum everything stayed the same forever, didn't it? Those statues of the Eskimos and the Native Americans stayed fixed in time and place. Wasn't this Maggie's problem too? And, like Holden Caulfield, Maggie resisted understanding this about herself. She preferred to jump from boy to boy, to keep herself isolated emotionally, to just behave badly without caring why she did what she did. Like running away to Paris.

"Right," Kiki was saying, "but what I want to say, or what I'm trying to say, is that I could have chosen *The Lord of the Rings* because a boy I loved in college not only gave me a copy, but he read me a chapter every night."

"Or *The Golden Notebook,*" Monique said. "I could have chosen that."

"I understand what you mean," Honor interrupted. "When I read *Wide Sargasso Sea* I was absolutely transformed. It mattered most to me then because of where I was in my life. So in a way, there isn't just one book that matters most, there might be several, or even a dozen."

Ruth got to her feet. "I still remember the

effect *Dinner at the Homesick Restaurant* had on me."

"You know what?" Cate said, her smile returning. "I'm going to start a list. I'll put all of these titles on it, and any other ones you think of, and I'll email everyone copies at the end of the year."

Everyone seemed pleased with Cate's idea. Still more were being called out. *The Leopard* and *Dr. Zhivago* and *The House of Mirth.*

"Don't forget Rabbit," Luke said.

"How could I?" Cate said. "Let's get back to Holden and Phoebe and Stradlater and the rest."

Hesitantly, John got to his feet. "Here's the thing that bothers me about the book," he began.

As the group listened, and then debated John's point about Holden being a phony, Ava looked at Kiki, who was sitting now, her folder in her lap. What Kiki had said about her own experience with the book had opened something up for Ava. That had been Maggie's problem all along, this sense of superficiality in the world, this phoniness. And Jim leaving had helped confirm everything Maggie had suspected about the adult world.

"Let's not forget his name," Honor was

saying. "A caul is the membrane that covers the head of a fetus during birth, isn't it? Therefore, the *caul* in his name might symbolize the blindness, the innocence of childhood."

"Jesus," John muttered.

"Hold on Caul field," Honor said. "Hold on to your innocence."

Innocence? Blindness was a better word. Wasn't that what Maggie felt now? The blindness she'd turned toward Ava and Jim's marriage, and maybe her own childhood? Another thought lodged in Ava's mind then. She'd also turned a blind eye on her marriage. No wonder *The Catcher in the Rye* still sold so many copies. Adults got something from it too. She imagined Maggie, somewhere in Paris, pictured her in front of an illuminated Eiffel Tower. Was she safe? Was she, maybe, a little happy?

■ ■ ■ ■

Part Nine: September

■ ■ ■ ■

But when the strong were too weak to hurt the weak, the weak had to be strong enough to leave.

— *The Unbearable Lightness of Being*
by Milan Kundera

AVA

Ava's father gripped her arm tight as they walked down the corridor to the family room. He had grown so old and shaky, she realized.

Her father stopped walking but held her arm even tighter.

"I wasn't there, you know," he said, his blue eyes huge above his sunken cheeks.

"Where, Dad?" Ava asked, thinking, *where are you now?*

He stared at her, his gaze fierce.

"That day that Lily died I was at work."

That day that Lily died.

The bright sun and blue blue sky. Her sister, blond hair tangled, blue eyes so much like their mother's, her purple shorts and pink shirt, climbing that tree. "Too high, Lily!" Ava had called to her. Had she really warned her? Or was this a trick of memory? Because if she had said, "Too high, Lily!" then wasn't she exonerated?

"I got a call from your aunt," her father said. "She said, 'Something terrible has happened and you need to get to the hospital immediately.' And I asked her if Charlotte was okay, because I had been worried about her, about your mother. So moody, so depressed. 'Just meet us at the hospital,' she said. And hung up. I kept wondering who *us* was. And then, the strangest thing, instead of going to the hospital I drove straight home. And I passed the ambulance coming down our street. No siren. No flashing light. That's when I knew. Someone had died."

Sitting at the kitchen table, Hank Bingham had given Ava a piece of paper and the stub of a pencil. "Draw exactly what happened," he'd told her. Ava had wanted to let him know that she wasn't a very good artist. She was good at other things — math and reading and geography. She could name the fifty states in alphabetical order and all of the capitals, even the hard ones like Tallahassee, Florida, and Albany, New York. Lily was the artist. She could fold slips of paper into origami cranes and boats. She could take an autumn leaf or a pansy and press it between two pieces of wax paper and magically preserve it.

"Lily can draw the picture," Ava had said

finally, the paper still blank, the pencil clenched in her fist.

Hank Bingham's eyes met hers.

"No, sweetie," he said. "She can't."

"I wasn't there," Ava's father said again. "I was at work."

"I know," she said, prying his fingers from their grip on her arm.

She took his hand — dry as parchment paper, bent from arthritis, cold as death — in hers. Ahead of them, the family room was all bright lights and orange plastic furniture. No families there, just patients staring at nothing. One stood hunched over a jigsaw puzzle of kittens playing with a ball of yarn, trying to fit a piece into an empty spot, any empty spot.

"I told your mother last night," Ava's father said. "I told her that Beatrice wanted me to go straight to the hospital instead of going home."

"Uh huh," Ava said.

"I told her that the ambulance didn't even bother to look like it was in a hurry," he said, his eyes blurred from tears.

Ava felt, suddenly, exhausted. She lowered herself into one of the orange chairs and closed her eyes.

"I told your mother and she said, 'I know, Teddy. Why do you think I had to leave?' "

Ava nodded but kept her eyes shut. The room smelled like boxed mac and cheese and alcohol and old people.

"She said, 'Didn't Penny Frost give you my note?' "

"Penny Frost?" Ava said, opening her eyes.

Her father got that confused look on his face, the one that broke Ava's heart.

"What do you know about Penny Frost?" he asked.

"Mom gave Penny Frost a note?" Ava asked him, even though she knew they had entered the place where he was lost to her.

"What do you know about it?" he demanded.

He waved his hand in the air as if he could make Ava disappear.

"You don't know anything," he muttered.

He was right, of course, Ava thought. She saw that big tree, abundant with green leaves. She saw that blue sky and a flash of purple and pink. She heard her own small voice calling, "Too high, Lily!"

"Dad," Ava said.

But he just stared off into the distance, at something she could not see.

Ava was in her bedroom, the air conditioner blasting so high that she'd put on a sweater, when she heard someone knocking, persistently, at the front door. On her lap she had a blank piece of copy paper and a box of colored pencils. Could she draw a picture of that day now, after all these years? She took out a green pencil, ignoring whoever was at the door.

She drew each leaf carefully, in the color called Grass Green, and then switched to Dark Green.

The knocking had stopped, but now Ava thought she heard footsteps on the stairs. She paused, Dark Green in hand, and listened.

The bedroom door opened and Jim walked in, looking pissed off.

"You still have a key?" Ava said, startled.

"It's like Alaska in here," Jim said.

He walked over to the air conditioner, bent to peer at the knobs.

"You got an air conditioner," he said.

"I like it cold," Ava said.

"I didn't even know you liked pink," he said, running his fingers across her pretty sheets.

"You can't just walk in here, you know."

"You're drawing? A tree?" Jim asked her.

Ava turned the paper over so he couldn't see it.

"I got a call," he said. "A troubling call."

He wasn't looking at her. He just kept

running his hand up and down the sheet.

"Okay," she said.

"From the police. In Paris."

Despite the air conditioner on low now, Ava felt chilled. She pulled her sweater closer around her.

"Oh God," she said.

She asked him, "Is she dead?" Even though she knew that if that were true he wouldn't have bothered with the air conditioner.

Finally Jim looked up at her.

"She overdosed on heroin and was taken to a hospital," he said. "It wasn't pneumonia."

"Heroin?" Her throat had gone so dry, Ava couldn't seem to swallow.

"Thankfully someone called for an ambulance instead of leaving her. They treated her at the hospital and gave her a talking-to and released her."

"You mean she's wandering around Paris? On drugs?" Ava was trying very hard not to fall apart.

"I don't know, Ava."

"Heroin. Jesus."

"Maybe it was just that once," Jim said.

They both knew that wasn't likely. But Ava nodded anyway, and said, "Maybe." Maggie had emailed her! She was supposed to be okay!

"They have her picture," Jim said. "And the police are going to look out for her in the areas where there's drug activity."

Ava thought of when she lived in that Manhattan railroad flat in Alphabet City in the eighties. Bathtub in the kitchen and the smell of roach spray. On the corner, above the bodega, was a shooting gallery, and all day and night she would see people going in and out. Men in business suits and scrawny teenagers and strung-out junkies and housewives and girls just like Maggie, from good families and good schools. Was that where Maggie was? In a place like that?

"Don't cry," Jim said, and that's when she realized she had started to cry.

He reached over and wrapped her in his arms. Ava pressed her face into his chest, felt the soft cotton of his t-shirt, a red one she didn't recognize with foreign words written across it. She inhaled his smell of minty soap and environmentally safe detergent and just Jim.

"We'll find her and we'll bring her home," he said.

She wanted to remind him that there was no more *we,* but she didn't. Instead, she just rested her weary self against him.

Ava

"You haven't found Rosalind Arden, have you?" Cate asked Ava.

They were in Cate's backyard, setting up for the Labor Day weekend barbecue that Cate and Gray always held. Ava uncovered the bowls of potato salad and kale salad and pasta salad, took the plastic wrap off a platter of deviled eggs, and ignored Cate's question.

"She's supposed to come in November," Cate said. "That's two months away."

Ava watched her stick bottles of beer and wine into the ice in a big silver trough. Beyond her, Gray stood at the grill shoving newspapers into a chimney. He refused to use a gas grill. *Changes the taste,* he always said.

"Is she dead?" Cate was asking. "Is that it? And you're afraid to tell the group?"

Ava took one of the red plastic forks sitting in a red basket of utensils and paper napkins decorated with red and black ants, and speared a corkscrew of pasta. The salad had sun-dried tomatoes and black olives and feta cheese.

"You're right," Ava said, plucking out an olive, "I can't find her. It's like she vanished. The publishing house doesn't even exist anymore."

"Which one was it?"

"White Swan," Ava said.

"They were in Boston," Cate said. "On Beacon Street. A small house with very few titles. Mostly New England writers. Poetry chapbooks. Accounts of the '39 hurricane. That sort of thing."

Ava looked at her, surprised.

Cate laughed. "I'm a librarian. I know these things."

"So they did exist," Ava said.

"I knew an editor there. Poppy Montgomery. She was ancient."

"The coals are white!" Gray called to Cate.

"Why doesn't he just use a gas grill like everyone else?" Ava said.

"He thinks it —"

"I know," Ava said.

First came the sound of voices nearing, and then a small gaggle of people appeared at the top of the driveway. Everyone clutched a bottle of wine, like an offering. Right behind them another head appeared.

"You invited Jim?" Ava said in disbelief. "And the yarn bomber?"

"Gray must have," Cate said. "I didn't."

But Ava saw immediately that Jim wasn't with Delia. He was walking down the driveway purposefully. Alone.

He looked sheepish when he reached Ava and Cate. But Cate immediately put on her good hostess voice, and welcomed him more enthusiastically than Ava liked.

"Ava," he said. "Hi."

"Hi," Ava said. Her mouth had gone suddenly dry. She hadn't talked to him since he gave her the news about Maggie a few days ago. Ava had made a timeline: the hospital, the email to Will, Maggie's email to her. How could Maggie have sounded so normal, so like herself?

"Let me put you to work," Cate said, guiding Jim away.

He glanced over his shoulder at Ava, sending her a look she didn't understand. It was very much like the kind of looks he would send her years ago when they had to part after a long night together in her small East Village apartment. Or, later, when one or the other had to be away for a night or a few nights and that absence felt enormous and impossible. Or when the children were babies and Jim had to leave for work, hating to miss even one minute of their babyhood. But surely he intended something different. Those looks had stopped even before he met — remet, Ava reminded herself — Delia Lindstrom.

Still, that glance over his shoulder was enough to send Ava up the driveway herself, and across the street to the refuge of her own house.

Unexpectedly, gray clouds moved across the sky, heavy with the promise of rain. With them, a cool breeze arrived, and Ava found herself shivering in her thin shift in her backyard, *The Unbearable Lightness of Being* in her lap. The book, with its explorations of light and heavy, art versus kitsch, and the various entanglements of love and marriage and adultery, had so absorbed her that Ava had almost blocked out the sounds from Cate and Gray's party floating in the air.

She uncapped her orange highlighter and underlined a sentence in the book: *A return after long wanderings.* That was what Franz's wife ordered for his tombstone after his death. *A return after long wanderings.* The words made her think of Maggie, wandering the streets of Paris. And Will alone in

Uganda, searching.

"There you are!" Jim's voice interrupted her.

Ava rubbed her arms to warm herself, but didn't respond.

He walked across their small backyard, sitting in the chair beside her, his elbows on his knees as he leaned toward her, smiling.

"You left," he said.

"I didn't feel like a party. Maggie," she added, and he nodded.

Jim cocked his head in the direction of Cate's house. "They've entered the dancing portion," he said.

Bruce Springsteen was belting out "Rosalita" and people were singing along. This was part of the Labor Day party at Cate and Gray's, and Ava could picture them, all the middle-aged couples stomping and twirling.

"You have goosebumps," Jim said.

He ran his index finger up her arm. Ava pulled her arm away from him, frowning.

"I need to read this," she said, holding up the book.

"Milan Kundera," he said. "The promise of socialism with a human face."

When she didn't respond, he said, "You should put on a sweater." He glanced up at the clouds. "A cold front is moving in."

"Time to go inside," she said, but he stopped her.

"Do you think," he said softly, "there's a chance we could be happy too?"

"You know," Ava said, "a year ago I would have said no. But I do think we can each be happy."

Jim was looked her, confused.

"I mean," she continued, "I've come to realize how very different we are."

"I thought opposites attract," he said ruefully.

Now Ava was confused. "What are you saying, Jim?"

"I meant, do you think *we* could be happy? Together. Again."

"What about Delia?"

Jim said, "This isn't about Delia. It's about you and me. I miss you, Ava. Sometimes I walk past the house and I pause and remember us being there, all of us. Our family. You."

Ava studied her husband's face. She had imagined this moment so often in those first months after he left. Surely, she used to think, he will come to his senses. Surely he will come back.

"Will you think about it?" Jim said.

Ava took his hand in hers. How familiar it still felt, soft and long-fingered.

"I don't have to," Ava said. "I don't want us to get back together."

Jim nodded slowly. For a very long time, he held her hand. Then he lifted it to his lips and kissed it gently before he stood.

As Ava watched him walk away, the line came into her mind again.

A return after long wanderings.

But he wasn't returning, she told herself as the familiar broad shoulders and shaggy hair disappeared around the corner of the house.

By the time the book club met, the heat of summer had lifted. Already Ava spotted red leaves among the greenery as she drove to work the morning of the meeting. It was the first day of classes, and she found it appropriate that the weather had turned autumnal. Ava thought of her children and their long-ago first days of school. How neat Maggie's braids were, how white and clean Will's sneakers. Soon enough sweaters were misplaced, tights ripped, zippers broke. But for that first day everything looked shiny and perfect. Now, Jim had hired a private investigator in Paris to try and find their daughter, who still blithely emailed her brief messages, signing off with #paree or #crepeheaven!!!

She found a parking place easily, another surprise. Could she take this fall weather and this gift of a parking spot as omens for a better year with Plouff? A better year all around? That PI finding Maggie? Ava hoped so. Like teachers everywhere, she thought of the first day of school as the beginning of the new year. She was a middle-aged woman, and needed to start acting like one. A middle-aged almost officially divorced woman, she reminded herself as she opened the large glass double door of Bagg, the modern languages building.

A single cryptic email had arrived this morning from Maggie: "Paris is always a good idea." To which Ava replied: "Stop quoting Audrey Hepburn. Dad and I are worried sick. Where exactly are you?" Of course she'd heard exactly nothing back.

Ava walked to the elevator and pressed the Up button, but immediately decided to take the stairs instead. If this was the first day of a new year, then she would climb steps, give up carbohydrates, drink more water and less wine. Maybe she would even get one of those fitness bracelets that measured steps and calories. Now all she had to do was stick with all her resolutions.

Her mood changed immediately when she saw Plouff standing at the top of the stairs, his arms folded, his hair looking even more Einsteinish than usual. She tried not to let him hear her hard breathing. How many steps were there, anyway?

"You're late," he said before she even reached him.

Ava stopped, four stairs from Plouff, and looked up at him. From this angle, his hair seemed even Einsteinier.

"Late?" she said. "But my first class isn't until eleven and it's only ten twenty."

"The ten o'clock faculty meeting?"

Ava frowned. What ten o'clock faculty meeting?

"You are reading your university email, aren't you? You got the memo that all correspondence as of September 1 would be only via the dot.edu account, didn't you?"

Ava moved her heavy tote bag from one shoulder to the other. She didn't even know her university email name or password. How was she ever going to get communications from the department?

"And you probably also didn't get the memo that all correspondence between you and your students must be on Blackboard, did you?" Plouff said. He didn't wait for a reply, but just turned abruptly and headed toward the conference room.

"Blackboard?" Ava asked his retreating back.

She hurried to catch up with him. By the time she entered the conference room, panting and sweaty beneath her new silk blouse, the one she'd bought in an effort to look more professional, Plouff was already talking. Ava slid into the first empty seat she saw. In the center of the table sat a tray of croissants. Ava took an almond one and bit into it. So much for the no-carbohydrate resolution, she thought, as Plouff droned on about the mission of the French department.

Cate went all out on the food at the book group that night. The table over which Emma — her hair dyed the color of car taillights — presided had platters of bread smeared with mayonnaise and topped with ham and sliced boiled eggs, bowls of beet chips the color of Emma's hair, sausages with mustard and ketchup, cookies cut into the shapes of houses, and poppyseed cake.

"Emma knows a Czech woman who made all of this traditional food for us," Cate told them.

John frowned. "Not a fan of beets," he said, putting three sausages on a paper plate.

"Makovec," Emma was saying. *"Pernik.*

Bramboraky."

Jennifer beamed at her. "It sounds like poetry," she said.

"What is it?" John asked.

He had a spot of ketchup on his chin and Ava had to resist the urge to wipe it off.

"Czech," Cate said. Then she added, "Because of the book?"

John's cheeks reddened, and Cate patted his arm as if to say it was all right.

When Ava caught his eye, she tapped her chin. He looked confused.

"You've got some —"

"Oh!" he said, reddening more. He picked up a napkin and rubbed his chin hard, then looked to Ava.

"Gone," she said.

Emma was happily handing out bottles of Czech pilsner.

"No wine?" Ava said. "Again?"

Emma shook her head, obviously insulted. "Kundera!" she said.

"Pilsner it is then!" Ava said with false cheer.

Her afternoon had deteriorated after the faculty meeting and she was determined to have a good night.

She took a big swallow of beer. Bitter.

"Mmm," she said to Emma, who had lost interest in her and was uttering more Czech words to Jennifer.

Monique sidled up next to her. "I don't like Blackboard," she said right away. "It's just one more way for them to monitor us."

"It gives me a headache," Ava agreed. "Why can't we just keep the old-fashioned way? Mimeograph the syllabus. Meet in person during office hours."

Cate was calling the group to take seats. Ava noticed Luke and Kiki sitting together, their heads bent toward each other, foreheads almost touching. Good, she thought.

Jennifer stood beside Cate. She was dressed in a lumpy hand-knit poncho and parachute pants.

"Jennifer wanted to begin with an explanation of Czech history and politics and how they affected Kundera," Cate said.

"Appreciated," Ruth said, nodding and already writing in her Moleskine notebook.

"The promise of socialism with a human face," Jennifer intoned.

Ava sat up straighter. That was what Jim had said that afternoon in her yard.

"The youthful members of the short-lived Prague Spring wanted to accomplish that promise back in 1968," Jennifer said.

Was she actually teary-eyed?

"1968," Jennifer repeated, and yes, she was crying. "Even though that was fifteen years before I was born, it affects me deeply."

She took a breath to compose herself.

"As you all know, the Prague Spring was a grassroots movement for human rights and freedom, not unlike grassroots movements today in North Korea and Bolivia and Myanmar."

She said the name of each country with its correct pronunciation, like someone who worked at the UN.

"Hear, hear," Kiki said, and Luke nodded.

"Milan Kundera was one of those young men," Jennifer said. "The arts flourished under Alexander Dubček, who outlawed political persecution and fought for basic human rights."

"Thank you, Jennifer," Cate said at last, and everyone burst into applause.

"I do want to say thank you too," Ruth said. "I remember when those Soviet tanks rolled into Prague. I was watching television with my grandmother and she started to cry. 'No more war,' she said. She was afraid of another world war."

"I'd love to talk about the dichotomy between lightness and weight in the novel," Ava said.

John looked relieved.

"That paradox can't be resolved though, can it?" Luke asked. "At least, none of the four characters in the book resolve it."

"What about Sabina?" John asked, surprising even himself.

"Sabina is the only one alive at the end, and she doesn't seem exactly happy," Kiki said.

"Yes, but she's the only one who lived her life in step with her principles, isn't she?" Ava said.

"That's true," Monique agreed. "She identified kitsch early in her life. She recognized that sentimental, insistently sunny art is propaganda and she stayed true to her own real art."

"She was my favorite of the lot," John said. "Even though I wasn't sure why she didn't understand Tomas's desire to get married."

"Because he traded his freedom," Kiki said.

"Let's not forget," Cate stepped in, using her let's-get-back-on-track voice, "Sabina's own desire for freedom makes her leave Franz, who she loved."

"Not just Franz," Ruth added. "She lost contact with everything and everyone from her past, didn't she?"

"Still," John said thoughtfully, "she's the

lightest character. I mean, the way Ava was describing."

Ava listened as the group discussed lightness and weight. Of course there was no right answer, but as she sat sipping the bitter beer her mind drifted away from *The Unbearable Lightness of Being* and back to that summer and *From Clare to Here.* At the end of the book, the mother chooses to stay with her dead child rather than return to the world of the living. Ava remembered how that decision had kept her awake at night. How could a mother do such a thing? How could a mother leave her living child who still needed her so desperately? Had she known at the time that it was the same choice her own mother had made when she left them and jumped off that bridge? Perhaps on some level she'd realized that, but somehow, sitting here tonight thinking about choices and the dichotomy of weight and lightness, she felt as if she understood it for the first time.

When the discussion finally broke up, Ava put on her coat and tried to slip away unnoticed. She was unhinged. She wanted to go home and crawl into bed and not think about anything at all.

But Cate seemed to be waiting to pounce on her.

"I've been trying to talk to you all night," Cate said, blocking Ava's path. "About Poppy."

"Poppy?" Ava said.

"Montgomery. The editor of *From Clare to Here,*" Cate said. "I did some sleuthing and you're never going to believe this. It's why I've left you five messages on your phone. Why didn't you call?"

"Maggie," Ava said.

"Oh, sweetie," Cate said. "I thought she was okay."

"We don't know. She sounds okay in her emails. But —" Ava stopped, unable to tell Cate anything more. "I call the embassy constantly," she added. "I just want them to find her."

"They will," Cate said. "Or she'll just show up at home like she does."

"What's this about Poppy Montgomery."

"Poppy Montgomery was Penny's mother," Cate said. "That's what I found out. Poppy died in 1997 and left two daughters, Penny and Helena, also both dead."

"That explains why Penny had a copy of the book," Ava said, more to herself than to Cate.

"You're welcome," Cate said. But she was smiling.

■ ■ ■ ■

Part Ten: October

■ ■ ■ ■

But she did look back, and I love her for that, because it was so human.
— *Slaughterhouse-Five* by Kurt Vonnegut

The Bookstore Owner

The girl was flopped in the leopard beanbag. It needed to be plumped up somehow, Madame thought. Refilled. She wondered what it was stuffed with and where she could find whatever it was.

The girl was reading *Treasure Island,* a slight smile on her face.

Madame watched her for a minute, then slowly went into the back room. It smelled of the lentil soup warming on the hot plate. And of mildew. Books lined the shelves along one wall. She reached for one on the top shelf. Once it was in her hands, she stared at it as if for the first time. There were over a hundred of them up there, collecting dust. *Thank God.* But sometimes she met someone who she thought — no, knew — needed to read it. Someone who might read it and understand.

She smoothed the jacket, and ran her fingers up and down the spine.

“Hello, little book,” she said softly. Then scoffed at her own sentimentality.

Out in the store, the girl was still in the beanbag chair, still reading *Treasure Island.*

“Stevenson,” Madame said. “His father and grandfather built lighthouses. Did you know that?”

The girl looked up slowly.

“Here,” Madame said, holding the book out to her. “Read this one.”

The girl hesitated, then took it.

Madame wanted to say so much more, but she didn’t. She just walked away.

AVA

The Frost mansion stood regally on Prospect Street behind a row of boxwoods so tall the brick house was completely hidden. Ava drove through the entrance, between the wall of hedges, and down the winding driveway. To the right bloomed an English garden, with a dazzling array of dahlias in pink and purple and yellow and maroon tipped in white, and other flowers Ava couldn't identify. In the center of it all, wearing an enormous straw hat, cropped pants, an oversized chamois shirt and lime green Crocs, stood Helen. She looked up as Ava neared, frowning above oversized sunglasses.

Ava stopped the car and got out, plastering on a smile and extending her hand toward Helen, who frowned even deeper.

Helen held up both hands, which were covered in dirt, and shrugged.

"What a gorgeous garden," Ava said. "I

always think of autumn as marigolds and mums."

"Will flower until frost," Helen said. "That's what Mother always said."

Ava took in the purple and red fuchsias and the cannas in every shade of orange imaginable.

"What are the big ones?" she asked, pointing to the purple blooms looming at least three feet tall above everything else.

"Salvias," Helen said matter-of-factly. "Mother planted them because she feared the others seemed too tropical for this time of year."

"Ah," Ava said.

Truth be told, gardening bored her. Jim always did their planting, the window boxes of pansies and vines of morning glories along the back fence. And the tulips, of course, for her.

"I should learn more about it," Ava said.

"Some consider it a waste of time," Helen said.

She didn't wait for an answer, just began to walk toward the front door. Ava followed.

As soon as they arrived on the doorstep, the door swung open and a butler appeared. He was old, seemingly even older than Penny herself had been. But he stood straight in his butler's uniform, and held a silver tray with a single glass of water on it. Helen took the glass and drank the water down without even pausing.

Through the grand foyer Ava hurried after Helen. Ahead of her, a jaw-dropping view of the statehouse with its imposing marble dome appeared.

Helen paused to wait for Ava to catch up. She pointed at the window and the state-house beyond.

"That's the fourth largest unsupported marble dome in the world," she said. "Did you know that?"

Ava did, but apparently the question was rhetorical because Helen was saying, "St. Peter's Basilica in Rome. The Minnesota state capitol. The Taj Mahal. And us."

"Impressive," Ava said, noticing the trail of dirt Helen had brought in from the gar-den.

"Stephen? Tea?" Helen called. To Ava, she said, "Sit."

Ava sat.

Despite the dahlias and the butler and the view, Ava saw now that the house was a bit shabby around the edges. Fine cracks in the ceiling. A draft coming in through the wall of windows. The upholstery faded. As if she knew what Ava was thinking, Helen ran her fingers over the worn fabric on the chair where she sat.

"I suppose this is about the book," she said.

"It's come to my attention that your grandmother published it," Ava said, relieved there would be no more small talk.

"Poppy Montgomery. Editor to New England's finest authors."

"That book was very important to me the summer I was eleven," Ava said. "So when the book club made us choose the book that mattered most to us, I immediately picked *From Clare to Here.*"

She waited, but Helen remained impassive.

"Your mother chose *Pride and Prejudice,*" she added, but Helen only nodded slightly.

Stephen the butler arrived, noisily wheeling a cart like a flight attendant's. After he served them tea — his hands shaking so hard that as much spilled to the floor as made it into the cups — and wheeled the cart out, Ava said, "The problem is, I can't find any copies of *From Clare to Here.* I know the publisher went out of business —"

"There *are* no copies," Helen said.

"But there must be."

"It went out of print rather quickly. The author refused to do any publicity for it, and Grandmother always believed that helped keep a book alive. No reviews to speak of, just the *Globe* and the *Journal.* Typically when a book goes out of print the author buys up whatever's left. I assume that's what happened."

"The note from your mother," Ava said. "Do you understand it?"

"She said she knew *your* mother."

"My mother owned a bookstore," Ava said.

"I remember when you first joined the book group, Mother told me that she'd once delivered a gift to you from your mother. A long time ago, when you were a child."

"My mother died when I was young," Ava said. "So I wouldn't remember that."

Helen shrugged.

"I should be going," Ava said.

Helen stood — a little too eagerly, Ava thought.

"I suspected you might want to see the records I have about the book," Helen said. "So I made copies for you."

She handed Ava a red folder with the logo for White Swan Books across it.

Ava thanked her, then made her way through the large rooms to the foyer and the front door.

Will flower until frost, she thought as she passed the garden. She paused to admire the dahlias, some of which were almost as big as her head. Then she got back in her car, the folder on her lap. She had to resist the urge to open it right there in the long driveway and read what it had to say. Instead, she made her way around the wide circle, past a chipped marble fountain of classical figures without any water bubbling from it, between the tall boxwood hedges, and back onto Prospect Street.

Ava drove a couple of blocks, then pulled over.

She opened the red folder. Inside, a thin stack of papers, neatly paper-clipped together. The top one read: "*From Clare to Here.* Synopsis." Behind it were copies of the contract. She scanned to the bottom, and what she saw there made her breath catch. Instead of the author's name being listed as Rosalind Arden, it read "Charlotte North."

Ava read the name again, and then again.

Charlotte North? *Charlotte North?*

She closed the folder and looked straight ahead at the yellow and red leaves on the trees, the sunlight dappling them.

She opened the folder again, as if perhaps she would discover she'd misread the author's name. But it read "Charlotte North."

Ava's mother had written *From Clare to Here.*

MAGGIE

From her perch on the stool at the cash register, Maggie saw the tour guide from the Musée d'Orsay walk by. Unexpectedly, Madame had directed Maggie behind the counter this morning when she came in. With no explanation, Madame said, "I assume you can punch these keys and make change?" and without waiting for an answer she walked away. Now a second surprise: Noah.

Maggie jumped down and ran to the door, flinging it open.

"Hey you!" she called.

He stopped and turned around. When he realized who it was, he brightened.

"I'm glad you're okay," he said.

Maggie chewed her bottom lip. She only had a hazy memory of seeing him at the café, remembering only that he'd bought her food and acted concerned. But what had she done or said that morning? How had she looked?

"I ran after you," he was saying, and now he was moving toward her, "but no luck."

"I wanted to thank you," she said. "I was so sick that day."

"No. You were completely wasted."

She started to argue with him, but stopped.

"Right," she said. "I was."

"I'm Noah," he said. "In case you forgot."

"Maggie," she said, and surprised herself by giving him a hug.

Noah hugged her back, wrapping her in his arms and holding on tight. She thought of solid things, like stone piers and hard clay. Things that held you in place.

"You're a good hugger," she said when he released her.

He grinned. "I aim to please."

They stood awkwardly for a moment, then Noah tilted his chin toward the store. "You work here?"

Maggie nodded.

"All day?" he asked.

"It's kind of loose," she said.

"Maybe we could meet up when you finish? Get a bite of food or something? My last tour ends at four."

Maggie hesitated.

"Hey," Noah said, holding up a hand.

"That's cool. I'm just glad you're all right."

He adjusted his backpack in a way that indicated he was leaving.

"Wait," she said.

She took a step closer to him. His eyes were nice, dark blue, like the ocean in a certain light. And he had that shock of hair that fell over his eyes. Maggie tried to find something false in his face, but he looked open, genuine.

Noah surprised her by wrapping her into another hug and holding her there.

"I'll be back around five," he said into her hair.

Maggie nodded against his chest.

"Falafel?" he said.

"Falafel," she said.

"L'As?" Noah said. "Have you been?"

Maggie didn't answer.

"On rue des Rosiers," Noah said. "They're super crisp and they put hummus, and this pickled red cabbage and salted cucumbers and fried eggplant and harissa. And the pita is enormous, like, you can't even hold the thing."

After he left, Maggie couldn't stop grinning. She went to the back room and wrestled the mouse enough to write to her brother.

Wills!!! I have an honest to God job! I met a nice boy. I have a friend. I'm practically normal!

Instead of signing it she sent a row of emoticons: a face with eyes popping, a dancing girl, the French flag, and then a dozen books followed by a dozen hearts.

Immediately after she sent it, Will replied.

Maggot. Stop playing games. Call Mom.

Without hesitating, Maggie did. She picked up the phone and dialed her mother's number. When she heard her mother's voice — "Hi, this is Ava. I'm not here to take your call . . ." — Maggie unexpectedly started to cry. After the beep, she took a breath.

"I love you," she said, and hung up.

Hank

Hank Bingham did his best thinking in his little spiral notebooks. When he wrote in them — the facts of a case, the descriptions of people and places, what people told him, his own unanswered questions — it was like he was figuring something out. He *was* figuring something out: the solution.

It used to drive Nadine crazy. "Put down the Bic, Hank, and let's have a conversation." She'd chop off every syllable in the word *conversation,* as if he might not understand it otherwise. He'd tried to explain it to her, how writing stuff down helped him think. But she didn't buy it. "It's called approach avoidance, Hank," she told him once. But when he looked it up in the *Merriam-Webster,* he decided she was wrong. Approach avoidance was when a goal was both desirable and undesirable. Nadine's we-need-to-talk conversations were never desirable to Hank. What he had was simple avoidance.

Miss Kitty was sitting right on his notebook, so Hank had to slide it out from under her, which made the cat hiss at him and jump off the table. Oh, if Nadine knew a cat was sitting on her kitchen table she'd go ballistic on him.

Hank sat down and took his pen from his pocket.

The idea of solving a problem — a case — still thrilled him, almost the way he used to feel right before he kissed a girl or put his hand inside her bra to touch her warm breast. He liked the *right before* part of things, when it was impossible to be disappointed. Sitting here now at the kitchen table where he and Nadine used to sit across from each other with their morning coffee, sometimes avoiding eye contact, sometimes sharing the newspaper, Hank felt it, the excitement of the *right before.* After all these years, he was about to solve the Lily North case.

Also on the table, besides his notebook and his cat, was *From Clare to Here.*

He opened that first.

He read the epigraph out loud:

Now go we in content
To liberty, and not to banishment.

It was from a Shakespeare play, *As You Like It.* Hank knew that, and knew it was called an epigraph, because when the book had first arrived in the mail all those years ago, when he'd been crazy with grief over Charlotte leaving him, he'd thought there might be a clue inside somewhere.

"What's this?" he'd asked Nadine, who was sick with suspicion over his melancholy.

"An epigraph," she told him, narrowing her eyes and studying not the words but him. All of him, like she was a human x-ray machine trying to read him and discover what was wrong. "A poem or a quotation the writer puts at the beginning of a book."

"And what's the point? I mean, you've got the book itself, right? Why borrow someone else's poem or whatever?"

"It suggests the theme of the book," she said.

"Don't you get that from reading the book?"

Nadine closed the book and handed it back to him. "Go read *As You Like It* and you figure out why the writer put this epigraph here. Okay?"

And he'd gone to the library for the book Nadine mentioned, but when he found out it wasn't a book really, but a play, by Shakespeare, written in language he couldn't understand, he'd given up.

Until today.

Hank opened his spiral notebook and flipped to the first empty page he saw. He licked the tip of his pen, and frowned. Something was written in a woman's handwriting across the top of the page.

He tapped his pocket to see if his readers were there, and took them out and put them on, squinting anyway at the unfamiliar handwriting.

Rosalind Arden.

He held the paper closer, as if the name might change.

Rosalind Arden.

"What the hell?" Hank said out loud into the empty kitchen.

The cat, still mad that he'd disturbed her nap, glared at him.

Then he remembered. Last summer in Home Depot. He'd run into Ava North buying an air conditioner and she'd asked him for help tracking down a writer. She wrote the name in his notebook, and as soon as he told her to do that he decided he wasn't going help her. He didn't like her.

Now here it was. The name she'd written down. The writer she was looking for. Had she figured out who Rosalind Arden was?

Hank reached for the mustard-yellow

phone on the wall and punched in Ava's phone number, which was written in small numbers beneath the name *Rosalind Arden.* She crossed her sevens. How weird was that? Hank thought as he listened to the phone ring.

When Ava answered, he didn't even say hello or who he was.

"I found your writer," he said.

Ava gave a short, harsh laugh.

"I don't think so," she said.

"Yeah?" Hank said.

"She's dead, Hank," Ava said.

"Maybe," he said. "That's entirely possible. But I think she's in Paris."

"Paris?" Ava repeated, and laughed again.

"You home?" he asked her.

"Why?"

"Jesus Christ," Hank muttered.

"I'm home," Ava said, like she was admitting something.

"I'll be right over," Hank said. "I'll explain everything."

He didn't wait for her to reply. He just hung up, grabbed his notebook and *From Clare to Here* and his car keys, and drove toward Ava.

Beatrice

That Morning
1970

Later, Beatrice would wonder if the idea took root that morning as she stood alone in the street watching the ambulance drive away with Lily's body. Was it possible in the midst of such sorrow to understand something vital? If so, she understood it somewhere deep inside her then: *Flee.*

They had been raised, Charlotte and Beatrice, on books. When they had a question, literature answered it. If they complained about being bored, their mother — a melancholy Parisian who used laudanum to assuage the pains of homesickness and her husband's infidelities — would hand them a book. "No one who reads can ever be bored," she'd tell them, propped up in her bed in her pink silk dressing gown. She was beautiful, and pale, with sharp cheekbones and circles like bruises beneath her eyes. "Darling," she'd say, "hand me my tincture, would you?" Her tincture was in a small glass bottle with a cork and a red skull and crossbones on a label around the neck. Crest Brand, it said on the front of the bottle. Poison. She always had a book open in her lap. She favored the Victorians: the Brontës, in particular.

Their father — an absent-minded, charming scoundrel — quoted Chekhov and Shakespeare and Dickens. "It was the best of times, it was the worst of times, my lovies," he'd say when they bickered. He'd hold his head and cry, "How, how, how?" when they felt confused. And Shakespeare. He could recite Mark Antony's eulogy to Caesar, Hamlet's "To be, or not to be" soliloquy, Romeo's "Good night, good night! Parting is such sweet sorrow, that I shall say good night till it be morrow" every night at bedtime.

Perhaps that was how Beatrice came to think these words that morning, standing alone in the street: *I was too young that time to value her, But now I know her. If she be a traitor, Why, so am I.*

As You Like It. One of their father's favorites. They always had a cat named Arden. One Arden would die and they'd get another. Arden, where Rosalind and Celia were banished.

She was instructed to stay there until Ted arrived, and then to go to the police station to talk to Officer Lee. "Just a few more questions," he'd said.

While she waited for Ted — and really, she didn't wait very long because he saw the ambulance leaving — she repeated the details.

Beatrice closed her eyes, as if she could block out the story. How she'd arrived late because she forgot she'd promised to babysit and had gone instead to the bookstore to set up the window display for *Jonathan Livingston Seagull.* How with all those white seagulls soaring into the sky stacked around her she'd remembered her promise and left right away, leaving the window in disarray and the hippie college student — long braids, gypsy skirt, no bra, bells around her ankles, reeking of pot — in charge for the day. How when she got there she saw Lily in that tree and considered making her come down, but shouldn't she make them lunch? Shouldn't she tidy up the still-messy-from-breakfast kitchen? She hesitated. She did. But then she went inside and looked in the fridge — egg salad, melon balls, tomatoes — and tackled the dried batter in the frying pan. Why didn't people soak their pans? That's what she was thinking when she saw, from the corner of her eye, something fall from the tree.

"Weren't you watching them?" Ted asked her when he arrived, wild-eyed.

No. She wasn't watching them. She was washing the frying pan.

Beatrice wanted a drink. No. She needed a drink.

She went inside and found a bottle of Johnnie Walker and poured a finger's worth into a juice glass left on the table from breakfast. Inside, everything looked so ordinary. A family's morning still on display. A cup half filled with cold black coffee. A child's purple sweater draped over a chair. A jump rope tangled on the floor. A book left open, face down on the table, *The Swiss Family Robinson.*

Beatrice sat at the table and sipped her scotch, feeling herself calm as it hit her stomach.

She thought: It's my fault.

She took another swallow of scotch.

She thought: We need a plan.

As children she and Charlotte had been so close they were sometimes mistaken for more than sisters, twins. Even then, they'd had their roles, their different personalities:

Charlotte was sensitive and beautiful, Beatrice rebellious and boisterous. Later that would mean Beatrice always got into trouble. At just sixteen she'd gotten pregnant by the son of her mother's friend in Paris, a boy who'd spent the summer with them. Her mother had arranged an abortion, almost resigned to the fact that of course this would happen to Beatrice. But Charlotte studied literature at New York University, and married well, and lived an exciting bohemian life until she got pregnant with Ava and settled in Providence, buying a rundown house and restoring it.

Already Beatrice had one marriage behind her, and had lost a scholarship to study theater, and had another abortion. It was Charlotte who convinced her to move to Providence and to open the bookstore together. Beatrice liked it, the two of them surrounded by books. Even as Charlotte's perfect life started to show cracks, Beatrice stood by her.

Of course, Charlotte would put it differently. *Had* put it differently. Charlotte would remind Beatrice how she'd warned her against marrying husband number two, how she'd worried over the drinking. Charlotte would say she'd stood by Beatrice. And it was true. It was.

But then came Charlotte's unhappiness, a slow unraveling not unlike their mother's. Except their mother had reasons to be unhappy. Their father's affairs. Her inability to fit in with the other mothers. Charlotte — Charlotte had a husband who adored her, and lovely children, and a profitable business, and a home with a goddamned historical plaque on it. Yet she was barely able to get out of bed for days at a time. And then Beatrice had to do everything: run the store, do the bookkeeping, deal with customers and salespeople and shoveling snow and paying bills and answering phones. Yet Ted — foolish cuckolded Ted! — would complain that Beatrice was edgy, or drank too much. A bad influence around the girls. Once, when she went to check on Charlotte, who was in bed with the shades drawn on a beautiful spring day, she'd found her sister had overdosed on sedatives. If Beatrice hadn't walked in, Charlotte would be dead. Afterward, Charlotte claimed it was accidental. She couldn't sleep, that was all. She lost track of how many she'd taken. But Beatrice didn't believe her.

Then a man walked into her life, and Charlotte told Beatrice that maybe her unhappiness had come from not loving Ted, or not loving him enough. "I'm *fond* of him," she'd said. This time, with this man, Charlotte assured Beatrice, it was for real. They loved each other. Her sister seemed younger, prettier in the wash of new love. Maybe this time it *was* real. But the idea of that made Beatrice angry. Why should Charlotte have such a love? She already had a family, a husband and children. A home. And all Beatrice had was a long line of mistakes.

Maybe that was why, after Lily died, Beatrice knew she had to fix their lives.

Charlotte was like a wild animal in those weeks and months following Lily's death. Her eyes seemed to burn with anguish. She grew thin, and erratic. Sometimes she would burst into unexplained laughter. Sometimes she would disappear for a day or two and Ted would fear that she'd done it for real this time, taken her life. But Beatrice knew better, because they had made a plan.

The affair continued, with even more passion because Charlotte knew she would be the one to leave. She'd always written poetry, old-fashioned poems and sonnets and villanelles. And short stories. But now she decided she would write a novel, a book that would explain why she had to leave everyone. Beatrice didn't ask questions; there was too much to do.

By fall she'd gone to Paris to find them an apartment and a small store. They would do the only thing they both knew how to do: lose themselves in books. In the midst of such grief over Lily, Beatrice's departure went virtually unnoticed. Besides, some people blamed her. *Ted* blamed her. He was happy for her to be gone. She secured an apartment that could house the bookstore on the ground floor and living quarters above. Then she began to acquire books. She bought paperbacks from backpackers for a few francs and asked hostel and B and B owners if she could have the books visitors left behind. People left books everywhere, Beatrice soon learned, and she combed the train stations and Métro cars for abandoned ones. Bodice rippers and classics and novels assigned for college English classes; bestsellers and paperback flops with their front covers torn off; guidebooks and children's books and slender volumes of poetry. She'd brought two suitcases full from the store on Thayer Street, and eventually with those and her finds the shelves of the small store began to fill.

But what a hodgepodge! When she tried

to put them in categories, they defied the usual Fiction, Non-Fiction, Bestseller groupings. On index cards in purple Magic Marker, Beatrice wrote her own categories: *"Books Our Mother Loved"* (here she placed *Indiana* and *The Devil's Pool, Jane Eyre* and *Wuthering Heights*), *"Books Our Father Loved"* (here she placed *The Lady With the Dog and Other Stories, Great Expectations,* and *Twelve Plays by William Shakespeare*), *"Books I Love"* (here she placed *Siddhartha, The Painted Bird, On the Road*), *"Books We Don't Understand Why People Like"* (and here she put *Peyton Place* and *Love Story* and *Hawaii*).

It took a year for all of this to be put in place in Paris, while back home Charlotte mourned and loved and wrote her novel that White Swan, a small publishing house in Boston, bought and she published under a pseudonym. The night before Charlotte was to arrive in Paris, Beatrice went out to the little café around the corner, a smoky neighborhood place known for its steak frites. Her hair had grown long and even wilder. Her arms were tanned, and muscular from hauling books and furniture and building shelves. That night Beatrice took the piece of wood she'd salvaged from someone's trash and painted the name of the store in purple, Charlotte's favorite color. GANYMEDE'S BOOKS. It was her own little joke. If anyone ever came looking for either of them, maybe they would figure it out. She stepped back and admired her work, smiling to herself. But if Charlotte did her part right, who would ever come looking for them?

AVA

"You ever read *As You Like It*?" Hank Bingham asked Ava.

"I think we can settle this pretty quickly," Ava said.

Hank looked like he intended to stay awhile. He had his shirtsleeves rolled up and he'd laid out a notebook and the novel *From Clare to Here* on the coffee table that sat between them. His long legs were stretched out, crossed at the ankles. Ava saw that he had on two different colored socks: one navy blue, the other black. What with the instant coffee and mismatched socks, she almost felt bad for him. Almost.

"That writer you wanted me to find," Hank was saying. He opened his notebook and flipped through the pages. "Rosalind Arden."

"That was a pseudonym," she said softly.

Hank looked up at her, surprised.

"You know who she is, this Rosalind Arden?"

Instead of answering him, Ava went and got the folder Helen Frost had given her. She opened it and slid it across the coffee table to Hank.

"She was my mother," Ava said.

The words felt strange in her mouth, and she had the strong desire to erase them.

"You want some wine, Hank?" she asked him as he studied the papers in the folder.

"I don't suppose you have something stronger? Whiskey?"

"I have some Bailey's Irish Cream," she said.

Hank scowled. "Wine'll be fine."

Ava went into the kitchen and looked at the wine rack. She reached for her basic thirteen-dollars-a-bottle house red, but then reconsidered. Why did Hank Bingham think her mother was in Paris when he knew she had jumped off that bridge?

"The hell with it," Ava said, pulling out the pricey bottle of zinfandel that she kept for big occasions.

When she returned with it and two glasses, Hank was tipping back in the chair, looking, Ava thought, smug.

"Could you not do that?" she told him.

"The chair. It's an antique and kind of fragile."

"Oh. Sure," he said, lowering it.

She handed him a glass of wine, then settled back onto the sofa, curling her legs up beneath her, and took a long swallow of wine.

"Did you look at all this stuff?" he asked, tilting his chin toward the folder open on the table.

"I saw the contract," Ava said. "That's how I know who really wrote the book."

He rifled through the papers and took one out, holding it toward Ava.

"What ever happened to your aunt?" Hank asked. "Beatrice?"

"She left. After Lily."

"Left," Hank said, staring into his wine. "Where'd she go?"

"I don't know."

Hank looked up.

"I do," he said. "She went to Paris."

"Uh huh. With my mother?"

"Exactly."

He set the paper he'd been holding in front of Ava.

"Your aunt bought up all the books after they went out of print. Why?"

Ava frowned. She picked up the paper and scanned it. Her aunt had bought every copy of *From Clare to Here.*

"I don't know."

Hank took a long swallow of wine, then put another piece of paper from the folder in front of Ava.

"They were shipped to Paris," he said, tapping the paper. "The address is right here."

Ava kept reading the order form, as if she could make sense of it. But it didn't make sense. Aunt Beatrice had gone to Paris? And had all of the remainders of *From Clare to Here* sent to her? Why?

"I've got a theory," Hank said. "They owned a bookstore here. They opened one there."

"They?" Ava said, her voice shaky. "My mother is dead. She jumped off a bridge."

Hank scratched his head. "Maybe," he said. "Except all they found was the car."

"The police told my father they might not find . . . her," Ava said. The words *the body* had always upset her.

Hank nodded. "Right. And if she didn't jump, that would eliminate finding the body altogether, wouldn't it? But it would make it easy for her to get on a plane to Paris, and meet up with her sister, and do what they did. Sell books."

"This is ridiculous," Ava said.

"Okay."

"I mean, you think Aunt Beatrice bought two thousand books to sell in a bookstore in Paris?"

Hank laughed. "I never thought of that!"

He poured more wine, still chuckling.

"Now go we in content. To liberty, and not to banishment," he said. "From *As You Like It.*"

Hank opened the copy of *From Clare to Here* that he'd set on the table and pointed.

"This is called an epigraph," he said.

"I know what it's called," Ava said.

"Now go we in content. To liberty, and not to banishment," he recited as Ava read it silently.

Ava had seen the epigraph before, of course. But when she thought a stranger named Rosalind Arden wrote it, she hadn't given it much thought. Now that she knew her mother had put that quote there, Ava had to make sense of it.

"I think she must have seen death as freedom," she said after a few minutes.

"Sure," Hank said. "But it says *we.*"

"Well, it's from *As You Like It.* That's what it says in the play."

"And your mother's bookstore. The one she owned with your aunt. That was called what?"

"Orlando's," Ava said.

"Like in the play!" Hank said with mock surprise.

"Okay, Hank. I give up," Ava said. "What is your bright idea?"

Hank leaned forward, close enough that Ava could smell the Old Spice on him.

"Your mother left us a clue, Ava. She and Beatrice went away so they could be free of guilt. They banished themselves for that liberty."

"No," Ava said. "That's ridiculous. A mother couldn't leave her daughter like that." To herself she added, *couldn't leave me like that.*

Hank's face softened. "But Ava, that's exactly what happens in *From Clare to Here.* She gives up her life with her living daughter and punishes herself by staying with her dead child."

"No," Ava said again, even though what Hank was saying made a certain sense.

Now Hank was taking another book from his bag. A travel guide to Paris. As he turned the pages, Ava saw that someone had highlighted parts in hot pink.

"Don't miss Ganymede's Books, a quirky cluttered bookshop in the hip Marais section. The American owner, who goes simply by Madame, is a mercurial dragon who opens and closes the shop at her whim,"

Hank read. "Ask her a question and she's just as likely to bite you as help you. But that's part of the fun. And her eclectic selection of books is worth the trip."

He closed the book, keeping his finger on the page.

"Ganymede," he said. "Also a reference to *As You Like It.*"

"When Rosalind runs away to the forest," Ava said, "she decides to disguise herself as a young man named Ganymede."

"Interesting, isn't it? And the owner is American," Hank added.

But Ava shook her head.

"Even if this Madame person is Aunt Beatrice, Hank, my mother jumped off that bridge."

Hank scratched his head again, a technique he used, Ava realized, not to express bewilderment, as it suggested, but to indicate he'd figured something out.

"What if your aunt bought up all those books not to sell them, but so no one figured this out?"

"That's crazy," Ava said.

Hank didn't answer her. He just kept his blue eyes leveled at her.

"Only one way to find out," he said finally.

Maybe she wouldn't have agreed if Maggie wasn't there. "I love you," her daughter had said. As she turned on her computer and typed in flights to Paris, two tickets, something Hank said came back to Ava. She left *us* a clue, he'd said. Why would her mother leave Hank Bingham a clue? And why would Hank Bingham look for her mother, even after everyone believed she was dead?

Helen Frost stood looking uncomfortable at Ava's door.

"May I come inside?" Helen asked, and when Ava said, "Of course" and opened the door wider for her to enter, she seemed relieved.

There was an awkward moment of the two women having to maneuver around the door in the small foyer, and then Ava — her coat already on and *Slaughterhouse-Five* in her hand — motioned Helen into the living room and onto the sofa. Ava sat across from her, just as this morning she'd sat across from Hank Bingham and listened to his theory.

"Oh, were you on your way somewhere?" Helen asked, noticing that Ava had on her coat.

"The book group," Ava said, suddenly missing Penny, with all of her writers' quotes and old-fashioned ways. "Your mother is so missed," she added.

"It's been hard, going through her things and Daddy's things. But actually, that's why I'm here."

Helen dipped into her black quilted Chanel bag and pulled out a folder much like the one she'd given Ava the other day.

"Your mother owned Orlando's," Helen said.

"A long time ago," Ava said.

Helen placed a black and white photograph in Ava's lap and said, "See?"

Ava looked down.

Staring up at her, beautiful, elegant, smiling, was her mother, with her Brigitte Bardot blond hair and wide blue-green eyes. In the photograph, she was kneeling and had one arm around Ava and one arm around Lily. Ava scowled back at the camera, arms folded, her barrette hanging by her cheek instead of in its place at her temple. But Lily beamed. Like their mother's, her smile lit up the picture. At the bottom was the date the picture was taken, just three days before Lily died.

"As I said," Helen said, "your mother always hosted book parties for my grandmother's writers. Obscure poets. New England history. I think Grandmother published a dozen books on Roger Williams alone. First novels. Orlando's always agreed to have a party. And your mother and aunt knew how to throw good parties."

The background was blurry, but Ava could make out the once familiar bookshelves, the dais where they stood behind the cash register, the ornate ancient cash register itself — they'd refused to get a more modern one; both her mother and aunt had loved the way this one looked and sounded. The partygoers appeared as a smear of gray as they moved across the frame.

"You can have it, of course," Helen said, standing.

"Thank you," Ava said. She stood too, but slowly. "I don't have any pictures like this."

Her father had packed them all away after they got the phone call saying her mother had jumped off that bridge, as if he could put their history away too.

Now Cate was knocking at the door, and there was a flurry of greetings and pleasantries and then Ava and Cate were alone on the sidewalk, turning toward Benefit Street and the library.

"You okay?" Cate asked Ava. "You look like you just saw a ghost."

"Want to hear something crazy?" Ava asked Cate as they walked along Benefit Street.

On their right, the stately Georgian-style John Brown House loomed. The street, with its faux gas lamps and Colonial homes, always looked lovely. But Ava thought it was even lovelier in autumn, when the leaves on its old trees turned yellow and red and orange. Some residents had already placed fat pumpkins on their stoops.

"Sure," Cate said.

Slaughterhouse-Five must have stymied her creativity — she was dressed like her usual self tonight, in wide-legged black cotton pants and a black turtleneck and her red Australian walking shoes.

"I'm going to Paris tomorrow night," Ava said.

Cate stopped walking. "Maggie?"

"Hopefully," Ava said. "But also . . ."

Cate waited.

"Rosalind Arden," Ava said.

"You found her?" Cate said, surprised.

"I think she's dead, actually. But there's a crazy chance she lives in Paris."

Cate put her hand on Ava's arm. "You don't have to go all the way to Paris, you know."

Ava started walking again, her face flushed.

"No. It's important," she said, and gratefully Cate let it go at that.

■ ■ ■ ■

Maybe Cate was just running out of steam this late in the year, Ava thought when she saw Emma, her hair unnaturally black, presiding over a table of ordinary cheese — the return of the Havarti! — and crackers, some grapes, and bottles of red table wine.

John was dressed in a blue blazer and khakis, and with his thinning hair bleached by the sun and his nose peeling from a sunburn, he looked boyish and less morose.

"Your big night," Ava said to him.

He lifted his glass of wine. "Courage," he said, smiling.

Had he always had that one dimple? Or maybe he just hadn't smiled very much.

"I'm so glad I recognize the food," John said. "*The Unbearable Lightness of Being* night kind of put me over the edge."

"Tell me," Ruth said, coming to stand beside Ava, "what's Rosalind Arden like? I mean, you've met her, right?"

"Yes," Ava said. "I've met her." Then she added, "She's lovely."

"I remember when the kids were in school," Ruth said, cocking her head as if to study Ava more carefully. "You weren't one of us."

"What do you mean?" Ava said. She'd brought in her share of pizzas, and attended all the off-key concerts and awkward school plays, and during the unit on Egypt had even come in and helped build a replica of the Great Pyramid.

"Well, you worked, for one thing," Ruth said. "No standing around gossiping for you. I remember you were always carrying a satchel full of papers to correct. I kind of envied you."

"What?" Ava said, surprised. Ruth had always seemed so content, so organized and confident.

"Here you are, with a career and a life, while I'm struggling to find my way after all these years. I mean, after my eight-year-old finally gets to high school, I won't have to help anyone with a Halloween costume or Colonial diorama anymore," Ruth said. "Then what."

"Oh, Ruth," Ava said, touching Ruth's arm gently. "You were the engine of those classrooms. Really, I'm so grateful."

"I think it's wonderful how you've embraced the book group and gone even one step further by inviting the author," Ruth continued.

"Thank you, Ruth."

"Could we take our seats?" Cate said from

the front of the room.

Ava made her way to the empty seat beside John.

To Ava's surprise, Luke was now taking Cate's place in front of them.

"So," he said when everyone quieted, "I just wanted to share some news."

He seemed to be looking right at her, Ava thought.

Luke held up his left hand.

"I got married this past weekend!" he said, grinning.

"What?" Ava blurted, that one word louder than all the oohs and aahs from the others. Loud enough that everyone turned from Luke to her.

"When your girl says fish or cut bait," Luke said, "you get married."

Some people laughed softly.

But Kiki jumped to her feet, her nostrils flaring. "You *married* Roxy?" she said.

"Isn't this wonderful?" Cate said in her save-the-day voice. "Our first wedding. Congratulations, Luke."

"Why is he looking at you?" John whispered to Ava.

"I have no idea," she said.

Cate started talking about Kurt Vonnegut, so Ava could ignore John's comment and pretend to be interested in the writer's life.

"As most of us know," Cate was saying, "*Slaughterhouse-Five* was based on Vonnegut's own experiences in World War II."

Monique started taking notes.

"Like Billy Pilgrim in the novel, he survived the Allied forces' firebombing of Dresden, Germany, and actually emerged from hiding in a meat locker beneath a slaughterhouse the day after the attack. Captured, he was made to find and bury and burn bodies."

John let out a low whistle. "No kidding," he said. "I didn't know he'd experienced what Billy Pilgrim does."

"In the first chapter," Honor said, opening her Moleskine, "he writes: 'It is so short and jumbled and jangled because there is nothing intelligent to say about a massacre.' "

"Bravo, Mr. Vonnegut," Jennifer said. "This book came out in 1969 during the height of the Vietnam War, yet massacres continued in Cambodia and Rwanda and Bosnia. They continue today."

"But history repeats itself," Diana said. She stood as if facing an audience from stage. "That's why I'm where I am. My mother and grandmother both had breast cancer. They both died from it, in fact."

"All these years sitting at the book group

together and I didn't know that," Ruth said.

"As the great George Bernard Shaw said, 'We learn from history that we learn nothing from history,' " Diana said ruefully.

"Could you say that again?" Monique asked, her pen hovering above a page in her own Moleskine. "I need to write it down."

Diana repeated the Shaw quote.

"Shaw was one of the great ones," she said. "Perhaps you saw me in *Major Barbara* two seasons ago? That play was written in 1905, long before the carnage of the world wars. Yet it feels relevant, doesn't it?"

"Shaw is worthy of an entire evening's discussion," Cate said in her let's-get-back-on-track voice. "But tonight is for Vonnegut. And John."

At the sound of his name, John startled.

"Did you want to lead the discussion?" Cate asked him. "Or should I maybe give a little more context to the book first?"

"Sure," John said.

Since it wasn't clear to anyone if he meant *sure, he'd lead the discussion now* or *sure, Cate should keep talking,* Cate kept talking.

Ava tried to concentrate on Cate. She tried to keep *Slaughter-house-Five* foremost in her mind. But it proved impossible. Tomorrow's trip to Paris, Hank Bingham's belief that her mother was alive and living there after all these years, the memories of that long-ago morning when Lily fell from the tree, the sad year that followed Lily's death, and the hope that she might find Maggie — all of it kept intruding, pushing at her mind and forcing her backward and forward in time without any warning.

"One of the most striking things about *Slaughterhouse-Five,*" Cate said, "is that Billy Pilgrim has become unstuck in time."

Unstuck in time. Yes, Ava thought. That was exactly what she was: unstuck in time.

"He travels between different times and places in his life, and can't control which period he lands in," Cate continued. "Billy Pilgrim travels in and out of the meat locker in Dresden, to his swimming lessons at the Y and his meetings at the Lions Club to his possibly imagined captivity by Tralfamadorians."

"Favorite part," Luke interjected.

"But they're hallucinations," Monique said. "Hallucinations that help him escape a world he cannot understand."

"A world destroyed by war," Jennifer said. "This isn't a science fiction novel. It's a moral statement. Billy can't grasp the destructiveness of war, so he makes up something to help him shape the world. Billy Pilgrim can't ignore the catastrophes of war, and neither can we."

Luke returned the discussion to the Tralfamadorians and their knowledge of the fourth dimension.

"Every moment of time is in it and keeps occurring and reoccurring simultaneously," he said, shaking his head in awe at the notion.

"Simultaneously and endlessly," Kiki said.

Ava couldn't speak. The idea of being unstuck in time, and the fourth dimension, seemed to exactly explain what she was feeling, exactly what she was experiencing. And realizing that brought her back to her childhood bedroom, Lily's bed across from hers a year unused, the sheets and thin summer coverlet still rumpled and turned down, as if she had just leapt from it or was about to climb in again. And Ava with *From Clare to Here* propped up on her lap, reading it and thinking it had been written just for her. Had it? she wondered now.

"I really have to thank John for choosing such an important book," Cate said.

Ava looked up and saw that the discussion was winding down. People were closing their notebooks and gathering their coats and bags.

"Um, I never got to say anything," John said.

"Oh no," Cate said, embarrassed.

No one else seemed to have heard him. They talked with each other on their way back to Emma and the wine and cheese.

"That's okay," John said. "I'm glad everyone liked it."

"No, no," Cate said. "I'll get everyone back in their seats."

John stood now too, and pulled on his lime green fleece vest.

"Really," he said. "It's fine. I don't love public speaking. So I kind of got off the hook. And I really liked hearing what everyone had to say."

Cate hesitated. "Are you sure?"

John grinned at her. With his toothy grin and that deep dimple and sunburned nose, he looked boyish, so unlike the sad middle-aged man who had sat here all year.

"So it goes," he said.

Cate grinned back. "Well, then. More wine?"

John nodded, but he didn't follow Cate. Instead he lingered by Ava as she slowly tucked the book into her purse and wrapped her polka-dot scarf around her neck for protection against the autumn chill.

"So it goes," he said again.

"Right," Ava said.

"I think the Tralfamadorians believed that

even though a person is dead in one moment, she's alive in all the other moments that are happening simultaneously, and we can visit those moments over and over," John said.

Ava paused. "I think so too," she said.

"You know why I picked this book?" John asked, holding up *Slaughterhouse-Five.* His copy was an old one, dog-eared and wrinkled.

Ava shook her head.

"1978," he said. "University of Miami. English 101. Me, a marketing major, whatever that is. I was there to be on the sailing team, not to read books or major in anything. The professor assigns *Slaughterhouse-Five,* and I'm telling you, I just don't get it. All the time-shifting and the aliens and the optometrists convention. And the cutest girl in the class, Marjorie Wells, comes up to me one day after I embarrass myself by not being able to answer the question: are the Tralfamadorians real? Marjorie Wells. Strawberry blond hair. Freckles. An Izod shirt the same color as her eyes. Cutoff jeans that show legs that don't seem to stop. And — I still remember this — those rubber flip flops? Orange ones. She says, 'John, what are you going to write your paper on?' And I say, 'Not the Tralfamadorians.' And she smiles up at me — she was only this tall —" John holds his hand to his mid-waist. "With this space between her front teeth that was so adorable, she smiles up at me, and says, 'Okay. Tonight. My room. We'll write that paper on the Tralfamadorians. And you'll get an A because I always get A's.' "

John looked away from Ava, somewhere off in the distance, maybe all the way back to the University of Miami, 1978.

"I went to her room that night, and she explained the book to me, and I got an A on the paper," he said softly.

"And you married her?" Ava asked.

"Three weeks after graduation. We were together from that night in 1978 until she died last year."

Ava took John's hand and squeezed it.

His eyes were wet with tears. "I never thought a book could help with, you know, life. But honestly, when I reread this one for tonight, and I thought about time travel and stuff, it actually made me feel better. Or maybe understand something?"

Ava realized she was still holding his hand. It felt awkward to drop it now, so she held on. That's when she saw that everyone else had been listening.

"I was hoping maybe it helped you too?" John asked. "All of you."

■ ■ ■ ■

Part Eleven: November

■ ■ ■ ■

What the mother knew was that she couldn't go back home. She would save her surviving daughter by staying away, and letting her guilt over what had happened be hers alone. Maybe someday they would be reunited, here, in Clare . . .

— *From Clare to Here* by Rosalind Arden

MAGGIE

"So," Noah said to Maggie over fondue at Le Refuge des Fondus in Montmartre, "do you know anything about art?"

"It's only my major," Maggie told him.

They were seated at a long wooden communal table and drinking red wine out of silly baby bottles. Surely, Maggie thought when they first sat down, Hemingway never ate here. But she found herself giving in to the fun of it — the dramatic waiter slamming their fondue pot onto the table, the tourists snapping pictures of one another drinking from baby bottles, and the convivial crowded atmosphere.

"Painting?" Noah asked her.

"Art history," Maggie said.

She thought of Florence, her brief time there feeling like she didn't belong. The other girls with their little pails to carry their toiletries down the long hall to the bathroom. The way they shared makeup and stories about high school and crushes on boys. Everything Maggie said seemed to be the wrong thing. One night she got drunk and threw up and said all kinds of stupid things. That was the night she met the guy she followed to France.

"Are you even listening?" Noah was asking.

"Sorry. No," she said.

"The company I work for is hiring," he said. "Your French is excellent, your English is passable —"

"Ha ha," she said as the waiter slammed two fresh baby bottles of wine in front of them.

"And apparently you know something about art?"

"I guess," Maggie said.

Noah dipped a piece of bread into the fondue and held it out to Maggie.

She hesitated, then bit it off the fondue fork. Noah smiled at her.

"I'm not good with people," Maggie said, remembering him with the little bratty kid that day in the Musée d'Orsay. "I repel them."

"You didn't repel me," he said.

Maggie frowned. Was Noah flirting with her? It felt nice to have a friend, someone fun and smart. Someone normal. Someone who didn't really want anything from her. But maybe he did?

"Look, think about it," Noah said. "It's a pretty easy job. And the tips are good."

Later, when they got off the Métro and were about to go off in opposite directions, Noah wiped some flyaway strands of hair off her face.

"I like you," he said.

Before Maggie could tell him "Don't," he turned and walked off, waving to her without even looking back.

Upstairs in Geneviève's apartment, Maggie looked through the pile of clothes on the floor until she found the book Madame had given her. *From Clare to Here.* She tossed it on the bed, made herself a cup of tea and then brought it with her back to bed. She picked up the book, and began to read.

She didn't stop until she'd read the last words.

Maggie closed the book and lay back on her pillows.

The mother in the book chooses to stay behind with her dead child instead of returning to her family. Beneath those stones it's dark and frightening. Above, the rain has stopped and light is shining. But still she chooses not to come back.

Maggie stayed very still for a long time. The book on her chest, her head on her pillows, staring up at the ceiling.

She heard Geneviève come home, but she did not call out to her or get up to greet her.

Much later, after Geneviève had gone to bed and a light rain had begun to fall, Maggie got up and went to the computer.

The first email she wrote was to Noah:

> So yeah, I could take rich American families around the Louvre and impress them with my vast knowledge of Art History. #threewholesemesters! Wanna drink wine from baby bottles and discuss????

Almost immediately, Noah wrote back. Consider the job yours, he said. He'd fill her in over fondue.

She smiled as she read it, and sent him back an emoticon of clapping hands, a round face with eyes popping, a baby bottle, and then she added one of a face with hearts for eyes.

The second email she wrote was to her brother, who had stopped reprimanding her long enough to tell her he'd fallen in love with an Australian zoologist.

Will the Pill? In love? My heart be still! (Hey! I just wrote a poem!)

Lots of exciting things going on in the life of your sister. So here's the scoop. I've decided to stay in Paris and work as a museum guide for this tour company that charges Americans too much moula to go see the Mona Lisa and The Thinker and all of the Impressionists. Using my great education! Maybe I will even write that novel I always say I want to write. I mean, that's why writers come to Paris, isn't it????

Email me details of this woman so I can properly vet her, k? U are a poor judge of women, bro. Oh wait. You actually only had one girlfriend!!! And she was . . . well . . .

And by the way. Speaking of love. I love u. Mags

Maggie paused, made herself another cup of tea, and then sat back at the computer. The third email was the hardest one to write.

Dear Mom,

You already know that I dropped out of the Florence thing, and I've really really made a lot of bad mistakes. I'm so sorry.

For wasting your money. For ruining your trust. For being such a bad daughter.

I'm safe and I'm okay. I've screwed everything up again, but I promise I'm going to fix it. I have a job in Paris as a tour guide for an American company. And I have an apartment with a nice roommate.

I don't expect you to believe me this time, but I really am going to fix things, fix myself. I read this book and I realized that we get to choose — darkness or light, life or death. I choose light. I choose life. I do. If you can come to Paris, that would be wonderful. I know a fondue place where they serve wine in baby bottles! I would take you there, if you let me.

I love you, Mom. Maggie

HANK

Hank Bingham decided immediately that he did not like Paris. For one thing, everything looked different than it did at home: the people and the signs and the buildings. It even *smelled* different. He supposed that people who liked to travel did it for this very reason. But Hank liked being home. He found comfort in knowing shortcuts, and where to get the best beer on tap. He found comfort in sameness. Here, nothing was the same, and Hank felt off-balance, as if he might at any moment actually tip over. Of course, having not slept — and he a man who needed his eight solid hours — didn't help. And Ava's lack of patience with him, telling him to *hurry up* or *watch out* or *let's go,* only added to his sense of confusion.

In the taxi from the airport, as Ava spoke French to the driver, exhaustion washed over Hank in waves.

"We could still go to the hotel first," Ava

said, and Hank realized he'd done that head jerk that people do when they fall asleep sitting up.

He shook his head. "Coffee would be good, though."

"I'm sure there's a café near the bookstore," Ava said.

There was lots of traffic and horns beeping, the driver hitting the brakes and then speeding up.

"You all right?" Ava asked him. "You've gone pale."

How could he tell her he just wanted to be back home?

"Fine," he mumbled, and concentrated on trying not to throw up.

Sure, the driver's stop-and-go driving and his own lack of sleep had made him queasy. But now that he was actually here, and Ava was nudging him and saying, "Look! The Eiffel Tower!," Hank let himself think for the first time about the fact that if he was right — and he knew he was, knew it deep in his bones — he was about to see the woman he'd loved more than anyone. More even than Nadine, with whom he'd built a life. Nadine, whose hand he'd held as she died. If he was right, then very soon he was going to walk into a bookstore in Paris and see Charlotte North for the first time in over forty years. And what the hell was he going to say?

"See?" Ava said as they got out of the taxi. "A café right there. And the bookstore there."

He followed her finger pointing first to the café, and then to the bookstore. Its purple sign read GANYMEDE'S BOOKS, and its narrow door was painted lavender. Hank began to sweat.

A light rain fell, and everything looked like it had been painted in watercolors. Hank let Ava lead him inside and tell the waiter they wanted a table.

He wanted to lay his head on that table and go to sleep, but instead he took one glance at the menu and, unable to recognize anything on it, told Ava to order for him.

Soon, two omelets appeared in front of them (not fluffy ones like he was used to back home, but flat thin ones), and large cups of milky coffee, and a basket of warm bread and butter. Hank dug in, and, as Ava predicted, it revived him.

He noticed that she just picked at her food, her eyes frequently drifting across the street to the bookstore. Was this the time to tell her about him and her mother? Did he need to tell her at all?

Hank cleared his throat.

"Ava," he said. "I need to tell you something. Something about your mother and —"

"Don't," she said. "What I have to think right now is that she's dead. Like she has been for most of my life. I can't even let myself believe . . ."

Hank nodded. Better to keep quiet, he thought.

For the first time since he'd figured out that Charlotte was here in Paris, Hank hesitated. He and Ava stood at the lavender door of Ganymede's. Through the windows on either side, he could see the warmly lit store, the crowds of people.

"Well?" Ava said.

"Right," Hank said, and yanked the door open.

A bell tinkled.

"Hank?" Ava said, because he'd opened the door but not taken a step forward.

"Hank," Ava said again.

He felt Ava's hand on his back, urging him forward.

And then he was inside. Beside him, Ava took a sharp breath.

"It looks the same," she said softly.

Hank scanned the place. Index cards with

quirky categories were taped to the shelves. Everyone spoke in a low voice, as if they were in a library. A hairy young man sat, looking bored, under a sign that said "Information." And to the left was the dais where the salesclerk sat on a stool, a perch from which to watch for shoplifters, just like Orlando's.

"Look," Hank said, actually turning Ava's head with his big hands. "That's the same cash register as the one in Orlando's."

"Oh my God," Ava said.

"I told you —"

"Oh my God," she said again, louder.

"Ava?"

But she wasn't listening to him. She was pushing through the crowd, frantically moving toward the register.

Hank lost sight of her for an instant. But then he saw her, standing in front of it, head tilted up.

"Maggie!" Ava said.

And then again, "Maggie," but this time the name was caught in her sobs. "My God, you're all right," he heard her say.

The missing daughter, Hank realized. Right here at her grandmother's store.

Maggie was shrieking with delight and relief. "You came! You got my email and you came!"

Hank too pushed through the crowd.

"Email?" Ava said, crushing her daughter to her. "I didn't get an email. I've been traveling since yesterday."

Maggie was crying now too.

"Let's go talk," Ava said, leading her out of the shop.

Then a voice cut through the quiet chatter of the crowd.

"What is all the commotion?"

Hank followed the sound of that voice, and there, standing at the door to a back room, stood Charlotte's sister Beatrice.

Beatrice didn't have the soft beauty of her sister, but rather a sexier, tougher look. Even now, all these years later, Hank saw that in the older woman moving toward him. She'd let her hair go gray but kept it long, and it fell in the same waves down her back that it always had. And there was no disguising those gray eyes. They were steelier now, which made them even more unnerving. Most women Hank had seen age had gotten thicker. Even Nadine used to complain about what she called her new muffin top. But Beatrice was actually thinner than she'd been as a young woman, revealing sharp cheekbones and a slender waist.

"May I help you?" she said when she stood in front of him.

"Beatrice," he said. "Officer Bingham. I'm sure you remember me."

Something changed in her eyes. He saw it. Was she deciding what to tell him?

She sighed. Resigned. "Hank," she said, "Let's go in the back."

Without waiting for an answer, she started to walk through the store to the back room. Hank saw a few people surreptitiously snap photos of her on their phones.

"You're a celebrity," he said when they were alone in the back and she'd closed the door.

"Of sorts," she said. "Coffee?"

She pointed to a beat-up metal pot sitting on a hot plate. Once more, she didn't wait for his answer and just began measuring coffee and water into it.

Neither of them spoke as the coffee began to perk. Beatrice heated a small saucepan of milk and carefully filled two white porcelain cups with café au lait.

"Good on a rainy day," Beatrice said, sitting down.

Hank didn't really want any more coffee. He stood awkwardly beside her, holding the hot cup in his hand.

"For God's sake, Hank, sit down," Beatrice told him.

When he did, she narrowed her eyes at

him, sizing him up.

"Why are you here? Or do you just happen to be in Paris?" Beatrice finally asked.

"Oh, I came looking for you," Hank said.

"Why? I haven't broken any laws that I know of. A person can move away and start a business and make a life, can't she?"

"Absolutely," Hank said.

"So?"

"Actually," he said, "I came looking for you, and for her. For Charlotte."

That same thing seemed to pass over her eyes.

"She's dead, Hank."

"Right," he said. "Jumped off a bridge."

Beatrice didn't say anything, but Hank kept watching her.

"What happened that morning?" he asked her.

"Is that why you've come here? To rehash all of that?"

Hank didn't answer her. He just leaned back in his chair and waited. He had learned long ago that when you interrogated someone, they talked more if you stayed quiet. People couldn't stand silence; they needed to fill it.

"I went to the store and worked on a window display of that seagull book," Beatrice began. "And right in the middle of it I remembered I had promised to babysit, so I kind of ran out, leaving the patchouli-smelling girl in charge. When I got to Charlotte's, Ava was reading and Lily was up in a tree. High. Too high. And I should have told her to come down but I didn't." She said again, quietly, "I didn't." Beatrice took a breath. "Instead I went inside and started cleaning the dishes."

"And?"

"And Lily fell."

"So it wasn't anybody's fault," Hank said.

To his surprise, Beatrice laughed.

"You fool," she said. "It was everybody's fault. Charlotte's for being with you, and Ava's for letting Lily climb the tree in the first place, and mine for not telling her to come down."

"No," Hank said. "It was an accident."

"Sure," Beatrice said. "Then why has guilt ruined all of our lives?"

"If Charlotte's dead —" Hank began.

"Hank," Beatrice interrupted, "trust me. Charlotte's been dead a long time."

She stood then, as if to tell him their conversation was over. Hank stood too, and followed her to the door that led back into the bookstore.

"Why did you buy all the books?" he said.

When she turned around to face him, he

added, "*From Clare to Here.* I know she wrote it, and I know you bought all the copies that didn't sell. The remainders, I think they call them?"

"To sell here," Beatrice said.

"Peculiar," Hank said.

They continued toward the door. Beatrice opened it, and held it so Hank could pass.

"Ganymede," he said. "From *As You Like It,* right?"

"You surprise me, Hank. I didn't take you for a lover of Shakespeare."

"Ganymede is the name Rosalind takes when she goes into hiding, isn't it?"

Beatrice studied his face for a moment.

"Enjoy Paris," she told him.

They stepped out of the back room, and almost bumped into Maggie and Ava on their way in.

Ava paused, studying Beatrice's face.

"Aunt Beatrice?" Ava said, her voice full of a combination of wonder and anger.

Beatrice sighed. "I guess we better all go sit down," she said.

AVA

Even as Beatrice talked to them about moving to Paris and opening this bookstore, Ava kept repeating to herself: *I am in Paris with Aunt Beatrice, I am in Paris with Aunt Beatrice,* as if saying it enough times would begin to make sense of it.

"All this time, my own great-niece was here, right under my nose," she said. "No wonder I took a shine to you."

Maggie sat up straight, her brows furrowed the way they did when she thought hard.

"This place felt so familiar, so safe," she said. "And sitting here I just remembered that I saw a picture of it once, a long time ago, in an old photo album. Except it wasn't this store, it was the other one, in Providence."

"Orlando's," Beatrice said wistfully.

"My mother," Ava finally managed to say.

"Did you know she wrote *From Clare to Here*?"

Beatrice sighed. "For six months after Lily died, that's all she did. All she could do. Write that book. I think it saved her, that story. And then when White Swan bought it, I thought she'd be happy finally. Or at least, on her way out of grief toward happiness. But instead, it freed her."

Ava didn't even try to hold back her tears. They fell, hot and fast.

"At your mother's request, the editor of the book, Poppy Montgomery, her daughter brought you the first copy. Do you remember that?"

Ava remembered the black Cadillac, the woman emerging from it, the package in her hand. *I knew your mother,* Penny had written to her.

"That was almost a year to the day after Lily died. The book was published, and your mother . . ." Beatrice let what she'd left unsaid hang there.

"The dedication," Maggie said. "It was to you, Mom. A was you. And T was Gramps, right? Teddy? And H was . . . who was H?"

Hank sighed.

"Me," he said. "H was me."

Ava looked at him, confused. "Why would she put you in the dedication, Hank? You were just the detective on the case. She hardly knew you."

Hank shifted his weight in the chair, and looked at Beatrice.

"It's not for me to tell," she said to him.

"I knew her," he said after a pause. "I knew her before your sister died."

"But how?" Ava asked, confused.

"I was in love with her," Hank said softly. "I was with her that morning. Planning our future together. That's why I couldn't let this case go. Charlotte couldn't forgive herself for not being at home. For being with me. It was my fault too that Lily died."

On that long-ago morning so many lives had been ruined: two lovers planning a new life, a woman scraping batter from a frying pan, a little girl reading a book beneath the shade of a tree.

Maggie finally broke the silence. "But it was an accident," she said, so matter-of-factly that Ava answered without hesitation:

"Oh, it was. A terrible accident."

When she looked at Hank, she saw tears in his eyes.

"How I wish my mother had realized that before she took her life," Ava said softly.

"Yes, well, there are some things we cannot change," Beatrice said brusquely.

Ava watched Hank watching her aunt.

"That's true," Hank said. "And then there are things we can change."

"Profound, Hank," Beatrice said. "Perhaps you'll become a philosopher in your retirement."

"Oh, no," he said. "I'm still a detective."

Maggie

Maggie, cross-legged on the bed, studied her mother's face: her brown hair just starting to streak with gray, her freckled chest above the scoop neck of a black t-shirt. She noticed for the first time that her mother's ring finger was bare, and the sight of that made Maggie's heart heavy. But the nails were still cut short and square, and her hands still moved with the same quick efficiency they did everything — comb tangles from hair, zip a snowsuit, touch a forehead to check for fever.

Her mother paused and cocked her head toward Maggie. "What are you looking at?" she asked.

"You," Maggie said, her voice cracking. "My beautiful mother."

"Oh, baby," her mother said, and just like that she was at Maggie's side, those hands rubbing her back the way they had when Maggie was a little girl needing comfort from bad dreams or fits of loneliness.

"I want to take you home with me," her mother said.

Maggie shook her head. "I need to do this myself. To stay here and make my own life. To not mess up this time."

"I'll worry," Ava said. "Every minute."

"How could you not?" Maggie said. "You have no reason to trust me. But you'll see, Mom. I promise."

Her mother sighed and returned to folding a nightgown, and placed it in the suitcase.

"What will you tell Dad?" Maggie asked her.

"That I saw you and you seemed well. And happy."

Maggie smiled. "Thank you."

"Don't be mad at him, Maggie."

"He ruined your life!"

"Our lives are our own to ruin or not, I think. No one can do it for us."

Her mother zipped the suitcase shut, then turned and pulled Maggie into a hug.

When her mother got into the taxi, she leaned out the window as it pulled away and yelled, "You will be fine, Maggie! I love you!"

Maggie stood beneath the umbrella her mother had given her, blowing kisses, even after the taxi disappeared in the traffic.

She took a deep breath.

Today, she thought, my life is starting.

Hank

Hank stood near the Musée de la Poupée on avenue Parmentier, watching the bookstore. The Musée de la Poupée was a doll hospital, and the window was filled with decapitated doll heads and random limbs. Unnerving. But he knew that eventually Charlotte would appear, and so he waited. Everything he'd learned from being a cop told him Beatrice was lying. Everything he knew in his gut told him she was lying. He was determined to stay and find Charlotte, no matter how long it took. Of course, he didn't tell Ava any of this. He pretended she'd been right all along, and allowed her to look smug and self-satisfied. Maybe, he thought as he stood in a light drizzle, maybe she was even relieved. Because what do you do with a mother who you have believed was dead for most of your life? Forgive her? Hate her? Let her in?

Three days and no Charlotte.

He was missing something. Something important.

In his hotel room the next morning — three o'clock! Would he ever sleep through the night again? — Hank went over every detail about his time inside the shop, every detail about Beatrice. He closed his eyes and imagined the crowded aisles, the layout of the store, the back room. And then the upstairs apartment, he could see from the back stairs.

The room. Those beat-up sofas. The cluttered desk. The shelves of extra books. The file cabinets.

Out the window, there had been a yard.

Hank opened his eyes.

There had been a yard.

He smiled. And finally he slept.

The rue Deguerry was a small street that ran behind the avenue Parmentier, and the back of the bookstore faced the rue Deguerry.

When Hank finally woke up — after noon! He'd never slept that late in his life — and had his coffee, he did not go to his usual spot near the Musée de la Poupée. Instead, he went around to the rue Deguerry, where he stood facing the fence that bordered the backyard of the bookstore. That fence had a gate that opened onto the street. And Hank knew that Charlotte was going to walk through that gate.

He leaned against a small wall across the street, and waited.

After only fifteen or twenty minutes, he heard footsteps coming down the street. He turned toward them.

An older woman was approaching. She had a kerchief over her white hair. A beige raincoat, belted at the waist. A purple scarf around her neck. She had on silver boots that stopped at the ankle. One of those net bags everyone here carried their groceries in, and from the top of that bag poked leeks and carrots. A worn leather satchel had papers practically spilling from it. The papers were all marked up in her own handwriting, like the pages of *From Clare to Here* that he'd seen so many years ago. *So she is still writing,* he thought as he watched her.

The woman saw him and stopped.

They looked at each other without saying anything for what seemed a lifetime.

Then she said three words: "Hank. At last."

AVA

"Do you want me to tell them?" Cate asked Ava as they walked up Benefit Street to the library.

"Yes," Ava said. "But I have to do it myself."

When they walked in, Ava saw the sign Emma had made that read: WELCOME TO PROVIDENCE, ROSALIND ARDEN!!! with a copy of the cover of *From Clare to Here* in one corner and a quill pen drawn in another. Maybe Cate should tell them afterward. Maybe Ava could slip away.

Even worse, there was champagne and strawberries dipped in chocolate and a brie that was properly runny rather than hard and cold.

John came up to Ava almost immediately with a glass of champagne for her.

"She arriving on her own?" he asked.

"Not exactly," Ava said.

Luckily, Cate started asking people to take

their seats.

"Can you believe it?" Cate began. "Our year of The Book That Mattered Most is actually coming to an end tonight. We've traveled from Prague to East Egg, from Brooklyn to a small town in Alabama, from Russia to Victorian England, from New York City to Dresden to South America. What a wonderful year of books!"

They all applauded, even Ava. Cate was right. They had traveled far, and Ava knew that despite her rocky start, this group, these books, had changed her this year, just when she needed it.

"I want to announce our theme for next year, and of course get a commitment from you that you'll be back in this very room, the second Monday of every month, talking about books with me."

"Excuse me?" Jennifer said. "Where's our special guest?"

"Ava will get to that as soon as I announce our theme for next year," Cate said.

"Drum roll please," Honor said.

Luke tapped out a drum roll on his chair, and everyone laughed.

"In 1888," Cate said, "a French newspaper referred to Alfred Nobel as 'the merchant of death' because he had invented dynamite. His intention was for it to end all wars, but instead it was viewed as a deadly product. Therefore, when he died, he left nine million dollars for the establishment of a prize given in six areas to those who conferred the greatest benefit to mankind. The first awards were presented in 1901, so you have a long list to choose from for next year's theme: Nobel Prize-Winning Literature."

Some people oohed and aahed.

"I've already got mine," Diana announced. "Alice Munro."

"Emma has a list of the winners for each of you," Cate continued. "When we meet next month, you'll tell us your choices. Except Diana, of course. Who has already chosen Alice Munro."

More laughter.

"We know that we have one spot to fill with the sad loss of Penelope Frost," Cate said. "And to that end you can email me recommendations. I must ask, please raise your hand if you'll be returning next year."

Everyone's hand went up immediately. Except Ava's. Would they still want her in the group when they heard what she had to say?

Ava stood and walked to the front of the room.

"Do you want me to stay up here with

you?" Cate asked her.

"No," Ava said. She squeezed her friend's hand. "This is for me to do."

When Cate sat down, Ava cleared her throat, and let her eyes settle on each of them before she began.

"You probably noticed that Rosalind Arden isn't here," Ava said with a nervous laugh.

She took a breath.

"Rosalind Arden died in 1971," Ava said. "I thought I could find her, and I went all the way to Paris on a hunch someone had that she had staged her death and was living there. But Rosalind Arden is dead."

"That's all right," John said. "You didn't know. You tried."

"But you told us back in January that she'd agreed to come," Jennifer said.

"I know," Ava said. "I shouldn't have. I was desperate. To be here. To fit in. To reread the book that truly did matter most to me."

To Ava, the quiet in the room seemed louder than any noise.

"But the book," Monique said. "*From Clare to Here.* It's a treasure. A gift you've given us."

"It is?" Ava said.

"The underground, where she finds her

dead daughter, represents its own unique thing for each of us. Do we choose darkness? Or light? To go on? Or to give up?" Diana said. "This book touched me in ways I can't even articulate."

"It's about all the big themes. Life or death. Love and sacrifice. Grief and hope," Honor said.

"At first," Ruth said, "I wondered if a mother could actually do that. Leave her child behind and choose death. But I was ultimately convinced by the writing, and by the character of the mother. Her guilt over the death of her child prevented her from continuing as a mother or wife. She had no choice in a way, did she?"

"And her guilt was unfounded," Kiki said.

"But when someone dies," John said, "we blame ourselves, even when we are blameless. Why wasn't I home with her? What if 911 had been called sooner? The would haves, could haves, should haves can drive you crazy."

"You all liked the book?" Ava said.

"I'm sorry the author died," Luke said. "I had a list of questions for her. Like how did she know grief so well? And guilt?"

"I can answer that," Ava said. "Rosalind Arden is a pen name for my mother, Charlotte North. In 1970, my little sister Lily fell out of a tree in our yard and died. My mother wasn't home, and she'd left Lily and me in the care of our aunt, who was in the kitchen washing dishes when Lily fell. I tried to get Lily to come down. She'd climbed too high, and I was afraid of heights so couldn't go up after her. And just like that, Lily fell."

"And where did you say your mother was?" Diana asked.

An image of Hank Bingham young and handsome in his uniform flashed through her mind.

"She was at work," Ava said softly.

"And she wrote *From Clare to Here*?" Monique was saying. "That's remarkable."

"She wrote it because she did it," Ava said. Her voice grew stronger. "She wrote the book as a way, I think now, to explain to me why she would leave us and take her own life."

"Oh, Ava," John said.

Cate came up to Ava and put an arm around her shoulders.

"Thank you for sharing all of this with us," Cate said.

"Yes," Ruth said. "Thank you."

And then they were clapping, all of them, even Monique, even John.

"I need a glass of that champagne," Ava said.

"Great idea," Diana said.

Emma had poured a glass for each of them, and as they all moved to the table, Diana raised hers.

"To Rosalind Arden!"

"Hear, hear," a few people said.

Ava looked around at these people who had brought her into this group, who had watched her struggle and try and fail and, finally, stand here with them, more confident. Even, she realized, hopeful. She imagined the year ahead, watching movies at Kiki's and bringing in snacks one night and helping Diana through radiation after her surgery. She imagined books, dozens of them, piling up on her shelves, growing dog-eared and worn, read and reread, highlighted and scribbled on. She imagined books and this book group getting her through whatever was coming next.

"Emma," Ava said, "I need one of those lists. Of the Nobel Prize winners."

Cate's eyes met Ava's.

Thank you, Ava mouthed. She saw tears in Cate's eyes, but Cate quickly looked away.

The door opened then, and surprised by the intrusion, everyone looked toward it.

Hank Bingham walked in, looking big and

uncomfortable. No longer that young handsome detective, still Ava could see what women had seen in him once — the way he held himself, the bright eyes and strong jaw, the easy smile.

Behind Hank was a white-haired woman, with a bright purple scarf around her neck and short silver boots on her feet.

"I haven't been in a library since tenth grade," Hank said. "But this is where Ava North's book club thing meets, right?"

"Hank?" Ava said, confused. "What are you doing here?"

The woman stepped forward. Her face was lovely, soft and pale with blue-green eyes. When she spoke, her voice was surprisingly strong.

"I understand you invited Rosalind Arden here to discuss her book, *From Clare to Here,*" she said.

Her gaze fell on Ava.

"Yes," Ava said. Something was swelling in her, a feeling like nothing she had ever felt. It seemed to fill every inch of her. Yet somehow she managed to say, "I'm Ava."

"I understand you've been looking for me," the woman said.

Memories came rushing at Ava with such intensity and speed that she had to hold onto the edge of the table for balance. Her mother and Lily and her own young self making fairy parties, reading in Orlando's, snuggling in bed as her mother read stories to them. Grief came too. Lily. The horrible year of grief that followed. Her mother's death.

How many of us want to stop time, change the course of events, get a chance to bring someone back? Ava thought. Wasn't that what *From Clare to Here* explored? Except now her mother *had* changed course. She'd spent decades grieving, hidden, in some ways with Lily. But now — now! — she was here, standing in front of Ava.

Ava took a step toward her mother. And then another. And then another.

Charlotte opened her arms.

"Ava," she said. "Forgive me."

And then the two women were embracing. Ava inhaled the scent she never thought she'd smell again: books and ink and violet water. Her mother.

Over her mother's shoulder, Ava saw Hank Bingham smiling at her.

"I wrote it for you," Charlotte whispered. "That's all I can tell them. I wrote it for you."

"I know," Ava said.

Ava had so much she wanted to say and so much she needed to ask. But for now, she couldn't let go. For now, she just had to hold on, tight.

ACKNOWLEDGMENTS

For several years, ever since the idea for this book was born, I asked everyone I knew what book mattered the most to them. The books selected here were chosen from those suggestions, so thank you to all my friends who indulged me in my quest. Thanks to my family, who give me so much love; to Andy Green, who helped me with an important plot point in the story, and to my friend Sharon Ingendahl, who is one of the smartest readers I know. Also many thanks to the Hermitage Artist Retreat for giving me the time and space to write, and Erica Sklar for doing the same here at home. And enormous gratitude to everyone at Brandt and Hochman and W. W. Norton, especially Gail Hochman and Jill Bialosky, for helping my words turn into books.

ABOUT THE AUTHOR

Ann Hood is the editor of *Knitting Yarns: Writers on Knitting* and the best-selling author of *The Book That Matters Most, The Knitting Circle, The Red Thread, Comfort,* and *An Italian Wife,* among other works. She is the recipient of two Pushcart Prizes, a Best American Spiritual Writing Award, a Best American Food Writing Award, a Best American Travel Writing Award, and the Paul Bowles Prize for Short Fiction. She lives in Providence, Rhode Island.

The employees of Thorndike Press hope you have enjoyed this Large Print book. All our Thorndike, Wheeler, and Kennebec Large Print titles are designed for easy reading, and all our books are made to last. Other Thorndike Press Large Print books are available at your library, through selected bookstores, or directly from us.

For information about titles, please call:
(800) 223-1244

or visit our Web site at:
http://gale.cengage.com/thorndike

To share your comments, please write:

Publisher
Thorndike Press
10 Water St., Suite 310
Waterville, ME 04901